TONS OF MONEY

Clark Shannon

LOST⁓
COAST
PRESS
Fort Bragg
California

Lost Coast Press
155 Cypress Street
Fort Bragg CA 95437
1-800-773-7782

www.cypresshouse.com

Library of Congress Cataloging-in-Publication Data

Shannon, Clark, date
    Tons of money / Clark Shannon.
    p.cm.
    ISBN 1-882897-53-6 (casebound)
        1.Computer industry--Fiction. 2. Avarice--Fiction. I. Title.

PS3569.H3347 T66 2000
813'.6--dc21   00-042400

Cover design by Mendocino Graphics
Cover image © Real Life Images/
Stock Connection/PictureQuest

Manufactured in the United States of America
2   4   6   8   10   9   7   5   3

To Jim, Mike, and Tracy — My three lifelines.

ACKNOWLEDGEMENTS

EVERY AUTHOR NEEDS ENCOURAGEMENT and acceptance. Mark Walsh and Chris Braddock certainly have been helpful. Without Mark, this work never would have been published. His support and assistance will forever be appreciated. Chris' insightful critique has added integrity and continuity to the story.

Larry Hauserman has been a friend and business associate for many years. His guidance through the monetary hazards of this work has been invaluable.

To all of these great friends and to my family. I thank you.

TONS OF MONEY

ONE

RYAN TIPTON STUDIED THE DOCUMENT. It was staggering: $75 million actual, plus $50 million for the punitive crap. No court in the country would allow this, but if any did, Patton wouldn't survive.

As he re-read the registered letter from Parker, Haslett and Thomas, he hoped what they were alleging wasn't true. The complaint involved massive patent infringement, misleading and fraudulent advertising and a host of other breaches of ethical and legal protocol. Before calling Patton, he did some quick calculations from the last quarterly report. God, it was worse than he'd suspected.

"I think you'd better come to my office and give me some background on what they're alleging, Ray. It's mind-boggling, and if it's true we have big problems. I'm looking at the latest quarterly, which shows bank payments on outstanding loans three months in arrears. Is that right?" Tipton asked.

"Yeah, and it could get worse. Look, just tell me what it is they want. I don't have time to screw around with bullshit from Mecham Temple," Patton bellowed. Typical, Tipton thought.

"There are twenty-eight pages to the complaint; bottom line could be as high as $125 million. I need to go over this with you. We've got thirty days to respond and this could take some time. Much of it is extremely technical," Tipton cautioned.

"Of course it's technical—that's what computers are all about. How long can we delay the process?" Patton demanded.

God, what a pushy bastard! I should be used to it by now. "Once we respond, it's up to the court to set a trial date. The venue is Boston, so there'll be some travel. Of course Temple could get some relief if the court believes he's suffering losses before the case comes to trial. We'll just have to see."

Attorneys! Patton was furious. For what he was paying this guy you'd think he could find a way out.

"I don't know that much about computers, but if what they allege is true we could have a very difficult time contesting this."

"Can't you lawyers figure out some loophole?"

"We'll try, but let's take this a step at a time. First, I'll need your technical response to all the items, and then I'll draft a rebuttal."

This was aggravation Patton didn't need. International Computer Corporation was his life. He'd struggled for ten years to get where he was. Sure, there'd been some setbacks, but on balance the company was successful. He sure as hell wasn't going to let Mecham Temple and Computer Corporation of America deprive him of what was rightfully his. Maybe he had cut it a little close, but by God he was selling computers. Lots of them: over a billion dollars worth last year. But the costs were eating him alive, and the debt—$80 million and growing! Maybe he should have waited to build his new plant in Atlanta. And he probably should have shelved the Singapore operation, but he couldn't ignore the Asian markets. Tipton had better stop this crap now!

RICHARD STEARNS TOOK THE ELEVATOR to the twenty-fifth floor. He walked to his office, which overlooked the harbor.

"Good morning, Jim. Is Parker in yet?"

"I think he's in the conference room with Mecham."

Richard strolled to the conference room, past the neat little offices of the other seventy-five associates.

"Good morning, Don, Mecham. Any news from Atlanta?"

"No. But I would guess it'd be soon. With the kind of money we're talking about, they'll want to come to terms as soon as possible," Parker announced. "Although it would be helpful if we knew something about their current financial situation."

Seldom did an ambitious young attorney have the opportunity to be involved in so visible a case. True, Don Parker was the lead attorney; would have total control, and share in the settlement, but Richard could bask in the warm glow of legal success. This was important—attorneys needed a track record.

"What he's done is a desperation move. Why? We need to get a banker's perspective on this," Richard suggested.

"How do we do that?" Mecham asked. "ICC's a private company."

"Well, we contact a banker. Not just any banker; one we know well enough to ask him to snoop. They all do it, it's part of the business," Richard speculated.

"Frank O'Connor comes to mind, but he's pretty straitlaced. I don't think we should presume on someone we do business with," Don Parker cautioned.

"Why not? We've made him a lot of money the past few years. He's not *that* straitlaced. Besides, we gave him one hell of a deal on his computer upgrades last year," Mecham snorted.

It was true. Both ICC and CCA had bid on the International Bank of Boston's computer modernization program, a sweeping renovation involving every computer the bank owned. CCA was the successful bidder.

"Do you really want to get Frank involved, Mecham? Surely he'd see it as presuming on our friendship," Parker suggested.

"Of course we're presuming on his friendship! He's a business associate. We bank with him. Call him."

Parker knew better than to argue with Mecham, especially with Richard in the room. If Frank had any apprehension about ferreting out information on Ray Patton and ICC, he'd tell them.

The International Bank of Boston occupied the entire ground floor. It was the largest bank in the state; Frank O'Connor was the CEO and an icon in Massachusetts' financial circles. The bank had been in the O'Connor family for decades.

"Thanks for returning my call, Frank," Parker began. "Would you have time to come up to my office? I'm with Mecham Temple and we have some questions I'd rather not discuss on the phone. Shouldn't take long."

It was a brief elevator trip to the twenty-fifth floor—nonstop on the express serving the top floors. The surge of power lifted O'Connor's spirit as well as his body. He loved the authority ownership gave him. The forty-two-story building was the best address in downtown Boston.

He stepped into the lavish reception area. It had been months since he'd been in Parker's office. The law firm occupied the entire twenty-fifth floor and a portion of the twenty-sixth. The receptionist led him up a spiral staircase to the conference room. God, he thought, Parker must be coining money! He made a mental note to check on when Parker's lease expired.

"So glad you could see us on such short notice, Frank. You know Mecham, and this is Richard Stearns, one of our associates. He's assisting on a case with me," Parker said.

"Actually, it's a case we want to talk to you about. We have a delicate situation with a competitor of Mecham's. I believe you know the company, ICC, the computer company in Atlanta, run by a man named Raymond Patton. We've completed all the paperwork on litigation involving serious patent infringement and other issues. The numbers are in the tens of millions." Parker stopped and glanced at Mecham. "It would be helpful if we knew what kind of financial condition this company's in. We know it's private but...we thought you might have some ideas."

It really was presumptuous to think Frank would breach any fiduciary trust. The O'Connor name was synonymous with integrity and ethics. His response was surprising. "Ray Patton? Yes I know who he is. Mecham will remember that the two of you bid on our computer system some time ago. He didn't get the job and I can tell you why. His bid was considerably below Mecham's so I had our people do some checking. ICC is a multinational operation and we still do quite a few offshore fund transfers for them. But their reputation for service and warranty work is appalling. In fact, Raymond Patton has found himself in trouble before. We felt safer with Mecham," O'Connor paused. "What is it you'd like to know about them?"

"We want to know if they have the resources to pay the large amounts of money we're suing for," Mecham began. "This could force them into bankruptcy. They're a major competitor, but we'd be interested in acquiring them if it came to that. Inside information would be very helpful."

If ICC was threatened financially it could put the International Bank of Boston in some jeopardy. No great danger, but Frank felt it warranted his attention.

"I can't say I feel much compassion for Patton. We'll look into it and see what we come up with. I'll get back with you tomorrow morning."

§§§

For Richard Stearns, what was happening just down the hall from the conference room would be almost as profound as the Patton case. There in the personnel office was Mecham Temple's daughter, Brooke. A recent graduate of Harvard Law, she had just accepted a job with Parker.

Her beauty dwarfed even her considerable academic credentials. Twenty-three, she held every male in the office captive. Mature, court-savvy attorneys stared in childish disbelief. Tall and curvaceous, she sauntered to her office. When Richard left the conference room he nearly collided with her.

"Oh, excuse me! I'm so sorry," he clumsily uttered, steadying himself. "Can I help you with anything? I mean, are you looking for someone?" Her blinding loveliness left him staring. "Let's start over. Whom are you here to see?" He felt like a ten-year-old boy.

"I work here and I think I can find my way, thank you," she said, then disappeared down the hall. His eyes followed her provocative departure. Works here? What in the hell does she do? Women who look like that don't work in law offices.

He quickly made his way to the personnel office. "I wonder if you could tell me who that attractive young lady I just ran into might be? She said she works here."

4

"Oh, you must mean Brooke Temple, Mr. Temple's daughter. She was hired yesterday. I believe she'll be working with Jim Ahern. Actually, her office is right next door to yours."

This would take a tactful approach. No smart-ass remarks or subtle suggestions, just wait for the right moment.

Back in her office, Brooke reflected on her encounter with the handsome man in the hall. His boyish behavior—not an unusual reaction—amused her. She enjoyed the effect she had on men.

Brooke was assigned to work with Jim Ahern. In his mid-forties, balding, married, he'd been with the firm for twelve years. It crossed Brooke's mind that he had long since been passed over for partner. His detached approach to her attractiveness was a welcome relief. This evaporated when Richard Stearns walked into Jim's office. Brooke was sitting at the conference table.

"Hope I'm not interrupting, but I want to apologize for my ill-mannered behavior earlier. My name's Richard Stearns. I hope you'll forgive me."

She looked at him. Tall, ruggedly handsome, well dressed, probably twenty-five or so. Could be intimidating, but that usually wasn't a problem.

"You have nothing to apologize for. It was a casual encounter in the hall; you didn't offend me." Enough, she thought. No need to encourage him. "Now if you'll excuse me, I have work to do."

Not the usual enthusiasm he'd come to expect. Meeting and charming young women was something he had developed into a form of art.

"Well, I'm sure we'll be seeing a lot of each other. I look forward to it." He slowly turned and left.

This might take some serious changes in tactics, he thought. Her sensuous face etched in his mind, he walked to his office.

TWO

FRANK O'CONNOR RETURNED TO HIS OFFICE and called Bill Wolford, president of the bank. Wolford had been with the firm for over twenty years, and Frank relied heavily on his sound, astute skills.

"Bill, would you see what you could find out about that company in Atlanta that bid on our computers awhile ago? Seems they might be in some trouble. Keep it confidential. In fact, give it to Shane. It'll take some sleuthing; he's good at that."

Shane O'Connor, Frank's only child, was a vice president of the International Bank of Boston. Shane's grandfather, Marcus O'Connor, launched the bank in the twenties. Thirty years ago Shane's father had succeeded Marcus.

"Shane, could you come to my office? Your father has a project for you."

The banking business could be painfully boring. After seven years of predictable and mundane performance, Shane wasn't at all sure this was the life for him. On an income in the mid-to-upper five figures, he barely scraped by. And his father was only fifty-seven. *I'll be close to fifty before I take over.*

"What does he want now, Bill? Apparently I've become his personal gofer."

"I don't understand your chaffing, Shane. Someday this will all be yours. Most people don't have it so easy. I've been in this business for over thirty years and I'm still just hired help. Count your blessings," Wolford said. "Remember that computer company in Atlanta that bid our upgrades a year ago? Apparently they're in some kind of financial trouble, and your father would like you to dig up what you can about them. He suggested you keep it confidential."

"You mean International Computer Corporation? Good God, they're one of the largest computer companies in the country. What kind of trouble?"

"I didn't ask. I've found it best not to question your father's directives. I'll see to it you have access to all our computer facilities and any other sources. They do business with us—check with Brian in offshore accounts—but again, this must be done quietly."

At least it was a departure from the usual dull assignments he was given. This could actually be fun, sort of like being a bank detective.

By the end of the day he had what his father wanted. Bill Wolford, one of the most meticulous and computer literate banking executives in the area, assisted Shane with some of the more delicate information gathering. The final results were not good: ICC was in the toilet. With sales approaching a billion dollars a year, their debt was enormous and servicing it was crippling. They had a current balance at the International Bank of Boston of a little over $400,000, mostly for use in offshore transfers. Why was his father interested in this? There was no obvious threat to the bank.

"The computer business must not be as good as I thought, Bill. These guys might not last out the year. What exactly is it my father needs this for?"

"No idea. It was his decision that you do the research. Why don't you take it to him yourself?"

Strange. The bank didn't routinely root around in the financial dealings of a privately held company. But it was intriguing: a billion-dollar-a-year company on the brink of disaster.

"Hi Dad. You asked Bill to have me do some research on ICC. If you're free, I'll bring it right over."

Shane walked the length of the enormous lobby to his father's luxurious office. If only he had access to the O'Connor wealth now.

"This took a little ingenuity but it's all here. What's this all about?"

"Well, give me a summary and I'll fill you in. How bad is it?"

"It's disastrous. Three bank loans ninety days in arrears and a negative cash flow projection. They're in pretty deep."

"This is confidential so keep it under your hat. Don Parker's firm is suing ICC for over a hundred million on behalf of Mecham Temple and CCA. Some patent infringement thing. They wanted to know if ICC had the resources to pay; obviously they don't. Could mean the end for them," Frank concluded. "Let me call Don and arrange for you to run upstairs and brief him."

Shane felt like an errand boy. His father had no idea how demeaning it was to be used like this. He always couched such assignments as preparation for the day when Shane would take over the bank. How the hell did tasks like this prepare him for anything?

He walked to the elevator for the trip to Parker, Haslett and Thomas. This was somewhat routine; he often met Richard Stearns in his office to plan their weekend soirees. Good friends, both enjoyed the single life. But today he was just a messenger. He stopped at the receptionist's counter and announced himself. He was to meet Don Parker.

"It was generous of your father to get the information so quickly, Shane. Let me call Richard in here to take some notes."

Shane led them through what he'd found. Parker frowned as the story unfolded, then turned to Richard. "They'll never survive. This is what Mecham suspected. Better get him on the phone."

The brief meeting over, Shane walked with Richard to his office. As they exchanged casual banter, Brooke Temple emerged from the ladies' room. Richard acknowledged her with a brief hello as Shane stumbled, nearly running over him. Once in Richard's office, Shane demanded to know who the hell she was.

"Calm down. She works here, another attorney. Better yet, she's Mecham Temple's daughter. A little inside track, wouldn't you say?"

"Well, how's it going? Been out with her yet?"

"No. She hasn't been here that long. Besides, she's a little cool, probably has a steady. Rejection isn't good for me. I'll bide my time. She isn't going anywhere. Why don't you meet me at Legal Seafood for dinner? I want to learn more about Mr. Patton and ICC."

"There isn't much more to tell," Shane replied, "though Wolford does have a dossier on his past sins. I'll bring it."

While returning to the bank, a recurring thought entered his mind, re-kindling an image of the endless spreadsheets he had methodically prepared. His position at the bank included responsibility for all the computers, net-working, and electronic fund transfers. In this regard Bill Wolford had been extremely helpful.

As recreational drug users, Shane and Richard had repeatedly specu-lated about the enormous amounts of money to be made in trafficking. They knew all the arithmetic and all the risks. The spreadsheets graphically por-trayed the speed with which the money multiplied. It was a fantasy: neither had the funds or the stomach for the reality.

As the only child of one of Boston's most influential and wealthy men, Shane knew it was only a matter of time until he would inherit it all. But he was thirty years old and time was slipping by. He was be-ginning to lose his hair. A modest salary, as calculated by his standards, barely allowed him the basic indulgences. He still drove the BMW his mother gave him when he graduated from college, and his father provided him with housing in one of his Back Bay residential develop-ments. His intellectual skills were adequate and he'd inherited his father's proclivity for details. His fascination with computers bordered on obsession and occupied much of his time both at the office and at home.

He dated a parade of stunning women. His average looks were offset by the O'Connor name. Much of his dating involved trysts with cocaine-using cocktail waitresses. They were impressed with his flashy appearance and ready access to drugs.

As his job at the bank became more unappealing, thoughts of trafficking in drugs and the enormous amounts of instant money consumed him. He had learned to love the affluent life, but had little sense of how to sustain it or to differentiate between inherited wealth and earned wealth. Maybe he could combine the two and hasten his arrival at the gates of Eldorado.

Shane rushed from the elevator to his office and booted up his computer. He pulled up Excel and made the initial entry; the columns instantly reflected the change. Using $400,000 to make an initial cocaine buy and parlaying it five or six times, the numbers became astronomical.

He printed the spreadsheet and stared in astonishment. The amounts of money blinded him. He checked the entries and re-examined the results: there were no errors, the totals were correct. He had stumbled into an unsuspected source of funds sufficient to solve any number of problems. His dinner meeting with Richard might take longer than either had planned.

THE WAITER WAS CLEARING THE TABLE as they ordered brandy. Shane began, "What's the suit all about? I mean, tell me what Ray Patton has done and what Mecham Temple wants."

"Simply put, Ray has infringed on a number of patents held by Mecham Temple and CCA. It's so obvious, it's pathetic. How he thought he'd ever get away with it is unimaginable. Of course, with what you found out today it might be academic."

"Maybe not. This guy is no saint. From what Wolford gave me, he's been in all sorts of trouble for some time. But listen, his skirmishes with the law could be a windfall for everyone—you, me, Mecham Temple, even Patton himself."

"What the hell are you talking about?"

"In a minute, but first tell me about the timing on all this. I mean, when does it all come down?"

"The short version is, about four weeks. They've got that long to respond. They'll want to meet with us for a possible settlement, but Mecham won't hear of it. Should all be over in about a month."

"When do they want to meet? Would it be here in Boston?"

"I don't know when for sure, but of course it would be here."

"OK, now listen, and don't give me any of that high and mighty attorney crap. I have a plan and I want you to hear me out. As I told you in Parker's office, ICC has over $400,000 in our bank." Shane pulled the spreadsheet from inside his jacket and laid it on the table.

"Here's my plan. I want to meet this guy when he's here. I intend to offer him a way out. Remember all the spreadsheets we've done on drug trafficking? Here's how it's going to work," Shane began. The excitement in his voice and the smug contentment reflected in his face were alarming. Shane had become obsessed. Every gesture and expression reeked of greed. It was behavior Richard had never before seen in him.

"I convince him to use his $400,000 to make a drug buy. If our calculations are even close, the first buy should triple his $400,000. By the time we've made the last buy, we will have netted us—you and me—over $80 million! I've worked it all out and we can do it in less than two months. Patton comes out in great shape. Even if he loses the lawsuit and has to pay the entire amount, he'll be able to pay all his bank loans and get on with his business. I don't know the guy, but he'd be crazy not to go along. What do you think?" Shane said, breathlessly.

Richard was shell-shocked. What made Shane think he'd go along with such a scheme? It was dangerous and illegal. Sure, it was fun to speculate how much money they could make, but that was just a computer game. The thought of the risks made Richard's skin crawl.

Shane laid the spreadsheet in front of him. It was arranged in columns for each buy. At the end of the fifth buy, Richard and Shane had nearly $82 million.

"At that point we don't need Patton's money anymore. I'll still need his bank account to run the money through, but we don't need him. From this point on, all the money is ours," Shane proudly pointed out.

The spreadsheet went on for two more buys without Patton, and showed a net to the two of them of over $600 million. It was unbelievable, Richard thought, $300 million apiece in a little over two months. That was more money than he could comprehend. At 5 percent, it was $15 million a year in interest alone. This was ridiculous, he thought. No one in control of his senses would even consider such a thing. He tingled with excitement.

"There must be more to this than you're telling me. How do you intend to get your hands on enough drugs to pull this off? We don't know anybody well enough to get involved."

"You know Sam, my source for our little weekend drug use? Well, the last time I made a buy from him he said his supplier was in town. He also said this guy is connected in South America and makes big buys for all his distributors. I know Sam well enough to get to meet the guy."

"Shane, I don't want anything to do with this. It's way too dangerous and the risks aren't worth the rewards. I've got my career to think about. If we were caught we'd spend most of our lives in jail. All those years in school down the drain. My folks would die. I just can't do it."

Shane wasn't deterred. He knew Richard well enough to know his needs. Maybe it was a little too much to lay on him all at once. He had a little time before Patton arrived.

"Don't dismiss it out of hand. We'll let it cook awhile. But promise me one thing: let me know when Patton is in town. If you don't want to get involved, I may want to approach him on my own."

RAY PATTON HAD STARTED HIS COMPANY ten years earlier. Since then he'd embarked on an aggressive expansion program to meet the increasing demand for his products. He was forty-seven years old and had struggled in his early attempts to make ICC a viable company. He held degrees in engineering and business from Georgia Tech, had been married twice and had no children. As ICC grew, there'd been frequent setbacks: On several occasions he was charged with deceptive advertising. He had twice been forced to recall over fifteen thousand computers that had defective components. At one time he pled guilty to the theft of ten thousand hard-to-get computer processors. He'd been fined $250,000 and got a two-year suspended sentence with a year's probation. None of this had thwarted Patton's intense desire to succeed. He'd persevered in the face of adversity. In the last five years his company had grown almost exponentially. Much of this he could attribute to the incredible growth in the computer industry.

When CCA's new lines had come out last spring, Ray Patton insisted his engineers take a hard look at the products. He probably didn't intend for them to go as far as they apparently had in emulating CCA's designs. In many instances, ICC's product was a virtual clone of CCA's. Suspecting he might be vulnerable to patent infringement litigation, he'd pressed on anyway. No one was surprised when Mecham Temple's attorney contacted Ryan Tipton.

Tipton had been ICC's corporate attorney since Ray Patton started the company. He was a board member and a close friend of Patton's. He'd watched the company grow from a small operation on the outskirts of Atlanta to become a major player in the industry. He also held substantial shares of its stock.

Over the past two years he had tried to caution Patton about his rapid expansion and the debt they were taking on. Patton convinced him that growth was essential in the computer industry.

THREE

Don Parker had been in the lawyer business for over thirty years, twelve of them in the same location. He was retained as Mecham Temple's attorney the day Mecham started his business. He knew Mecham well and respected his business judgment. He'd watched CCA grow from a small local manufacturer to national prominence. He liked Mecham's prudent, pay-as-you-go approach to expanding his operation. Mecham abhorred debt, and his company was virtually free of encumbrances. CCA was growing faster than anyone had projected. It enjoyed an excellent reputation in the industry, its product lines among the best in the business.

Mecham had founded his company eight years before. Though not as large as ICC, it was gaining rapidly. Mecham insisted his engineers provide their customers with the very latest in speed and ease of use. They had delivered. He now had the fastest-selling computer in the industry. His plant, just outside of Boston, worked round-the-clock to meet demand.

Mecham had never liked Ray Patton, whom he saw as arrogant and self-serving. During the past few years he had become an embarrassment to the industry, Mecham felt. Patton's ethics problems were well known. Despite all this, ICC had grown to be a major force in the industry. Patton had nearly tripled the size of his company in the last couple of years. For Mecham's part, he was content to grow his company carefully, relying on quality, service and some of the best products on the market.

After graduating from MIT, Mecham had found his first job with a small local telephone company when he was twenty-four, leaving after twelve years to start his own company in the electronic components business. For the next eight years he struggled in a highly competitive and capital-intensive environment. He considered himself fortunate to have been able to sell the business at a small profit.

The sale had enabled him to start his computer company. That was eight years ago and he'd never looked back. He'd caught the industry at the time when no single corporation dominated it, and had capitalized on the rapidly growing acceptance of computers. At age fifty-two he was at the peak of his professional career. He had been married for thirty years to Hanna.

They had one daughter, Brooke, who had just graduated from Harvard Law.

Brooke Temple had known she wanted to be an attorney since high school. Her devastating good looks and quick mind set her apart from her peers. Nothing was much of a contest: she'd had her pick of all the young men and was at the top of her class in most subjects. She needed a challenge. Mecham indulged her as his only child and she'd become accustomed to having the best, and lots of it. Cruising through law school, it became apparent that if she was to realize her dream of independent wealth, she must affiliate with the most prestigious law firm in Boston. There she hoped to develop contacts that would pave the way for all she envisioned. Her view of the future included not just a suitable marriage to a virile, wealthy young man with a connected family. No, she had seen how the wives of such men were soon relegated to a life of quiet motherhood and social insignificance. The Junior League was not her idea of power, and power was at the top of her list. But power meant money—money in quantities few people could even comprehend. She doubted Richard Stearns could possibly be such a candidate, but his roguish good looks might be an interesting diversion in the interim. His cavalier approach to her was a challenge. Rarely did men succeed with this passive behavior but she had no current commitment. She viewed him as a project. It would be entertaining to watch him succumb to her ample charms.

IT DIDN'T TAKE LONG. The proximity to Richard's office made the initial encounter inevitable. As he studied the Patton papers his thoughts wandered to Brooke Temple's face. She certainly was one of the most attractive women he'd encountered in recent months. Her detachment was unnerving and made approaching her uncomfortable, but hell, most women behaved that way. They loved to be chased, especially the ones who looked like Brooke. Rejection was only temporary; once he managed to overcome his apprehension, she'd warm up—they all did eventually. It was nearing noon, and a lunch invitation might work. Sensing she was alone, he casually wandered into her office. She was seated at her computer, her back to the door. His greeting startled her.

"Oh, damn it, you scared me," was all she could manage. Collecting herself, she turned to face him. "Don't you knock? I was absorbed in my work and you frightened me. Please don't do it again."

Not a good start. The anger in her eyes heightened her seductiveness. Her long black hair framed a chiseled face highlighted by piercing blue eyes. Her mouth, while not smiling, curved in a slightly suggestive pout. Her perfect teeth completed the portrait as she sat facing him.

"I'm not making much progress. Every time I approach you it's so confrontational. Sorry to bother you," he said and turned to leave. He didn't need this crap. Either she'd come around or she wouldn't. He had plenty of other female friends.

"You didn't bother me, you scared me. There's a difference. Please excuse my abrupt reaction, but it was unnerving. Please, sit down."

Well now, this was better. Maybe she was just being assertive. A lot of women behaved that way these days.

"I really should have alerted you. I know how disturbing that can be. Shall we bury the hatchet and get on with more pleasant things?" God, why did women demand such contrition?

"It's almost lunchtime. There's a delightful little cafe near here. Care to join me? I promise not to anger you in any way."

Why not? She'd established her position. Whether he honored it would soon be evident. Men were so transparent.

The restaurant was a short walk, allowing a flow of casual chitchat. Her tall, exquisite body moved with sinuous ease. She looked up at him with impish confidence. He hoped his manner reflected the pride he felt: it was important to be seen with women like this.

Seated in a secluded corner of the restaurant, they ordered, then looked at each other. She saw an extremely handsome, confident, well-mannered young man, impeccably dressed and comfortable with himself. His dark hair and tanned face accentuated his broad white smile.

"This is a stylish restaurant. I've lived here all my life and never been here. Do you come here often?"

"My good friend Shane O'Connor and I do occasionally. You ran into him briefly a couple days ago. His father owns the bank on the ground floor. Actually he owns the entire building. Where do you usually dine out?"

"Well, my parents live in Andover so I usually stick to that area. We also have a place on Martha's Vineyard, which I love. Great seafood! How about you?"

A little rich for his tastes. He usually gravitated to Legal Seafood and other downtown bistros.

"Oh, I live near the Common so I pretty much stay close to home. Shane's father has a place on Martha's Vineyard. We spend some time there when we can. Like you, I enjoy it."

It was going well, Richard thought. Don't rush it. But it was hard not to cut to the chase. Bedding her could be a challenge.

"I've come to know your father over the past few weeks. Seems like a great guy. Not at all like the one we're suing." He didn't want to dwell on business but it was difficult to avoid their mutual place of employment.

"Do you have brothers or sisters?"

"No. I'm the typical spoiled only child. And yes, my father is a great guy. We're very close. In fact, he was instrumental in my joining Don Parker. I wanted to connect with the best. I have great plans for my future—like you, I suspect. How long have you been with the firm?"

"About two years. When I graduated from Harvard I was elated that Parker wanted me, though my plans for the future include my own practice. Could be a few years, but I'll get there."

God, she thought, it could take more than a few. No, there were faster ways to achieve what she had in mind. She'd find the right man to pave the way. Richard Stearns could languish at Don Parker's firm for an eternity. But he did have a seductive demeanor. It had been some time since she'd had a fulfilling physical relationship.

"What do you do besides lawyering? I mean, do you like theater, sports, travel? You look like the active type."

"I like the Celtics and the Red Sox, theater sometimes, love to ski. And I've developed a yen for boating—been on a couple of cruises to the Caribbean. You?"

"I love skiing. Mostly in Colorado, Aspen actually. My dad has a forty-two-foot sloop at Martha's Vineyard that I adore. We travel to Europe at least once a year. My mother likes that. We all enjoy the theater, and the concerts too."

Good God, the woman lives in a dream world. How could he ever hope to entertain her like that? On his salary he was lucky if he could afford to ski in New Hampshire three or four times a year. But if he was going to even consider pursuing her, he needed some background on her current situation.

"You're a pretty busy girl. Any serious suitors?"

It was a little blunt but he wanted to know now. In the forty-five minutes he'd spent with her, his interest had grown well beyond casual. In fact, this woman had some depth, and her seductive beauty was mesmerizing.

"No, I haven't met anyone who has what I'm looking for. I date occasionally, but nothing serious." She looked at her watch. "I'd better get back. Thanks for lunch."

"I have tickets for the Sox game tomorrow night. Any interest?"

Baseball wasn't one of her favorite pastimes, but she thought it might be fun. At least it would give her a chance to get to know him better.

"Sure. What time?"

"If you'll tell me where you live, I'll pick you up around 6:30. Or we could have an early dinner right after work."

"Let's do the early dinner."

It was the beginning of what Richard thought could be the end of his womanizing. She was startlingly different. Beautiful and bright, yes, but beyond that, insightful and congenial. The conversation was stimulating.

That evening she laughed at his jokes and kidded him endlessly about the dream of his own practice. She listened, but with subdued interest. It was obvious to both that the lengthy process was a daunting one.

During the next few weeks the relationship grew beyond casual dating. Richard was beginning to view her as a long-term possibility. For her part, Brooke enjoyed spending time with him. His sexual performance stirred her womanly instincts, but her strategy didn't include life with a struggling attorney.

Spending more and more time with Brooke, Richard was rapidly coming to the conclusion that her needs would far outpace his ability to provide. Her clothes alone could consume his entire annual salary. At the same time, his attraction to her was growing. They liked the same things, enjoyed being with each other. He'd never been in love, didn't know exactly what it was, but he knew that time away from her felt endless. Losing her was unthinkable.

FOUR

RICHARD AGONIZED FOR DAYS about his last conversation with Shane. At the time he'd dismissed all thoughts of any involvement in Shane's insane plan. The risks simply were out of the question. But as he began to assess his developing relationship with Brooke and the needs it might present, he reconsidered Shane's proposal.

Shane was encouraged when Richard called. He'd spent hours refining the spreadsheet he prepared for their first meeting, and the numbers now literally leaped off the page. He called his local drug source to confirm the possibility of meeting with the man's supplier. It was arranged.

"Apparently your new romance hasn't closed the door on all your old friends. What's happening?" Shane asked.

"Why don't you come up for a minute? I have some news for you," Richard said carefully.

When Shane arrived in his office, Richard closed the door and stood at his desk, hand on his chin, thinking through what he was about to say.

"I've given some thought to your scheme. I'm not promising anything, but I've decided to listen to the plan. I want to know every detail and what my role would be. I want to know when it would start and when it would end. I want to know what the risks are and how you intend to mitigate them. Most importantly, I want to know how much money I could expect to net when it's over," Richard said as he walked to the window, his back to Shane.

Shane had gone over the plan a dozen times. He knew every risk and wrinkle. He knew all the players, not by name but by the roles they would play. Most of all, he knew the numbers.

"Great! I hope you've got some time right now, because this could take awhile. First, everything I'm about to tell you depends, of course, on Mr. Patton. There are inherent risks at the very beginning if he gets righteous and walks out threatening to go to the authorities. I think I've sized up the magnitude of his problem well enough to believe he won't. But if he does, I've planned the meeting between just the two of us in a neutral setting where I can deny everything. I intend to tell him this at the top.

"So, to get started, let's assume he goes along. It may take more than one meeting with him, but let's go on. One of the things that make this work is my position at the bank. For the amounts of money I'm talking about, we must be able to launder it all. Further, it's important we have a legitimate enterprise to pass it through. Patton's company provides that. In order to control the acquisition of the drugs and their subsequent sale to a major distributor, we need a reliable source and a fail-safe method of transportation. Let's take those one a time."

Richard returned to his desk and studied Shane. He'd known him for at least two years and never had he seen such intense focus. He was usually carefree and a bit cynical about his position at the bank. It was both refreshing and frightening.

"Through my local source, I met with his supplier two days ago. His name is Marty Stinson. He assured me, and we'll have to confirm this, that he can put us in touch with growers in Colombia who can provide a flow of material necessary to meet my financial projections. He also assures me he can unload all we can bring in.

"One of the biggest risks is logistics. I have friends at Logan who've assured me they can set up the leg from Miami to Colombia and back. They can also arrange a rather clever midair rendezvous maneuver just outside Miami to get the material into the States. Once inside, we arrange a second rendezvous with Marty to unload and collect the cash. We then fly the cash back to Boston, and I prepare the necessary fund transfer documents for moving the money into Swiss accounts.

"We have other risks at the bank. If anyone were to carefully analyze the large amounts of cash I expect to transfer to the Swiss account, there could be questions—even investigations. But because virtually all of this is done through computers that I control, any paper trail can be concealed. You'll have to trust me on this, I've been through it every way possible.

"The next risk is when we rendezvous near Miami. The material will be transferred in midair and then we land at the drop-off point to meet Marty. This entails two separate sets of risks. First, there's always risk with the Feds: if they intercept our plane we're dead, but that's unlikely because of the confusion we create with the midair transfer. Second, there's the risk that Marty's buyers at the drop-off point may get greedy. They could off us and take the material. I consider that unlikely: they're domestic suppliers, and they don't want to become involved in importing drugs into the country. Further, they'll want a sustained supply, and we're making them a fortune.

"Next is getting the cash from the drop-off point, through the bank and on to the Swiss. Once the cash is in Boston and off the plane, I'll take care of the rest. That's it. You can see by this spreadsheet that after five buys we'll have over $82 million. Think of it, Richard, over eighty-two million dollars!" Shane concluded. God, even he found it hard to believe.

"You forgot to tell me what my role is," Richard snapped.

"Simple. On each buy, you fly with me from Boston to the drop-off point and back. One of us will have to go with Marty to Colombia to evaluate the material and arrange the payment procedure, but that's a one-time deal. I thought you could do it while I'm arranging everything with the planes and at the bank. I think we can get everything in place in a week, including Ray Patton. The first shipment could arrive two days after that," Shane said.

Richard sat down behind his desk and loosened his tie. "At the end of all this, tell me what my share will be," he asked, eyes closed.

"That depends on how aggressive we want to get. The numbers I quoted you earlier assumed we went for five buys, after which we'd have the $82 million. I would vote we stop then. It seems to me the longer we stay in the business the greater our chances of getting caught. Of course, if we want to continue, the numbers just keep getting bigger. If we deal Patton out after five buys and take our share for two more we'll each have over $300 million."

The figures continued to numb Richard's mind. He couldn't even envision so many zeros after any number. But he imagined Brooke could.

"OK, let's do this. I'll let you know when Patton arrives in Boston and where he's staying. Assuming you do get to talk with him, let me know how it goes. If we both decide it looks feasible, we'll continue. Of course if he walks out, it's over and I'm in no way involved," Richard said.

What the hell was he thinking of? Just the idea of trafficking in drugs was repulsive, and what would Brooke think if she knew? Of course she'd never know. And the money, God, what the money would buy!

Shane took the elevator down to his office. He was delighted Richard had decided to go along with his plan. He would be a great asset as the operation began to unfold. Shane would be taking most of the risks. Getting the material into the country was dangerous, but he felt he had the perfect plan. The real risk of exposure came from the bank. A number of people were involved in the handling of large sums of money leaving the country. There were procedures in place to document all transactions, and there were signature requirements for moving certain amounts of money. In his role as vice president of operations, he knew the process well, but it would take a good measure of luck. Any curious computer operator or some overzealous supervisor—even Bill Wolford—could intercept documents or interfere with the plan. Shane would need to be attentive every moment.

Richard sat in his office, excited and apprehensive. The money was mind-boggling. What would he do with $300 million? He could live in luxury on the interest alone. But he had worked hard to educate himself for a life as a legal professional. He liked being a lawyer, it gave him a sense of accomplishment and pride. But it would be a long road lawyering to provide the things he thought Brooke might expect from him.

Richard had grown up in the Boston suburb of Newton with his parents and his younger sister, Sharon. Lester Stearns was parsimonious to a fault. He saved for his only son's education with a discipline that yielded sufficient funds to enroll Richard at Harvard. This was a source of great pride to the entire family. Richard was duly grateful for the opportunity and studied to keep his grades respectable.

Outgoing and socially comfortable, he cultivated campus friends with influential local connections. His striking good looks and athletic abilities endeared him to a host of university women—even some of the faculty. However, his limited financial resources and academic abilities constrained his success.

He devoted what time and money he could to pursuing the less academically endowed young women. This presented fewer intellectual challenges but offered more physical conquests. It also led him to explore the casual use of recreational drugs. The small amounts he found available were enough to impress upon him both the allure of the high and the dangers of addiction.

Graduating at the middle of his class and making use of his impressive cadre of legal associates, Richard had been able to convince Parker, Haslett and Thomas of his potential.

Friendship with Shane O'Connor was inevitable. Shane was older and had access to his father's "toys." Both single and with offices in the same building, the two converged on available young women with considerable success. Richard lived in Beacon Hill, drove a late-model Ford and knew the importance of fashionable attire.

As Richard reflected on the affluent life he'd enjoyed around Shane's father, an inescapable yearning began to take shape.

RAY PATTON SAT IN RYAN TIPTON'S office, the first draft of their response to Mecham Temple's attorney in his hand. They'd spent the morning carefully examining each item; Patton was growing impatient and questioned Tipton on each one.

"They've thrown in everything but the freaking kitchen sink. Why do we have to defend some of this stuff? It's in the public domain. No one can claim patent protection for a lot of this. And how," Patton shouted, "do they determine these outrageous amounts?"

"They obviously think otherwise, but we've stated our reasons for disallowing much of it. If we succeed, it will greatly reduce what they're asking for. We can discuss it with them next week when we're there. That's the purpose of the meeting," Tipton reminded him.

Patton was livid. He certainly had many more important things to do than run off to Boston and argue with Mecham Temple and his attorney. His business needed him here every day. He made every decision and in his absence there was no one really in charge.

"How long will we be there? I can't be gone all week—we have sales meetings and financial reports to go over; I can't just delegate these things to others," Patton snorted.

"Two, maybe three days should do it. If it takes longer than that we've got much bigger problems. If it goes smoothly we could do it in a day. We'll just have to see," Tipton said, calmly.

Tipton and Patton flew to Boston on Monday morning. They took a cab directly to their hotel, where Tipton called Don Parker's office. It was almost ten o'clock and Parker suggested they get started right away. They arrived at the International Bank building at 10:30 and took the elevator to the twenty-fifth floor.

They convened in a sumptuous conference room overlooking the city, and completed the introductions. Present, in addition to Patton and Tipton, were Don Parker and Richard Stearns.

"As counsel for the defendant, I would like to go over certain claims in the complaint. Mr. Patton and his staff have compiled information refuting many of them," Tipton began.

Little progress was made during the next four hours and the meeting was adjourned until the following morning. Parker announced he would have minutes of the meeting delivered to their hotel. Patton and Tipton left.

"I'll take care of preparing and delivering the minutes if you'll tell me where they're staying," Richard volunteered.

"Thanks Richard, they're at the Ritz. How do you size up their opposition to our claims? These guys are all over the map. Of course, we're not technically knowledgeable enough to make a judgment one way or another, but it seems to me they don't have a very well organized plan. I think Mecham or someone from his office should be here tomorrow. I'll call him," Parker said.

"They're limiting their objections to those items that would, I think, have little monetary impact on any judgment. They haven't challenged any of the major stuff. Maybe tomorrow they will, but it looks to me like they're groping," Richard said.

He wasn't impressed with Ray Patton. The man was rude and contentious, and appeared uninterested in much of the proceedings. When he did speak he was loud and animated; when he questioned Don Parker, he seldom listened to the response. But Richard did learn where they were staying.

"Shane, could you come up to my office?" he asked. He was still apprehensive about the whole deal. Maybe Patton would refuse Shane.

"OK, Patton's staying at the Ritz Carlton. Good luck with him. He's not someone I'd want for a friend. On the other hand, for your purposes he's a sitting duck. He doesn't stand a chance; I'd guess we'll get very nearly all we're suing for," Richard said.

"Great. I'll call him this afternoon. What's the amount you think you'll get? I won't tell him, but it would help to give him some notion of the trouble he's in. Also, I can use it to schedule his share of the proceeds. He should be ecstatic."

"Anything I suggest is only an estimate, but I'd guess over $100 million."

Ray Patton and Ryan Tipton sat at the hotel bar, Patton in a rage. What he had worked so hard to put together was in imminent jeopardy. He'd been through some difficult times before, but if Mecham Temple prevailed, together with the bank debt, his company undoubtedly would fail. He thought if he could talk to Mecham alone, perhaps they could work out a settlement. He wanted to get this all behind him. He didn't have the time to deal with it and run his company.

As they ordered another round of drinks, the bartender turned and asked for a Mr. Ray Patton. Patton raised his hand and the bartender slid a phone across the bar.

"Mr. Patton, my name is Shane O'Connor. I'm sorry to disturb you, but I have some information that may be of great value to you. If it's at all possible, I'd like to meet with you this afternoon or evening," Shane said, nervously awaiting Patton's reply.

"Do I know you?" Patton demanded.

"You might remember me. My father owns the International Bank of Boston. A few years ago you bid on a computer upgrade for us," Shane responded.

"Ah, yes, I do remember. What kind of information is it you have?" Patton asked.

"I'm not able to discuss it over the phone, but considering your current financial situation, I believe what I have to tell you may be of considerable worth," Shane said.

Patton really didn't remember this young man. He did keep a small balance at that bank for occasional offshore fund transfers, but aside from that he did no business with them. What on earth could Shane O'Connor know about his financial situation?

"When did you want to meet?" Patton asked.

"I can be at your hotel in fifteen minutes if that's convenient. But I must see you alone."

Hanging up the phone, Patton turned to Tipton. "Some guy from the International Bank of Boston wants to see me. Says he'll be here in fifteen minutes and I have to be alone. I don't have a clue what he wants. Why don't you get lost? I'll call you when we're through," Patton said, dismissing Tipton.

Shane walked the short distance to the hotel, his mind racing. What if Patton dismissed him as some off-the-wall crazy, or called the police? He doubted Patton would do that. The plan he had put together was virtually fail-safe.

He walked directly into the bar and saw Patton standing near a barstool. He was older than Shane remembered, slightly balding, wearing a suit that didn't fit well.

"I'm Shane O'Connor. Glad you agreed to see me. Let's take a table over in the corner." Gathering all his courage as they sat, Shane looked at Patton, trying to assess his interest in their meeting. He saw only anger.

"Mr. Patton, what I'm about to tell you is highly confidential. Some of what I know is public information; the balance I've pieced together myself. The litigation between you and CCA is a matter of public record. Anyone could access that information. I have other sources that suggest to me that if you were to lose this case you might not survive financially. I also want to tell you that if what I am about to suggest is of no interest to you, if you're outraged by it or threaten to go to the authorities, I will deny ever having said anything," Shane said, looking for some signal in Patton's eyes.

There was none; Patton stared at him contemptuously. As Shane outlined the entire scenario, emphasizing the speed with which he could accumulate huge sums of money, Patton's expression changed to one of thoughtful interest. He nodded his head frequently as Shane asked him for clarification of specific items. About to conclude his proposal, he felt sure Patton had taken the bait.

"That's essentially it. We could start within the next week if it's acceptable to you."

Patton was about to smile—something he rarely did. What a gutsy presentation! This guy had done his homework. His financial situation was probably no secret in the banking community, he thought. He was impressed with Shane's candor. It was obviously illegal, but then, O'Connor was taking most of the risks. He himself could claim he'd known nothing about it. But he would have to take precautions: he also knew nothing about Shane O'Connor.

"A very interesting proposition. How do I know I can trust you?" Patton asked.

"You'll have to decide that for yourself. I have a great deal to lose, probably more than you."

Patton sat stroking his chin, looking past Shane. If what he was hearing was possible, it would completely erase his financial problems. He was ignorant about the drug business. Not that it was beneath him—not at all—he'd successfully engaged in illegal activities before. He'd have to think this through before he could give Shane an answer.

"I leave for Atlanta tomorrow evening. Where can I reach you the day after? I don't want to discuss what I'm thinking over the phone. Could you meet me in Atlantic City on Saturday?" Patton asked as he checked his schedule.

"If you call day after tomorrow, you can reach me here," Shane said, handing Patton his card. "Tell me where and when to meet you in Atlantic City; I'll be there."

"I'll tell you when I call," Patton said.

Full of hope, Shane left the hotel. It had gone better than he'd expected. If Patton hadn't wanted to get involved, he would have said so immediately. He looked like the type of man who made quick decisions—yea or nay— and would stick with them. Saturday seemed an eternity away.

RICHARD STEARNS GAVE CAREFUL THOUGHT to his conversation with Shane. He knew that his obsession with Brooke was driving him to a dangerous decision. But as Shane unfolded the plan, it sounded plausible. Shane was taking most of the risks; his own role was minimal. The money was even more than they discussed earlier. He would be independently wealthy with no need to worry about money ever again. He could give Brooke the life she obviously yearned for. When Shane called to brief him on the meeting with Patton, Richard felt mixed emotions about the eventual outcome. The danger in what Shane was proposing gnawed at his sense of reason, but the prospect of the enormous amounts of money overshadowed second thoughts.

"I think we're in. He didn't dismiss it out of hand. He wants me to meet him in Atlantic City on Saturday. He'll call me day after tomorrow. Meet me for lunch and I'll go over the whole thing with you."

They walked together to the same cafe to which Richard had first taken Brooke. It was a short distance and little was said. Shane was deep in thought.

"If Patton agrees to go along, we'll have to begin setting up the entire operation quickly. The first item is to meet with the grower in Colombia. Marty Stinson has agreed to introduce us and help negotiate price and confirm quality. We'll also need to arrange for payment to the grower, and assure ourselves that he can deliver the quantities we're talking about. I think you could be very helpful with all that while I'm making the arrangements with the pilots and setting up everything at the bank. We can both work with Marty in establishing the drop-off points and planning the trip back to Boston with the money. That much cash is damn bulky."

"How do we know the grower is reputable? I mean, how will I know about quality? I assume you and Marty know what the price should be; what is it, anyway?" Richard asked.

"The price should be $10,000 a kilo. We want forty kilos on the first buy. The quantity goes up significantly each time: by the fifth buy we want over 10,000 kilos. That's a hell of a lot of cocaine. Marty will be able to assess the quality. It's his neck with his distributors if it's not top grade. They'll also assist in loading the planes. You'll have to work out the method of payment with the grower. He'll want cash, but find out how. You should be good at that, " Shane said.

"How long do you suppose this might take? I can't be away from the office too long."

"I would think a couple days should do it. Allow two days for travel. You ought to set that up right away," Shane announced.

This is dangerous, Richard thought. He'd heard of Americans going to Colombia and never returning. He didn't know a thing about Marty, or the grower either, for that matter, but if he was going to get involved, he had better be prepared. What kind of people were they? Would they hurt or kill you if they didn't trust you? Why would they want to do business with us? They were in it for the money, just like he and Shane, he decided.

"What's the arrangement for paying the grower? How do we get him his money?" Richard asked.

"You and Marty can work that out. I suspect he'll want the money deposited in some Caribbean bank—probably the Cayman Islands. He'll want to make sure it's there before he releases the load. Marty should know. I'll ask him before you leave."

Shane's contacts in the banking industry would make it easy to do whatever the grower wanted. He would first have to move Patton's money to a Swiss account. From there he could transfer it anywhere.

FIVE

NEGOTIATIONS WITH MECHAM TEMPLE'S attorneys were going nowhere. In fact, at their meeting the next day, Ryan Tipton threw up his hands and suggested to Ray Patton that they leave. The technical items were bogged down in semantics, which Patton wanted to debate. It became clear to Tipton they were losing on all fronts. Now was the time to retreat and strategize anew. The meeting was adjourned after three hours. Patton and Tipton left for Atlanta.

"The bastards won't relent. They've got us, Ryan, on just about every count. The courts won't have much trouble with this one. How does it work? If Temple wins—and my guess is he'll get close to what he's asking—how much time do I have?" Patton asked.

"If he succeeds with the litigation, the court will decree a judgment against us. We'll have twenty days to satisfy the judgment. If we're unable to do so, Temple can force the sale of assets, seize bank accounts and receivables, and generally put us out of business. We could forestall the proceedings by filing for Chapter Eleven bankruptcy, but that could severely damage the business. You could lose considerable amounts of trade because of customer reluctance to buy based on uncertainty about your ability to honor warranty and service. I sincerely doubt that would solve the problem. With the judgment, the bank loans and other payables, the company could be declared insolvent. In that case you'd be forced to liquidate. It's messy no matter what," Tipton said.

This was without any doubt the biggest crisis Patton had faced in nearly twenty-five years in business. If the scenario Tipton described came to pass, he'd be ruined. The business would be gone. He couldn't start over—he would have no assets and no credit.

As the flight attendant brought them a snack, Patton pondered his conversation with Shane O'Connor. It was a wild solution to his problems, but it could be his only way out. The illegality didn't bother him, and the $400,000 in Shane's bank would be gone anyway. If he decided to get involved, Shane would have the money moved before the suit was completed. If the numbers he'd been told were even close, he could be totally out of debt, pay Temple, and get on with his business. The way he figured it, there was little risk; he could deny everything. He decided to call Shane O'Connor first thing in the morning.

Shane was in his office when the phone rang. His secretary announced Ray Patton on the phone.

"Why don't we meet at the Taj Mahal in Atlantic City tomorrow morning at about eleven? I'll be in the main restaurant," Patton said. "Bring all your latest financial data."

Shane was elated. What other choice did Patton have? This was his only way out. Shane had him right where he wanted him. He called to get Richard started for Colombia.

"Yes, I meet him tomorrow morning." Shane could hardly contain his excitement. "Also, Marty Stinson, the distributor I told you about, is still in town and you and I are going to meet him tonight. Be at the Cruise Bar on Northern Avenue at eight o'clock."

This was the same bar where Shane usually picked up his weekend drug supplies. Shane was intrigued with Marty's appearance: he looked like a thirties mobster—dark suit with a black shirt and white tie. He was probably forty-five and had a swarthy complexion. He truly looked like a drug dealer. As they sat at a corner table, Marty looked at Richard with some apprehension.

"Who's this guy? I don't meet with people I don't know," Marty began. "You didn't tell me we'd have company."

"Relax," Shane said. "This is Richard. He's part of the deal. You can trust him—he's an attorney," Shane laughed. "Things are moving faster than we expected. That's why I wanted to meet with you tonight."

Richard was sure he'd made the biggest mistake of his life. Just the look of Marty Stinson made him uncomfortable. How the hell had he let Shane talk him into this?

"You told me last time we met that you'd introduce us to the people in Colombia. We need to set up a lot of things: price, quality, and how the grower gets paid. I'll take care of transportation. Also, can he deliver the quantities we're talking about? As I told you, we'll need ten thousand kilos in about a month."

Marty hoped this guy knew what he was talking about. Going to Colombia on a flyer with someone he knew little about could be very dangerous. If the cartel got wind of ten thousand kilos leaving Colombia without their involvement, things could get dicey. Maybe he'd better just help them get started and get out. He'd play it by ear.

"The price in Colombia is $10,000 a kilo. I'll verify the quality when we're there. I'll have to find out how he wants his money. I don't see any problem with the quantities you're after, but we'll have to confirm that with him. I know I can move all you can get. I'll give you $40,000 a kilo and you do all the delivery work. You get paid in cash when I see the merchandise," Marty said.

It was exactly what Shane had projected on his spreadsheets. The numbers flashed in his mind and he saw an endless source of money. "Sounds OK to me. We should get you and Richard to Colombia as soon as possible. This has to move fast—you should be there in the next couple days, OK?" Shane asked.

"I don't see any problem with that. Tell me about Richard."

"Richard's an old friend. I've known him for years. His office is in my building. He's been very helpful in finding a source of money," Shane hedged. What the hell, all Marty wanted was good stuff and lots of it. "I'll vouch for him. He'll be with me when we meet you at the rendezvous point."

Richard watched Marty. He was everything Shane said he was. He never smiled, and talked with a sneer. Richard felt he was looking right through him. He wasn't sure he wanted to travel anywhere with Marty. God, what had he gotten himself into?

SHANE WALKED THROUGH THE LOBBY of the Taj Mahal. It was crowded, but he could see Patton talking to a security guard near the restaurant. As he moved to join Patton, the guard walked away.

"Glad you could make it," was all Patton said.

They took a table away from the entrance and ordered breakfast. As they waited, Shane looked at Patton. He looked haggard and tired—the look of a desperate man, Shane thought. "Why don't you walk me through the whole scenario?" Patton asked. "I know you intend to use my balance at your bank, but how does it work after that?" Shane outlined the entire plan. When he finished the logistics, he took out his latest spreadsheet and placed it in front of Patton.

"Here's a summary of each buy. The plan is to parlay the proceeds from one buy to the next. At the end of the fifth buy, as you can see, you'll have over $300 million. Our share is 20 percent, and at that time we'll have over $80 million. We take care of all transportation and money movement. If you wanted to continue, the increase becomes almost exponential, but so do the risks. I don't think we want to go on much past five or six buys," Shane said firmly.

This was incredible, Patton thought. In about a month he could be completely solvent, settle with Mecham Temple, and bring all the bank loans completely current. He could continue his business almost as if nothing had happened. And if they continued? He'd cross that bridge when he came to it.

"How do I know the money will be there when the last buy is made?" Patton asked.

"Your share of the money will be in a Swiss account for your use at the time we all agree to stop. Obviously, it's a cumulative thing—that's how a parlay works. The gross from one buy is used to purchase the next. I'll agree to give you notes from the bank for your paper profits but I will continue to control the Swiss accounts. When you want out, give me back the notes and I'll release your share," Shane said.

"What are my risks?" Patton asked

"We're using your account essentially to launder money—a lot of it. If the bank was audited and this discovered, we would both suffer, but because I'm in charge of this function, I can arrange to subvert any ugly paper trail. You see, while there's some risk on your part, the risks to me and to my father's bank are far greater. It's sort of a self-leveling situation: I have every motivation to see to it that nothing goes wrong, thereby protecting both of us. You have the protection of knowing just as much about me as I know about your account. You could even deny you knew anything about what I was doing with your account. Beyond what I've told you, you have no other risks," Shane said.

Patton was impressed. He'd have to trust Shane's assurance that nothing would go wrong at the bank. If Shane were just another employee it would be different, but with Shane having to consider his father's interests and the bank's reputation, it sounded pretty safe to Patton. "When could you get started?" he asked.

"I have everything set to begin as soon as you agree to the plan," Shane replied. "Our first buy could be as soon as four days from now."

"Who else is involved in this with you?" Patton asked.

"Only one other person of any consequence: Richard Stearns, an attorney with Parker, Haslet and Thomas. I'm sure you know who they are. In fact, it was Richard who first told me of your problem with Mecham Temple. Of course, the litigation is a matter of public record, but I would never have known without Richard. He's an eager player and a good partner. He'll be no problem."

"I don't like that. What if Richard goes to Temple and unloads what he knows about our deal?"

"Not likely. First, it would jeopardize his position at the firm. Second, it could be cause for disbarment: he'll have compromised his attorney-client confidentiality arrangement. And last, he's an active player in the enterprise. No, if Richard spills his guts, he implicates himself. He's safe."

Patton pondered what he had heard. The decision was easy. He had no other options.

"Let's do it. Keep me fully informed of your progress and any potential problems. You can reach me at my office most of the time. If I'm not in, leave a message with my secretary."

That was it. Deceptively simple, Shane thought. How easy it was when you found a man in a desperate situation. He had seized the moment and, with a little luck and a lot of work, he and Richard would realize their dream—independent wealth. It was simple arithmetic, he thought, to understand that after the fifth buy he and Richard could go it alone. They wouldn't need Patton anymore. They would need his corporate account, but they wouldn't need him. Even if Patton closed the account, Shane could find ways to perpetuate it. And if he and Richard continued for, say, five more buys, they could parlay their $80 million into hundreds of millions. As he flew back to Boston his mind raced with dreams of homes, cars, girls and beaches.

SIX

RICHARD STEARNS WAS TORMENTED. His obsession with Brooke had taken on a life of its own. His share of the drug proceeds would provide him with all he needed to secure a place in her life—if he survived. He couldn't believe he was taking such risks. What if it all blew up and he was arrested, or worse?

He had worked damn hard to get through school and secure a position with the best law firm in Boston. Why couldn't he be comfortable with that? Why had Brooke put such pressure on him? As he thought about her—her face, her form, her voice—he made up his mind.

But there would be a price to pay. Never in his lifetime could he disclose to her the origin of his wealth. Not only would that jeopardize his safety, it would demean his self-assurance and professional abilities, which he'd worked so hard to impress upon her. No, he'd need to find ways to circumvent any questions she might have. It would take some fancy footwork to cover his absences and the vast amounts of money he envisioned, but he knew it would be worth it.

Brooke Temple kept herself busy with the case she was working on with Jim Ahearn. Her evenings, of course, were spent with Richard. He was exciting, but she questioned the long-term prospects. Mecham had seen great success in his business. He had given her virtually every material thing she'd ever wanted—and material things were what she wanted most. That, and an endless source of funds. Richard's dreams of his own practice, while they were endearing and provided pleasurable hours of speculation, made her wonder if he understood the lean years involved in establishing a profitable enterprise. She had her own agenda, and with her looks and intelligence she could be selective about any commitment. In the meantime, he was a great diversion—and he was only twenty-five.

Richard arranged to be gone from his office for most of the following week. Don Parker agreed to his absence inasmuch as the Mecham Temple-Ray Patton litigation was coming to a close. Creating a plausible story for Brooke was another matter. She knew him well enough by now to be knowledgeable about most of his personal life. His professional life was open to those who worked with him. He saw his family infrequently and had few relatives he felt close to. His best friend was Shane O'Connor.

The best story Richard could come up with was a trip to San Francisco to visit an old college classmate who was in some difficulty regarding the sale of unregistered stock. It was an outright lie. He wasn't admitted to practice in California and he had no classmate living there, but it was virtually fail-safe as far as Brooke was concerned. He didn't know where he would be staying and didn't have a phone number. He would call her when he arrived. He could easily cover the few days he would be gone.

IT HAD BEEN YEARS SINCE MARTY STINSON had traveled to Colombia. The contact he knew was safe enough, but any hint of dealing around the cartels was risky. The initial amounts Shane was proposing might be no problem, but if the larger deals materialized there could be real danger. On the other hand, if what Shane proposed was true, it could mean enormous amounts of money. He had distributors around the country begging for product. If Shane could deliver the amounts he suggested, Marty could quit scrounging for small quantities and concentrate on the larger dealers. True, there was some danger in dealing with so much cash, but it was definitely worth it. He'd deal with the cartels somehow.

SHANE CALLED RICHARD FROM THE AIRPORT in Atlantic City to make sure he had arranged to be gone the next week.

"It's all set with Patton—he went for it with both feet. It's important you get to Colombia early next week, preferably on Monday. I'll call Marty to let him know the plan is on. How's everything at your end?"

"I'm set. I can leave anytime. Tell Marty I can meet him at Logan. I've checked the schedule and there's a flight to Bogota leaving at 8:30 Monday morning. Let me know if that's OK with him."

"Good. If I can reach him, I'll call you right back."

During the long flight, Richard and Marty became better acquainted. Marty talked about his lengthy involvement in the drug business. He had been arrested twice long ago as a youngster in Brooklyn. Since then he had managed to avoid the authorities, and boasted about his ability to ply his trade with impunity. He didn't divulge his contacts but talked at length about his friend Salvatore, whom he had met some years ago while putting together a series of buys for his contacts in New York City, who were later arrested. Since then he had kept in touch with Salvatore and had done a few small deals with him.

As the plane touched down, Richard felt a little better about his role in the operation. He was to let Marty make the introductions and verify quality. Once the price was established, Richard would determine how Salvatore wanted his money. The two of them would negotiate for future quantities.

Salvatore met them at the gate and loaded their bags into an old station wagon. It was hot and just getting dark as they left the airport. Salvatore and Marty sat in front, renewing their friendship. They conversed in Spanish, which annoyed Richard and rekindled some apprehension. He was in a strange country with people he scarcely knew, didn't speak the language, and was on a mission that was dangerously illegal. He had no way to protect himself if something went wrong, and he wasn't even sure he'd know if things started heading in that direction.

He gripped the armrest as the station wagon bounced along a gravel road. Trees and bushes grew along the roadside, nearly brushing the car. He fully expected to see wild animals dash across the road. After an hour the terrain became hilly, then mountainous. Salvatore slowed as the winding road became difficult to traverse. After another hour they came to a clearing on what appeared to be a plateau. As they rounded a sharp corner, Salvatore pulled into a driveway that led to a large open area.

Here there were six large buildings with roofs supported only by posts. Bright lights illuminated the interiors, where dozens of people bent over long tables, filling clear plastic bags with a white powdery substance. Richard was sure he was witnessing the preparation of the material he was here to buy.

The car pulled in front of a smaller, enclosed building and stopped at a large, roll-up garage door. To one side was a smaller door for pedestrian entry. Salvatore motioned them in as he switched on the lights. Inside was a large, sparsely furnished office with three desks and chairs. Salvatore went to a cabinet at the far end and removed three clear bags of a white material. He placed them on the desk in front of Marty and sat in a chair, watching.

Marty smiled and said something in Spanish. They both laughed and Marty reached for one of the bags. He pulled a flap to open it, wet his right index finger and touched the contents. His finger went to his tongue and he tasted the white powder. He smiled, and repeated the process with the other two bags. This must be the quality control process, Richard thought.

Marty sat down at the desk and tapped out a two-inch line from each bag. He then rolled a dollar bill into a tube and inhaled the lines. Finished, he sat back in the chair and began to speak in English. "Is this the quality we can expect with everything we buy from you?" Marty asked. This was mostly for Richard's benefit.

"Precisely. We have been processing *coca* here for many years. We have refined our methods and deliver only the finest product. We are sure you will be pleased with it," Salvatore said proudly in perfect English. Richard was relieved to hear the exchange.

"How do you deal with the cartels? I mean, don't they keep an eye on you?" Marty asked, afraid of the answer.

"My attitude toward all the so-called cartels is one of respect. If they show an interest in what I'm doing, I will work with them. We're all in the same business, and they have never interfered with me."

"What's your price for this quality?" Richard asked, timidly.

"Ten thousand dollars per kilo here at our plant. We will assist you in loading your planes, and you may verify the quality before your pilots leave. We will also confirm the weight in your presence. We leave nothing to chance. If you intend to purchase the quantities Marty has indicated, we want you to be happy. We seek a sustained market. We are no longer interested in small, one- or two-time purchases. We are looking for a long-term relationship with people who can take our entire production," Salvatore said. Richard was impressed with his articulate speech.

"I'm sure we will be able to take the quantities Marty has told you. We also need to know how you prefer to be paid," Richard asked.

"We have an arrangement with the Island Bank of Cayman. We have known the owners for many years. We insist that certified funds in American dollars covering the amount you have ordered be in that bank one day prior to shipment. As I understand it, your first order is forty kilos; you must deposit $400,000 in that bank one day before you intend to pick it up. I think that makes it easier for both of us, don't you agree?" Salvatore asked with a smile.

Richard was beginning to like him. He had a pleasant voice and an engaging smile. He appeared to have the business end of the enterprise well under control.

"Fine. Do we need an account number or something to direct the funds to your bank?" Richard asked.

"I'll give you that information when we leave. Now, we're all going to *mi casa* for something to eat, and then I'll show you to your rooms," Salvatore said proudly.

This wasn't so bad, Richard thought as they were driving to the airport the next day. Salvatore was much more civilized than he'd expected, and the accommodations at his home were excellent. His wife had prepared a tasty Latin dish, and his daughters—both in their early twenties and very attractive—had joined them for dinner. One, Constancia, spoke acceptable

English and had joined in the conversation. The other, Delia, was shy, but kept her flashing eyes riveted on Richard throughout the meal. It was difficult to eat and keep his eyes off her ample bosom. His thoughts drifted to future trips.

The journey back to Boston was tiring, and Richard slept most of the time. Before they left, Salvatore had given him the account information and the banker's name.

"I'm impressed with Salvatore and his family. I expected to meet a group of armed *banditos* waiting to attack us. He seems refined, and comfortable with his business. Does he have no fear of the authorities or other growers?" Richard asked Marty.

"I've known him for almost twenty years and he's always been exactly as you saw him. He's a very religious man and devoted to his family. If he's had any trouble with anyone, he never told me," Marty said.

Richard felt he and Marty had accomplished what they set out to do and he was comfortable with all the arrangements. He was sure Shane would agree. As they approached Boston, the reality of what they were involved in surged in his chest. If it was all going to be this smooth, he might begin to relax.

He called Shane the minute he arrived home that night. It was close to ten o'clock and he was exhausted but he couldn't wait to give Shane the good news.

"Everything went great. The grower is a guy named Salvatore Diaz and he's much more civilized than I would have dreamed. Spoke perfect English and we were able to close on every item on our agenda. He wants the money transferred to a bank in Cayman. I have all the information you'll need. Even Marty was enjoyable. I'm impressed so far," Richard said.

"Good. Everything is set up at the bank. I can make the transfer tomorrow morning and set up the pilots. We should have the first buy complete in less than three days. I'll contact Marty for the drop," Shane said as he hung up.

SEVEN

RICHARD WALKED INTO HIS OFFICE feeling a new sense of security. How long would he stay with the firm? After five buys he and Shane would have over $80 million in the bank. If they continued, it would approach $650 million. God, the risks were beginning to haunt him. The numbers were mind-boggling. In the years since he had joined Parker, his mission was to have his own practice. He'd spent many hours pondering just how he would do it. Now it was within his reach. Or did he really need it now? There was so much to sort out.

He was anxious to see Brooke. They'd been apart for nearly a week, the longest since they had met over a month ago. He missed her terribly but he obviously couldn't call. He had put together the pieces of his story about the trip to California, and was rehearsing it when she walked into his office. "Hello stranger. Your old classmate must have kept you pretty busy. Were you able to keep him out of jail?" she joked.

She was impossibly beautiful. How had he managed to be away from her for almost a week without even hearing her voice? He had missed her more than he wanted to admit. She was the object of all his current activity but he couldn't utter a word about it. He'd better make the California story convincing.

"Hello angel," he said, closing the door and taking her in his arms. Her perfume was intoxicating and the smell of her hair warmed his whole body. Her moist lips struck at his very soul. God, he was sure he loved this woman!

"I missed you. Sorry I wasn't able to phone, but it was a busy time. The flights were long and the time difference made calling impossible. I think I was able to help him, though. I wasn't fully aware of his situation until I got there. He's married now and has two beautiful children. He'd made some foolish mistakes with a client but I think I was able to help. He needed a friend to help sort out his options. But it's great to be home," he finished, relieved.

He tried to detect from the look in her eyes whether she believed him. It was impossible to tell. For just a moment she held his eyes in her gaze, then looked away. She walked to the window and folded her arms, her back to him. "I thought the least you could do was call. I missed you. Maybe I've misjudged our relationship. I couldn't dream of being away from you for almost a week without hearing your voice," she said, turning toward him. His handsome face and tall, lean frame excited her. Maybe she was being too harsh. Don't overdo it, she thought. "But I forgive you," she smiled as they rushed to each other.

The crisis was over, Richard thought. It was cruel to lie to her, but he had succeeded in forestalling further questions. He knew it wasn't the last time he'd have to go through this.

As Brooke returned to her office, she pondered their conversation. An uncomfortable twinge of misgiving churned her stomach. Something was off center. Her legal mind wouldn't let it go. She filed it in that mental hinterland where unfinished business languished—sometimes forever.

THE NEXT THREE DAYS WERE FILLED with tension. Shane arranged for the pilots from Miami to be in Colombia on Tuesday night. They would return to the Miami area in the early hours of Wednesday morning for the midair transfer. Shane was particularly proud of this daring maneuver. He and the Miami pilots had contacted a former air force pilot who had flown KC-135 refueling planes. He managed to find one and they tested the concept. It was a little dicey, but they were able to transfer small sandbags—simulating bags of cocaine—down the tube into a waiting DC-9 as it flew beneath the KC-135. They were just outside the controlled airspace near Miami, and the DC-9 was on the fringe of radar control. Technically it had never left the United States. This was a fine point, but it worked during practice runs. The KC-135 was available to make the flights to Colombia.

Shane and Marty established the rendezvous point in the States—a small airfield near Tampa. Shane and Richard would fly from Boston to meet Marty and collect the cash. If all went well they would be back in Boston before Wednesday morning dawned. It would mean Richard would be away the entire night. He and Shane would leave Boston three hours before Marty was to meet them at the rendezvous point. The transfer would take an hour, then the return flight to Boston.

THIS WOULD MEAN MORE DECEPTION, of course. What would he tell Brooke this time? And the next, and the next? He had to come up with an ongoing reason to be away overnight once or twice a week for at least the next month.

He invented the Martha's Vineyard hotel story. Shane and Richard had kidded for years about owning a small hotel on the little island. It had become a pastime for them long before Richard met Brooke. Neither was very serious but it was fun to speculate. They had gone there often to spend weekends on Shane's father's boat and to enjoy the beach house. They frequented Carly Simon's trendy and expensive club in Oak Bluffs.

If he structured his story properly, he could easily attribute his absences to lengthy negotiations. Shane would be his partner and could confirm his whereabouts. It was clumsy, but it should work. Brooke would have little choice but to believe it, Richard thought.

The day Richard returned from Colombia, he and Brooke had dinner together. They had put aside his California trip and it wasn't discussed. Both were relieved that their relationship was back on the exhilarating level; neither wanted to dredge up past unhappiness.

During dessert, Richard began to unfold the Martha's Vineyard hotel yarn. He was at his best taking a listener through tales, either real or imagined. He put the best spin on the financial aspects of the investment. There were enormous amounts of money to be made with the right property, and he and Shane had spotted one. In fact, they were going there next Tuesday night to begin negotiations. Shane's father had agreed to finance the entire purchase, he lied.

Deceitfulness was difficult for Richard; it wasn't his basic behavior pattern. He was an honest, forthright and charming individual. In fact, those were the very attributes that had prompted his interest in a legal career. Lying to Brooke was very distasteful. He was sure she saw right through him. It pained him when she showed great interest in the hotel scheme.

"That's wonderful. What a delightful little island—I've spent many pleasant summers at my parents' beach home. Which hotel do you have in mind?" she asked, her eyes full of anticipation.

He wasn't ready for such a cooperative response. He expected suspicion and questions about the viability of such an investment, not enthusiastic acceptance and support.

"I'm not sure. Shane has all the details. I should know more after our meeting Tuesday night. I think he's looking at more than one. He knows far more about the island than I do. I'm glad you like the idea," he said, somewhat confused.

He was set for the first pickup, convinced that Brooke had bought the hotel story. She even seemed to like it. He'd have to make sure Shane was briefed.

H_E MET S_HANE AT L_OGAN AT ELEVEN O'CLOCK Tuesday night. The Lear was gassed and ready for takeoff. They were to meet Marty and the rendezvous plane at Tampa at 3:30 A.M. This was the first payoff for all the planning and risks. It was exciting, and the air of danger heightened the intensity of the flight.

As they landed at the small airport there was little activity. When the Lear rolled to a stop, they deplaned to the tarmac and spotted two large vans parked in the shadow of the small terminal. There were no commercial planes and few people about. They watched as Marty emerged from one of the vans and walked briskly toward them. They met him about halfway and stopped to exchange greetings.

"Everything set?" Shane asked.

"My people are here. Where's the other plane?" Marty demanded.

"Should be here momentarily. We've planned this down to the last minute, but weather could have delayed them," Shane said, searching the black sky for a sign of the other plane.

Richard looked at the vans, lined up like military vehicles. He saw no one inside, but suspected they were full of armed thugs. He knew that was where the money must be.

Moments later, a DC-9 dropped from the sky and they heard the screech of rubber on the runway. As it rolled near the Lear and stopped, the vans slowly moved into place. Had this been Miami, hordes of customs agents would have descended on them. No such greeting occurred at this remote airport.

The transfer took less than fifteen minutes. Each van was equipped with a scale and what looked like a small chemical lab. Richard and Shane looked on as the material was inspected and weighed. When the process was complete, Marty brought them two black attaché cases. The three of them climbed into the Lear and inspected the contents. Here was their first look at what they hoped would be the beginning of untold wealth. They were looking at $1,600,000 in cold, hard cash.

"My people are pleased with the transaction and they're anxious to get the next shipment. Let me know when you're ready," Marty said, and left.

Not one hitch, Shane thought. This might go on longer than he'd originally planned. "What do you think? Not bad! We've doubled our combined annual salaries in one night," Shane announced proudly. Richard looked on speechless. Was he really a part of all this?

P_ATTON WAS IN A SALES MEETING when his secretary put the call through.

"I'll take it in my office," he said.

"Give me some good news, Shane."

"Perfect. You've tripled your money and the next buy is scheduled for

Friday night. I'll send you all the paperwork. We should complete the fifth buy in two weeks," Shane quickly announced, a little nervous about explaining all this on the phone.

Patton was overjoyed. In two weeks his financial nightmare would be over. It was easier than he'd ever dreamed. In fact, he thought, why stop after five buys? He'd talk to Shane about that.

Shane was pleased with the way everything turned out. His planning had been superb and everyone was happy. He moved the money to the Swiss account and prepared deposit slips for Patton. He also prepared an official bank promissory note for $400,000 to Patton. He signed his father's name to the note and FedExed the slips and the note that afternoon. He prepared files of the transaction for Patton, Richard and himself, and locked them in his desk. He then went to the computer room and coded the transaction so only he would know the password. The first buy was 100 percent complete. He then set the second in motion, hoping it would go equally well. He needed a drink.

Richard wanted to tell someone about the incredible journey they'd taken. Of course that was impossible, but his exuberance showed. Brooke was the first to see him. He'd had no sleep; had barely had time to shower and shave. Now he had to shift gears from being a drug trafficker to being an attorney and hotel purchaser, and make it believable.

"Well, are you the proud owner of a hotel? You look like the proverbial cat. Did you get your canary?" Brooke joked.

"It was a very fruitful meeting. The owner wants to sell but his wife is having second thoughts. We meet with them again Friday night. I'm sorry I have to be gone again so soon, but we want to complete the deal as soon as possible. These things take longer than either of us thought," Richard said, feigning disappointment.

"Which hotel is it?" Brooke asked.

Richard was ready. He and Shane had discussed the hotel scenario just last night. Shane had kidded him about being a henpecked single man.

"It's the Oak Bluffs Inn. It's a small place but we think it has great potential. It's just up the street from Carly Simon's 'Hot Tin Roof,'" Richard said.

Brooke knew exactly where it was. Oak Bluffs was a little community near Edgartown. Mostly tourist facilities, but quaint. There weren't any hotels of any size, but it was popular in the summer. It would be interesting owning a small hotel in such a trendy place, she thought.

"Are you close to a deal? I mean, money-wise."

"We're not sure," Richard said. "We'll know more after the meeting Friday night." He wanted to end this conversation as soon as possible: it was phony and he felt he was beginning to sound that way.

EIGHT

THE NEXT BUY WENT AS SMOOTHLY AS THE FIRST, even with the increased amount of material. Richard and Shane were elated. The long flight was tedious and the transfer fraught with tension, but the reward was worth it. Their accounts were growing. Shane once again completed all the paperwork and re-coded the computer, then sent each player an accounting of his balance.

Brooke was mildly interested in Richard's hotel endeavors but she was more concerned about his behavior. He was less forthcoming about his personal life than he had been. She never pried or intentionally queried him about his friends or activities. Their relationship seldom allowed time for such conversation.

In the time since they had become almost inseparable, they shared everything. Richard's trip to California and the nights he was away for his hotel activities were beginning to annoy her. He seemed defensive and sometimes evasive about his activities, almost as though he was hiding things. She had begun to view their relationship as worth developing for future exploitation, something she almost always did with people she didn't quite know what to do with in the immediate. Eventually she could sort out where he fit in her long-range plans. She did hope, though, that his indifferent behavior would change.

BY THE TIME THEY COMPLETED THE FOURTH BUY, the whole operation had become almost routine. Richard sat at his desk, looking at the latest accounting from Shane. The two of them had over $20 million in the Swiss account, and Patton must be well on his way to $85 million. As he reviewed the account, he became acutely aware of his share of the money. It had always been just a number; now it was beginning to feel like real cash. He wanted to spend some of it. If Shane was right, and it looked more and more certain that he was, by this time next week he would have over $40 million for himself. It was amazing how fast it was growing!

He needed some new clothes, maybe even a new car. Certainly he deserved some pleasures after all the risks he'd taken. He called Brooke to meet him after work. He left early for an appointment with his tailor—he wanted to order at least two new suits and a few custom shirts. The tailor was near the restaurant where he would be meeting Brooke, so he walked the short distance. All the measurements and material selection took an hour. As he reached for his checkbook, he realized he had left it in his desk. What a stupid thing to do, he thought, but he wanted the clothes as early as the tailor had promised them. If he paid today, he could have them by the weekend.

He called Brooke to have her get the checkbook from his desk. He would get her settled in the restaurant and run back to the tailor. It would only take a few minutes and it was faster than going back to his office.

Brooke was looking forward to seeing Richard. The longer she knew him, the more attached she felt. God, she wasn't getting gaga, was she? She closed her office door and went next door to Richard's desk. He had said the checkbook was in the center drawer. As she opened it, a bundle of papers fell to the floor. She found the checkbook and, as she was replacing the papers, noticed that they were on International Bank of Boston letterhead and signed by Shane O'Connor, She couldn't help seeing they were statements of an account in Richard's name. The balance was astounding! He was doing much better than she suspected, and much better than most attorneys his age. Maybe she should reevaluate Richard's abilities. How on earth could he have amassed this kind of money so quickly? The date on the letterhead was only two days ago and all the deposits had been made within the last three weeks.

As she walked to the restaurant, her mind wouldn't leave the numbers on the statement. Richard had never mentioned anything about having so much money. If a relative had left it to him, surely he would have told her. She could think of no rational explanation. He probably had some investments, but nothing like this. She debated even mentioning that she'd seen it. The magnitude of the account and the time of accumulation were very strange indeed. Was he into something illegal? That could explain his recent behavior. But what? She sometimes wished her legal training didn't demand answers for everything. Why did things have to be black or white? But it wouldn't leave her. She knew that sooner or later she would have to ask him.

She found him waiting at their favorite table. As always, his virile good looks stimulated her. Whatever he was doing to accumulate the money couldn't be that bad. She could probably forgive him for not telling her, whatever it was.

Mecham Temple was very close to his daughter. She was his only child and he had indulged her all her life. They confided in each other and became not just father and daughter but the best of friends. She could tell him anything—and often did. When she was growing up, they'd entertained the notion of her joining his company, but it was early in the company's growth and he'd had his hands full just managing day-to-day operations. When she graduated from high school, they both decided that a law degree was more appropriate. She liked working with people and felt her future was in law. When Don Parker insisted she join his firm when she finished school, the decision was made. She graduated from Harvard Law in the top 5 percent of her class and couldn't wait to get to Parker's office. She was on her way and she knew her father was very proud.

Brooke hadn't visited her parents since Richard began his California mission. She told them about her developing relationship with him and they suggested she bring him to dinner. She hadn't been able to find the time with all of Richard's soirees on Martha's Vineyard. With her discovery in Richard's office, she had to talk to her father.

"Richard will be gone this Friday night and I wonder if I could spend the night with you guys. It's been too long since I've done that and I miss you both. Besides, I'd love some home cooking," she told her mother.

Brooke and Hanna were close. Because Mecham had no sons, he had dealt with Brooke on a man-to-man basis most of her life. He sometimes thought that even if she were a son, they couldn't be any closer. It was a great arrangement for both of them.

She arrived with a change of clothes, and sat in the den with her father while Hanna prepared dinner. After they'd exchanged chitchat, Brooke got down to the real reason for her visit.

"I've told you about him and of course you've met him. He's attractive and fun to be with. We do have some things in common but I need to know a good deal more about him. I'm not interested in his long-term struggle to build a practice of his own, but something else has come up. He asked me to get his checkbook from his desk two days ago..." She told Mecham what she had found, including all the numbers.

"Do you know any way he could make that much money in just three weeks?" she asked.

"Not in my business, but I suppose he could have invested in some commodity or something. It does seem extraordinary. What do you suspect?"

"I don't know. He's been acting strange for over two weeks. He's evasive and comes up with rather odd reasons for overnight absences. I'm not jealous; I don't suspect he's seeing someone else, he seems committed to me.

But his behavior is almost bizarre, and now this insane plan to buy a hotel on Martha's Vineyard. He says Shane's father, Frank O'Connor, will finance the purchase. Why would he want a loser like that with his apparent resources? I do care for Richard but I've got to know more about what I've discovered."

"You said the account was with the International Bank? I suppose I could prevail on Frank O'Connor to look into it. It's a little unusual and he's pretty straitlaced about confidentiality, but I know him fairly well. After all, it's my daughter we're talking about. Let me think about the best way to approach him. I don't want him to think this is some lover's inquisition; he wouldn't find that very convincing. I could suggest that you're considering marrying Richard and want some financial background. Apparently that's done rather routinely nowadays," Mecham said, with a wink.

"That sounds great. And it is, as you say, done routinely 'nowadays.' That's a perfect entrée. He couldn't refuse you. How soon could you talk with him?"

"I'll call you tomorrow and let you know."

FRANK O'CONNOR LED A VERY ACTIVE LIFE. His bank was his life and he loved it. He was also very good at it. It was a family enterprise and had been for decades. He looked forward to the day when Shane would take over. His social and business connections enabled him to develop invaluable associations with powerful and influential people, whom he cultivated with casual ease. When time permitted, golf and boating were his recreational activities. He entertained lavishly at his home or at the Summerset Club, on Beacon Hill. He and his wife were members of the area's most prestigious country clubs, at which they dined often.

Most Wednesday afternoons, he and Mecham Temple played golf, but today Mecham had called to say he wouldn't be able to. He asked whether Frank could meet him at the downtown club for lunch instead. They had known each other for over a decade and lunched together often.

Mecham felt some apprehension about presuming on Frank O'Connor for such a personal matter. True, Frank had managed to get him and Don Parker some rather confidential information on Ray Patton and ICC, but that was a business issue. On the other hand, Frank had known Brooke since she was a very young girl. Mecham and Hanna often entertained Martha and Frank in their home. Surely, Frank would understand his need.

They were settled at a corner table in the sumptuously furnished club, and drinks were served.

"Frank, I have a favor to ask of you. As you know, my daughter Brooke is now working as an attorney in Don Parker's office. Not long ago she met a fellow attorney, also with Parker's firm, whose name is Richard Stearns. You met him a few weeks ago. I know him because he's working with Don on our litigation with ICC, Ray Patton's company."

"Yes, I remember meeting him in Parker's office a few weeks ago. Seems like an ambitious and solid young man."

"To the point. Brooke is quite smitten. Marriage might be in the cards. In any event, young people do things a little differently these days. She wants to know more about his financial situation before she gets any more deeply involved. I'm led to believe this is done routinely, or I wouldn't even ask you. Brooke has reason to believe he keeps large sums on deposit in your bank. In fact the amounts mentioned were considerably more than one might expect given his age and his time with Parker's firm. I thought if you could confirm the amounts and their possible source, I could put my daughter's mind at ease. I hope this doesn't cut across the grain of confidentiality," Mecham said.

"Normally we don't discuss our clients' balances, but in this case I suspect I can make a discreet inquiry. I'll have Bill Wolford look into it and get back to you in a couple of days. What balance are we talking about?" Frank asked.

"Apparently, it's a pretty sizable amount—almost $10 million. I admit Brooke is somewhat materialistic and if this account can be confirmed, Richard won't have a chance. She's a pretty determined little gal once she makes up her mind."

When Frank returned to his office he summoned Bill Wolford.

"Bill, I need another little favor for Mecham Temple," he said and outlined what he needed. "When you find the account, just give me a longhand status."

Wolford was a stickler for organization. Every department head in the bank reported to him and he always delegated specific duties to the appropriate individual. Frank's request would fall in Shane O'Connor's area of responsibility. "Shane, would you please stop by my office when you get a minute?" Bill asked. "Your father asked me to get some account information," Wolford said as he passed a handwritten note to Shane. "He didn't sound like it was terribly important, but would you see what we have?"

On the note, Shane read the name and the amount followed by a question mark. His hands froze, his face turned white, and he thought he might pass out. What had happened? Why information on Richard Stearns? He thought quickly. He had sent Richard an accounting of his share, but

Richard wouldn't show it to anyone. Not Richard, who'd been so worried about getting involved in the first place; who wouldn't even talk about it on the phone. Something was terribly wrong. How would his father know anything about Richard's account? It wasn't even an account, really. What he sent Richard was only a statement showing his share of their Swiss account, but the Swiss account number was shown on it. "Sure, I'll take care of it," Shane managed to say. "Anything else?" All he wanted to do now was call Richard.

Back in his office, Shane was palpably shaken. Everything had gone so smoothly. It didn't make any sense. His father rarely got involved in this type of issue. Was Wolford leveling with him? Maybe he had stumbled onto something. Was this a subterfuge to get more information? Shane's mind raced, searching for some reasonable explanation. His mind was a torrent of possibilities, none connecting. No one knew anything, he was sure. He had been so careful. He should call Richard, but first he wanted to go over every detail of what he had done. Richard would panic—God only knew what he might do.

As the reality began to sink in, he knew that somehow, someone else must have seen the information he'd sent Richard. But he knew Richard would never jeopardize his own position: he was too careful; too concerned about being caught. He should have cautioned Richard how sensitive the statement could be. But Richard's an attorney—he should know!

"Richard, meet me in the coffee shop around the corner right away. I've got to talk to you," Shane said, ominously. Richard's heart was pounding as he entered the elevator. He had lived in terror of this moment. He knew something was wrong. Shane had convinced him the plan was fail-safe; it didn't sound that way now. "Don't get nervous. It might not be as bad as it looks," Shane said and told him what had happened.

"How would your father even know about any account I had at your bank? The account isn't with your bank anyway. What the hell's going on?" Richard whispered, loosening his tie.

"Where do you keep the records I send you?" Shane asked.

"In my desk, top drawer. I'm the only one who's ever in there."

"Do you keep it locked?"

"No, I never have. We don't have that kind of problem at the office."

Shane thought for a moment. He kept all his records locked in his desk. Why would Richard be so careless?

"At the completion of each buy, I send you and Patton summaries of the transaction. I do that because Patton insisted on it. I included you because you're part of the team. It seemed fair to let you know where we stood, particularly because you were so damn worried about how much money you were going to have. I assumed you knew how delicate the information was and how important it was to keep it in a safe place.

"The only other possibility is Wolford. As careful as I've been, he could have stumbled onto something. The computer would be the only source of information, but I've coded it carefully, and he could only have accessed it by some freak accident."

Both men shook their heads. Neither knew what had happened, who was responsible, or what danger they faced.

"Wolford asked to see what we have on your account. You have no account. That will be the first thing I tell him. If his behavior is any indication, it didn't sound like anything urgent. I'll also double-check all my computer tinkering to make sure it's safe. In the meantime, I want you to get those papers out of your office. Take them home or get them into a locked box."

Dazed, Richard returned to his office. The euphoria he'd experienced just hours ago had turned to bitter fear. His gut ached. His suspicions were confirmed—he never should have let Shane talk him into this insane scheme. He'd be ruined and Brooke would be history.

He went directly to the center drawer of his desk. As he frantically pulled it open, he willed the papers to be there. They were. They had completed the fifth buy and Shane had given him the last summary. He went through them three times. They were all there. He glanced at the last entry; he had over $40 million in the Swiss account. A lot of good it would do him now. He folded the papers, put them in his inside jacket pocket and sat down at his desk, his face buried in his hands. He thought of taking the money and skipping to Colombia. Maybe he could live with Salvatore and his beautiful daughters. What a mess! If Shane couldn't cover for them at the bank, it was over, he thought.

NINE

R̶AY PATTON SAT IN HIS OFFICE, looking at the last statement from Shane. It was incredible, he thought, over $300 million in the Swiss account was his.

Just five weeks ago his world was ending. He did a quick calculation. After settling with CCA and bringing all his bank loans current, he would have plenty to get on with his business. He wasn't sure how he would explain it all to Ryan Tipton, but that was the least of his worries. As he mused, looking at the statement, the same old thought crossed his mind: Why did Shane want to stop now? If he could make this kind of money in five weeks, what would the next five net? He had no idea of the agony Shane O'Connor was suffering at this very moment.

Ryan Tipton was in touch with Don Parker. The trial date was only days off, and there was apparently no hope of a settlement. It was obvious Temple would prevail, and for close to what he was asking. Tipton had tried to get some relief, but Parker was adamant. In his mind, it was a slam-dunk; they'd have Patton out of business by the end of the quarter. Tipton called Ray Patton.

"I just got off the phone with Don Parker. We have no plausible defense and they know it. This thing goes to trial in three days. I don't know why we would even show up. They'll get their judgment. I don't know what else to do, Ray."

Patton knew exactly what to do but he couldn't tell Tipton—not just now.

"I agree it would be a waste of time. When the judgment comes down, let me know how much time we've got. I can call in a few favors. Maybe we'll survive this yet. I want you to call the banks and get a status on all our loans and what it will take to bring them current. Then I want you to talk to our financial people and get a summary of all our payables. Add it all up and see what we need, including Temple. Then get a solid projection of the cash we need for the next six months. I might have a solution."

Tipton was shocked. He could do a quick calculation himself. What Patton was looking at was nearly $250 million to cover all the bases. Where in hell would he get that kind of money? Certainly not from the business. He'd seen Patton perform miracles before, but now he'd need divine intervention—and soon!

Shane was on his way to Wolford's office with an answer about Richard's account. He would tell Wolford there was no record of any account and, as far as he could tell, there never had been. It was the only thing he could say. He wanted to get a response from Wolford.

"Our records show nothing on Richard Stearns—no account, nothing. What's this all about, Bill?" Shane asked nervously.

"I don't know. Your father asked for it. I'll tell him what you've found. He's probably forgotten all about it by now."

Shane hoped so. Maybe it would all blow over, but not knowing gnawed at him. When Richard called, the news got worse.

"I know what happened now," Richard said, and told Shane about having asked Brooke to get his checkbook.

"It's the only answer. It dawned on me as I was going over our conversation. I never dreamed she would go through my papers, but she's the only one who had access to my desk. It has to be her. How it got to your father would have to be through Mecham. He's the only connection. She wouldn't go to Don Parker. What I've pieced together is—on second thought, meet me in the coffee shop in ten minutes," Richard said.

"I get nervous talking on the phone. Anyway, I think when Brooke saw the papers it shocked her. That's a lot of money. I also think Brooke views me as a 'possible,' but she foresees years of hard work and little money. That's not her style. She's told me often what she aspires to, and it's not struggling with me starting my own practice. That's the reason I got into this in the first place. When she saw the numbers, she wanted confirmation; probably wanted to know where the money came from. I know her and her legal mind. My guess is she went to her father, who went to your father. What have you found out?"

"Nothing," Shane replied. "I told Wolford we had no record of any past or current account in your name. From what he said, and his seeming indifference, your story could be correct. He didn't sound like it was any big deal. But what happens when Brooke finds out you have no account here? Where is all that money? Has she ever asked you about it?"

"No, but she will. Since I got involved in all this, I've gotten pretty good at lying to her. I hate all the deception, but I'm in too deep now. I'm going to tell her I made it trading in commodities. At least that's plausible. Those markets change drastically, up and down; I can fabricate any scenario to fit the situation."

Frank O'Connor called Mecham to tell him there was no account in Richard Stearns's name, and whimsically suggested Brooke might want to reconsider any matrimonial thoughts. Mecham had some misgivings about Brooke's infatuation with Richard, and was quick to inform her of the bank's findings.

Brooke was confused. What were the statements all about? No one kept bogus accounts of nonexistent funds. Richard might not be the man in her future but she wasn't going to give up access to a fortune.

As Richard suspected, Brooke launched into a litany of questions. He had his story well in mind. There would be no need to belabor it. Over dinner, he carefully explained that he'd made the money investing—through a client—in cotton and pork bellies. The transactions passed through the International Bank of Boston. He now had the money deposited in a savings account. End of story.

"I wanted to tell you sooner but I was in a few contracts I couldn't get out of and there was some concern that I might lose a ton. Today I liquidated everything and parked it in my savings account," Richard said, relieved.

He had no way of knowing how much she remembered of what she'd seen in his desk, but this should close the issue. He could now bask in the glow of her knowing about his wealth.

"That's a lot of money, Richard. Shouldn't you have it in the stock market or something? Savings accounts don't pay much interest. You'd do better with money markets or mutual funds," she said.

Her smug assessment of his investment acumen was a blow to his ego, but he didn't want to pursue it. He had accomplished his mission. She knew he had lots of money; he was anxious to see how it would affect their relationship. He didn't have long to wait.

Brooke had mixed feelings about his revelation. She accepted his commodity market story and said she was glad he had it in a safe place.

Over the course of their relationship, she was sure he had evaluated her need for economic independence and concluded it was beyond his reach. That should play into her hand now. She sensed that Richard was thoroughly infatuated. With the magnitude of his apparent wealth, he was now a target. She'd polished this tactic with other men, but the stakes paled in comparison. If Richard wanted her, the price would be his fortune. But this strategy would require great care: Richard was an intelligent, sensitive man. He was also immature and easily manipulated.

"I've got some time now to decide what I want to do with it. It's the first time I've been faced with investing so much money. At least it's safe where it is. Let's order, I'm starved," he said, trying to change the subject.

"Richard, I didn't mean to criticize you for the way you handled it. I just blurted it out. My father taught me a few things about investments, and I enjoy the subject. You'll figure it all out soon enough. But that's not the important thing here." Brooke had to neutralize some of the materialistic things she had said over the course of their time together.

"I suppose during the time we've known each other I've blabbed a good deal about how I intend to live my life: money for everything—clothes, travel, sumptuous homes, beach houses and all that. That's how my family has lived in recent years, and I've become accustomed to it."

This must be done with diplomacy. She mustn't portray herself as a predator, or a money-crazed bimbo.

"I want you to understand that while my tastes are definitely champagne, I'm just as interested in the goblet. My continued interest in our relationship will depend exclusively on my feelings for you. Your money has nothing to do with it. Am I making sense?" she asked with a pouting little smile.

He wasn't sure she was. Most of what she said, he'd agonized about many times. Maybe he had misjudged her. He'd sure gone to a hell of a lot of trouble to assure himself sufficient funds to give her what he thought she wanted. Well, he was in it now and the crisis was over. He knew where he stood with her, and that was just as important as the money.

TEN

SHANE WAS SETTLING HIMSELF DOWN, slightly. The account crisis seemed over. According to Richard, he and Brooke had resolved the question of where the money had come from. In fact, things were almost back to normal. His fascination with the drug business, which had been on hold during the past week, was beginning to resurface. His wild swings from abject fear to euphoric delight left him confused. How could he possibly want to get further involved, considering what he and Richard had been through these past ten days? On the other hand, where else could he make $40 million in five weeks?

THE JUDGMENT CAME DOWN much as expected. With attorney's fees, it would cost Patton $125 million. He called Ray Tipton.

"Did you get that information I asked for?"

"I have it all," Tipton said. "As you know, the CCA settlement is for $125 million. Eighty million will bring all the bank loans current, and your financial people tell me it'll take $30 million to get us through the next two quarters—a conservative estimate predicated on sales of $1.5 billion during that period. That totals $235 million. Any solutions?"

"I should have it all in three days. Don't ask me any questions right now, but I've got it covered. And it didn't cost me any equity. Just tell me the mechanics of getting CCA paid and I'll take care of it. I'll get enough in our bank to cover the rest. Send us your bill while it's fresh in your mind. This should put us back in business so I can get on with building computers," Patton said triumphantly.

Tipton was astonished. He knew Ray Patton well and he knew his current financial condition. During the past few months they had pondered going public, but their balance sheet, together with the litigation, made that impossible. Where Ray could put his hands on $235 million, Tipton had no idea. He had seen the man bounce back more times than he could count; apparently he had done it again.

Patton called Shane O'Connor. "OK, Shane, here's what need: I want

$125 million for the CCA settlement and another $110 million transferred to our bank in Atlanta. That should leave me over $100 million in the Swiss account. I'll let you know in a few days what I want done with that. Call me tomorrow when you've done all the transfers."

Shane had anticipated Patton's call. In fact, for any of them to get their money from the Swiss account, care must be taken not to recreate a paper trail. He had successfully laundered all the drug revenues through his father's bank by electronic fund transfer and clever computer tinkering. The odds against anyone detecting this were astronomical. Now the trick was to get the money back and legitimately into domestic accounts. This involved a little more ingenuity.

Through his offshore banking connections he was able to create corporations in a number of foreign locations. He did the same domestically. He then prepared phony promissory notes due the domestic corporations from the offshore ones. The phony foreign corporations used the Swiss funds to pay the bogus American ones. It was simply the repayment of a loan with no tax consequences. The money was now in American banks, available to each of them. It took considerable paper shuffling, but it worked. He used three different American banks for their separate accounts.

Shane explained this to Patton and identified the name of the United States bank used for his funds. The money would be there in two days and he could make the transfers himself, directly from the bank.

"Before the domestic account will be activated, I'll need you to return all the notes I've given you. I suggest you move the funds to your regular bank in Atlanta as soon as it's convenient. Let me know when you want the balance transferred," Shane said.

It sounded complicated to Patton, but Shane knew what he was doing. Everything had worked so far. He'd have Tipton take care of paying CCA. He'd love to see the look on Mecham Temple's face when the check arrived. He was also anxious to get clean with his banks and start spending more time with his business.

He had an overpowering yearning to explore further drug buys with Shane. Patton knew he had made it possible for Shane and Richard to accumulate a veritable fortune with no up-front funds of their own. True, they had taken all the risks, but their payday was more than they had expected. The bond of greed was surely something he could exploit.

"Shane, Patton here. I'm wondering if you might be interested in continuing our little scheme. I might be willing to negotiate a more favorable split with you. Why don't you think it over and get back to me."

Shane created endless spreadsheets with his and Richard's money. It was awesome how they could parlay it. They didn't need Patton's money but they could use his corporate account. On the other hand, they could use his money if he upped the split. Fifty-fifty wouldn't cut it. If he increased it to an 80/20 arrangement, and they used their own funds as well, it might make sense.

"Ray, Richard and I have given your suggestion some thought, but with all the risks we take, the split would have to be in the range of 90/10 or 80/20. It's still damn lucrative for you. If you can live with that, we may have a deal."

"You're getting greedy, Shane. Let me give it some thought. I'll get back to you," he said and hung up.

It was a hell of deal for Patton, Shane thought. He and Richard had all the machinery in place, and had made all the contacts and the myriad computer and bank arrangements. It really was a shame to abandon it now. All Patton had to do was put up his money. Between Patton, Richard, and himself, they had nearly $200 million. If Patton agreed to anything close to his offer, he'd convince Richard to continue.

Patton didn't know all the numbers but he could come close: he had $100 million to invest with Shane. It looked like if he gave them a 75/25 split he could triple it on the first buy. After another four it would approach ten figures. He promised himself, if Shane agreed, that this would be the end of it. He couldn't press his luck forever, even for this much money.

Don Parker was astonished when a draft for $125 million showed up in his office. He and Mecham Temple had fully expected Ray Patton to default. Information from Frank O'Connor had suggested that ICC was in desperate financial straits. In fact, Parker and Temple discussed the possibility of gaining control of ICC should Patton default. Nothing would please Mecham Temple more than the demise of Ray Patton. Thoughts of merging the two companies had occupied much of Mecham's time. It would give him virtual dominance in most computer markets. It would, however, take a considerable amount of cash. This meant debt, which Mecham abhorred.

"This is unbelievable, Mecham. Our information was unimpeachable—this man was on the verge of collapse. It's unthinkable he was able to come up with the payment. I checked with Frank O'Connor this morning to get a current credit report. He's dead current on all his bank loans, and all his payables are 100 percent. He's clean as a whistle; even shows positive cash flow projection for the next two quarters. Whatever his financial illness was, he's totally recovered. It absolutely defies gravity," Parker said, throwing his arms in the air.

"He's obviously found a source of cash," Mecham said. "I suspect he sold some equity; maybe he's lost control. We'll know in the next few months. Keep an eye on his performance as best you can. We could still have a shot."

ELEVEN

THE CRISIS PAST, RICHARD'S NEWFOUND WEALTH was no longer a subject of conversation. Brooke accepted the source, and their relationship flourished. The overnight trips to Martha's Vineyard had been curtailed after the fifth buy. He told her the hotel caper was on hold for the moment, but that he and Shane hadn't abandoned it. Their romance now included weekend trips to New York and Miami. Richard saw no reason to slacken his pursuit of the woman he intended to marry.

He was in a receptive frame of mind when Shane called to invite him to lunch. "I talked with Patton a few days ago and he wants to fire up the operation again," Shane said. "He's got the itch. With the results of our operation he's been able to turn his life around. All his debts are paid and his business is coming alive. To be perfectly honest, my interest is returning too. I never would have believed it after that scare with Brooke, but with what you've told me, she's pretty much settled down. Is that so?" he asked.

"Absolutely. She's totally convinced my fortune came from the commodities market. Even her father believes it. Of course, I've been able to spend all my spare time with her lately—no more overnight trips to Martha's Vineyard. To tell you the truth, I think the idea of being involved with a man of substance has put our relationship on solid ground. She's more comfortable with the longer term. There's no doubt the money has a lot to do with it. I know that makes her look like a money-grubber, but I don't see it that way. She's a solid lady," Richard said. How naive, thought Shane. The money was *all* Brooke was after; women were all alike.

"Then how do you feel about Patton's proposal?"

"I really haven't given it much thought," Richard replied. "I know that Don Parker and Mecham Temple were absolutely overwhelmed by Patton's settling the litigation. You should know that they asked your father to check Patton's credit and financial situation. Of course Mecham was delighted to win the settlement, but he and Parker have some suspicions. I hope this doesn't cause us any problems. What exactly is Patton's proposal?" Shane went through what he and Patton had discussed. As usual, he had prepared a series of "what-if" spreadsheets.

"After our conversation, he came back with a 75/25 split. I've done the numbers using his current balance of $100 million and our combined balance of $80 million. Parlaying it all for another two buys, it's absolutely unbelievable: Are you ready? Five or six weeks from now, Richard, you and I could have a combined total of over a billion dollars! Over a half-billion each! I know it sounds preposterous, but look at the numbers. Some of it comes from our share of the Patton deal, the rest from our own funds. We don't share any of that with Patton," Shane said, falling back in his chair, arms in the air.

Richard looked at the spreadsheets. He had seen these many times before. Shane was usually very precise with his numbers, and the first five buys fell almost exactly where he had predicted. There was little reason to question his arithmetic.

"How do we know Salvatore can deliver these quantities? It looks like the second buy is for over fifteen thousand kilos. That's a hell of a lot of cocaine. And how do we know Marty can unload that much?" Richard asked.

"I've checked on that. It might take Salvatore a little longer to arrange— he'll have to lean on other growers—but he can deliver. Marty, of course, says he can sell a trainload. I'm not worried about him. From what he says, his distributors are pissed because we haven't delivered in the past three weeks. We've got all the pieces in place; I vote we do it. I know the numbers are hard to believe, but it's all there. With this kind of money, Richard, we don't work the rest of our lives. Can you imagine having over $2 million a month from interest alone? Money-grubber or not, Brooke won't have any problem with that," Shane concluded.

Richard was numb. There were risks, of course: to amass this much money there had to be, but everything had gone so smoothly before. Why not? He felt like someone else was speaking for him.

"Let's do it. I'll need some advance notice to set up something with Brooke. I guess the Martha's Vineyard story is as good as any. I've told her it's on hold, but I can rekindle it."

Shane got busy setting everything up. He had to restart every aspect. Again, the biggest risk was the bank. The amounts would be getting larger with each buy and he'd have to keep separate accounts for the Patton part of the deal. It was much easier with computers, but it took a lot of his time.

BROOKE TEMPLE FOUND HERSELF READJUSTING to her relationship with Richard. The fact that he now had a measure of financial security made her feelings for him seem more practical. She could stop her subconscious search for Mr. Right: he had become Mr. Right, at least for now. She knew that had a materialistic ring, but it was only natural—she was materialistic. She had spent many years forming that image and now Richard met every test. And with her business savvy, she was sure she could nurture his fledgling wealth to even loftier heights.

Richard didn't look forward to further deception. Trying to prepare Brooke for his upcoming absences, he became withdrawn, drifting into periods of indifference, the guilt preceding the event. Her reaction was the same as before—incessant questions: Why did he want a tiny hotel that obviously couldn't provide much income? He'd get himself into a situation that would require a lot of his time for very little return. There were other, much safer, investments that required little time and returned greater rewards. Why didn't he let her help him?

Richard had little choice. He had no other options that would allow him to be gone overnight. He wasn't going to endure fabricating another phony alibi. He became hostile and told her it was a closed issue. It was something he and Shane wanted to do and he wasn't going to debate it any further.

They left it that way. He would be gone the nights he and Shane were negotiating for the hotel. She was upset, but at least not suspicious, Richard thought. On the night of the next buy, he left his office early. He told Brooke he wouldn't be seeing her that night, and met Shane at the airport for the long flight to Florida.

Everything went without a hitch. Marty was there with his vans, and they brought back nearly $300 million in cash-close to four tons of hundred-dollar bills! Because the quantities were getting larger, the next rendezvous was set for the following week. That would give Salvatore enough time to gather the material. It would also ease the tension developing anew between Richard and Brooke.

Upon his return to the bank the next morning, Shane began the laborious process of moving the funds to the Swiss account, doctoring the computer trail and preparing documentation for Patton and Richard. He cautioned Richard once again on the importance of keeping his records in a safe place. As always, he personally delivered Richard's statements.

"Put these in a safe place. Your $40 million just grew to $160 million overnight. Your girlfriend might find that most interesting. You'd have a hard time explaining that in the commodity markets," Shane said smiling.

"Are you kidding me? We couldn't print it that fast," Richard whispered.

"Wait till next week—you'll have over $500 million. My spreadsheets never lie. Where are you keeping these now?" Shane asked.

"I had a lock installed on my bottom desk drawer. I keep it all there and I'm the only one with a key. Don't worry, I'm probably more careful now than you are."

Having the lock installed was a simple thing. He'd called the office manager and requested it to protect confidential legal papers. Grace Alden had taken care of it the same day. It was done while he was in a meeting in the conference room.

In her office, Brooke heard the sound of drilling next door, but dismissed it until the workman peeked into her office and asked directions to the men's room. What was he doing in Richard's office? It was unusual to hear the sound of power tools in a law office. She picked up the phone to josh Richard about what was going on, but he didn't answer. She decided to see for herself.

As she came around his desk she saw the lower drawer on the floor, the drill beside it—cord snaking to the wall outlet—and a scattering of wood shavings on the floor nearby. Also on the floor was a small, clear plastic envelope containing a lock and two keys. Richard was securing his desk. Why? Not unusual, but why now? What did he intend to keep there? Her instinctive need to know prevailed. She bent down, removed one of the keys and left the office. She wasn't being nosy; she just had to know.

The next buy went off as smoothly as all the others had. The huge amounts of cash were getting even bulkier, and Shane needed bigger containers to handle them. Once at Logan, they transferred it to their cars and then drove to Shane's home, where they could safely bundle it into smaller packages.

"Well, Mr. Stearns, with this buy we each have over $500 million. I vote we quit. We have enough for the rest of our lives, wouldn't you say?" Shane asked proudly.

Richard certainly thought so. The long flights to Florida and the deceptive preparation with Brooke were wearing on him. The hotel scenario was becoming a joke: how long does one negotiate for a tiny hotel in a small tourist community? He left for his own home to shower and get ready for a day at the office. These nights without sleep were starting to take their toll.

Brooke smiled when Richard told her of another night of hotel bargaining. As neither wanted to press the issue, it was dropped. It had become obvious to her that he was using the hotel deal as a cover for something. She still didn't think he was seeing anyone else, but he continued showing signs of indifference and evasiveness. A tenacious lawyer's need to know drove her. She'd needed a reason to learn what Richard kept in that locked drawer. Now she had one.

TWELVE

O N NIGHTS WHEN HE MADE THE NECESSARY TRIPS to Florida—allegedly on his quest for the Oak Bluffs hotel—Richard went directly home from his office. Brooke didn't see him until he came to work the next morning. This night she worked late, well after everyone but the people who cleaned the offices had gone. She listened from her desk as the vacuum cleaner was turned off in Richard's office. When she heard the woman leave, she quietly walked into the darkened room, stopping at his desk to listen and wait until she felt it was safe. Then, she turned on the light and used her purloined key to unlock the bottom drawer.

She found a bundle of papers and took them to her own office, where she carefully examined each one. Some she had seen before, others were dated within the past three weeks. All on the same bank letterhead, they appeared to be statements of money belonging to Richard. The amounts were staggering. On the most recent, the balance was over $300 million. She couldn't believe what she was seeing. Only a month or so ago she had seen papers showing a balance of about $10 million. There was no way on earth Richard had parlayed that into this amount in any commodities market scheme. Brooke was frightened: whatever Richard was doing, it had to be illegal. This wasn't brain surgery; it was drugs. He sure as hell can't be interested in buying some rundown fifteen-room hotel with $300 million!

It was getting late. She took the bundle of papers to the office copier and photocopied each one. She then returned them to Richard's office, locked the drawer and left the building. At home she went over the papers again and again, writing down all the dates and amounts. As near as she could remember, most of the dates coincided with Richard's trips to his "dream hotel." As she laid it all out and calculated the rate of growth, the next statement should be for over $500 million. She knew nothing about drugs, but she knew something about geometric growth. Each statement was almost three times the previous one. If Richard continued this for another two weeks or so, the amount would be over a billion dollars. She needed a drink. This must be some Internet game he's playing with someone in Cleveland. It's like "Monopoly." Where *is* all this money?

She knew he would never tell her what it was all about if she confronted him. If it were illegal, he'd deny it. But most important, she thought, if it is illegal, it's only a matter of time until he's either caught or killed. God, what a dilemma! She wanted someone with financial security, not someone with a financial death wish. But Brooke was a realist, too, and now she knew she'd never let Richard get away from her.

THE LAST BUY WAS DONE. Even to Shane and Richard, the amount of cash they were flying back to Boston was unbelievable. They were glad it was over. It was frightening being alone with this much cash, like floating in a crystal sphere that could shatter at any time. It was eerie: they could almost hear a chorus of Benny Franklins singing "Nearer My God to Thee."

It took Shane all of the next day to process the money and document the transaction. When it was complete he took the elevator to the twenty-fifth floor and walked to Richard's office. He felt both a sense of relief and a nagging fear. The dangerous part was over but the wondering whether something might go wrong never left him.

"Well, old buddy, that's it, and this is the last for me. We've had a phenomenal run of luck and I'm not going to press it. If we can get past the next six months, we should be home free. The biggest danger now is some clerical or computer glitch, or some overzealous clerk. I'll watch that closely. Here's your last statement," Shane said, exhausted.

Richard looked at the balance. He, too, was dog-tired, but the nine figures at the bottom of the page leaped at him like flashing neon. He was truly a multimillionaire—at least on paper. All of Shane's spreadsheets came together in one giant, gilt-edged certificate displaying the number he was looking at. For now, at least, it was worth all the risks.

As Shane left, Richard put the statement in his desk drawer and locked it. He called Brooke and asked if she was ready to leave. He wanted to enjoy a big lobster dinner with her sitting across from him. It seemed so complete now. She was cemented in his life. She would be his wife, the mother of his children, the keeper of his fortune.

Brooke kept her secret from everyone, even her father, to whom she usually told everything. She had to come to terms with what she thought she knew. Should she confront Richard? It could end their relationship; she didn't want to risk that. As she watched him across the table, she knew she would stick with him no matter what he was involved in. It was pointless to embarrass him about his "trip to Martha's Vineyard" last night. She was certain that was not where he'd been.

RICHARD WAS TO SPEND THREE DAYS at a seminar, arranged weeks before by Don Parker, who felt it important to keep his most talented employees abreast of all changes in current law. Routinely, he paid to have them attend, and required a full written report upon completion. This seminar was held at Harvard. Richard could see Brooke every night.

Brooke called her father to have lunch with her the next day. They met at the same downtown restaurant where she and Richard had had their first date.

"This could take awhile, Dad. What I have to tell you involves Richard, and I need your sworn promise you won't speak of it to anyone. It is of the utmost importance that you honor this request. Have we got a deal?" Brooke asked, looking him straight in the eye.

"Of course."

"I've given a great deal of thought to what I'm about to tell you. Richard doesn't know it yet, but I've appointed myself his attorney. He'll undoubtedly need one. I have no proof, but I think once you've heard me out, you'll agree."

In the next thirty minutes, Brooke unfolded the story of all she had learned, leaving nothing out. She hadn't brought the photocopies but she did have her own calculations of the massive amounts of money and the dates. Mecham was shocked. He sat slumped in his chair, chin in his hands.

"It numbs the brain. The amounts of money are incredible. I'm sure you have some theories."

"It's patently obvious. The only way one amasses so much money in so little time is . . . drugs. Who else is involved and how Richard's done it, I have no idea. What I do know is that he's very vulnerable. Apparently he's gotten away with it thus far, but the odds of something going wrong are great. It appears that the International Bank of Boston is involved somehow. Why else would the statements be on their letterhead?

"There's more. From the papers I have, there's no record of where the money is. When he was pushing the commodities market story, he told me that it's safely in a savings account. Assuming the money actually exists somewhere, if he's apprehended it would be confiscated. The Feds would keep the money, Richard would go to jail, and my world would end.

"Further, if the money does reside somewhere, the transactions are complete. The drugs have been sold and Richard has the money. It's an irreversible process. From the authorities' point of view, the only thing left to do is apprehend the guys with the money, seize it, and jail the bad guys— in this case, the ones with the money. The people who did the grunt work are long gone. No one will ever go after the grower, the people who transported the drugs, or the people who distributed and sold them. That trail's too cold. They'd go after the ones with the money. That is, if they can establish that they are, in fact, the bad guys. Unless the Feds had a mole or were tailing them, that could be hard to do. Of course, if Richard continues whatever he's doing, his chances of being caught are far better than even."

The next part was more difficult for her. She had given it endless thought, not only from a legal point of view but from a practical and monetary perspective as well.

"Now comes the hard part: Neither you nor I are criminals, nor could we ever become criminals. We don't want to be part of any illegal acts, but there is some middle ground. If we go to Richard, convince him to stop this suicidal activity, and make every effort to protect him, the money could stay intact. If he's never apprehended—and as time goes on that becomes more likely—he could salvage his life. Would we be harboring a criminal? As his attorney, I don't think so. He's only a criminal if he's convicted of a crime.

"It seems to me unconscionable for the government to take millions of dollars they had nothing to do with. Granted, it was gained illegally, but from whom? If the Feds were doing their jobs, they would have intercepted the mules or the dealers—the ones peddling the dope. What Richard and his friends were doing was enabling the process. I know I'm rationalizing, but I see a way to save a man I care about and, at the same time preserve a sizable estate. I'm sorry, but that's the way I see it," she finished.

Mecham was shocked. Not only was her lover involved in drug trafficking, but his daughter was proposing to protect him and, worse, keep his ill-gotten gains.

"Are you sure you know what you're getting into? Isn't what you're proposing in violation of your creed of ethics? Weren't you charged with upholding the law? Don't you have responsibilities to the citizens of Massachusetts?" Mecham demanded loudly.

"Now don't get religious on me. Of course I'm responsible for all that, but I'm now this man's attorney and my first responsibility is to him. If, in the process, I'm able to allow him to keep his money, who'll get hurt? If it comes down to Richard getting the money or the Feds—who'll blow it on some ill-conceived boondoggle—I'd rather it went to Richard. I'm not saying he deserves it, or that he earned it or that it belongs to him. I'm saying that given the available choices, the government or Richard, I vote for Richard. I also think that if we prevail, Richard and I are responsible for seeing that the money is used in a constructive way. If you conclude that I'm saying I know better how to spend this money than the government does, you're correct."

Well, maybe she had a point, but it frightened Mecham: he was a law-abiding man and this sounded like breaking the law. But his daughter was the lawyer; he'd let her make those decisions. His guess was that if what she'd said was true, Richard would be arrested and sent to jail, the Feds would get the money, and that would be the end of that—and of Richard. There wasn't any exposure for Brooke, except she'd lose the only man he'd ever seen her so attached to.

"What do you want me to do?" Mecham sighed.

"I want you to meet with Richard and me. If you agree, I intend to tell him what I believe and convince him to get out. I want him to know we're behind him. I also want him to know what his options are. I see no need to get into the money thing right now. If they nail him, it's academic. If we're able to steer him out of this, we'll settle it then, OK?" Brooke asked.

"I just hope you know what you're doing. I'm not suggesting you don't, just be careful. You're the one I'm concerned about. And you needn't worry; I won't repeat a word you've told me, not even to your mother."

She felt better. At least she had an ally. She wasn't at all sure Richard would go along, but it was certainly better than the way he was headed. She arranged a meeting at her home the next weekend for the three of them.

THIRTEEN

SATURDAY WAS A BEAUTIFUL NEW ENGLAND DAY. Brooke had set the meeting for noon and wanted it to be casual. As soon as they finished with lunch, she wanted to get into the fray. It would probably take all afternoon.

Richard was the first to arrive. He looked puzzled and asked immediately what the purpose of a meeting with her father was. She dismissed the question with a flip of her arm and said he wanted to get to know his future son-in-law better. Mecham arrived within minutes and they sat down to eat. The conversation was light and it was evident Mecham and Richard liked one another. They had met formally during the Patton litigation but never really got to know each other. Richard used his considerable social skills, engaging chitchat, and amusing stories. Brooke almost forgot why they were there.

"Anyone like a drink?" she asked. "I have some delightful Duckhorn Merlot." Both men did. This should help, she thought.

Brooke joined them in the study, and sat facing Richard. It was a tactic she had learned in school: face the opposition eye to eye. Not that Richard was her opponent, but with what she had to say to him today, he might think so.

"Richard, you're not going to like what I'm about to say—you might even walk out—but I'm going to say it, all of it, and you'd better listen."

Brooke carefully outlined everything she thought she knew, then filled in the gaps with what she surmised. It comprised a chronological summary of Richard's activities over the past few months. As he listened, he stared past her. She was spectacular! He couldn't have stated it any better. Of course she didn't know the other players, but that could come later. After thirty minutes she finished, exhausted. Mecham had begun pacing the floor soon after she'd started. He was at the window now, facing both of them.

"That's all I know, Richard. I'm sure you'll be angry about all my sleuthing, but please know I did it because I was worried about you. If what I suspect is true, I want to help you; we both want to help you," Brooke said, as she glanced at Mecham.

Richard got up from his chair and stood with his hands in his pockets, looking at the floor. What could he say? She had him nailed; it would be absurd to deny it. He was reluctant to involve Shane and Patton, but eventually they would know. He slowly unfolded the entire scenario: how it had started, who was involved, the Colombian connection, Marty Stinson and the pilots, the Swiss accounts, the phony documents, all of it. When he finished, he confirmed the amount currently in his account: $750 million.

"Shane made it all sound so simple, and it was. As we speak, I know of no glitch. It all worked so smoothly; we were never challenged by anyone. Of course, Shane points out that we're not out of the woods yet. There are a lot of documents floating around and a lot of computer information he has secretly coded, but he suspects time will obliterate much of it. And we're through. We all agreed the last buy was the end of it," Richard said, falling back down in his chair.

"So that's where Patton got the money to settle with us," Mecham reflected. "I knew there was something crooked about that. He was in too deep to come out as clean as he did."

"Richard," Brooke interjected, "I told my father because I needed to talk to someone before I talked to you. He has sworn to me that he wouldn't tell anyone. Also, I have appointed myself your attorney. I don't know whether or not you'll need one, but you can now trust that anything you tell me won't leave this room. I think I can help you."

She took Richard through the same logic she had explained to her father, regarding the authorities and the money: how they could better be the keepers of the funds if, in fact, there were any to keep. It was an interesting concept; one Richard had never considered. As he thought about it, he liked it. It certainly made sense considering all the risks he'd taken. Of course, the entire scenario depended on not getting caught. All that really had changed was, he now had partners he hadn't planned on, but who better than his future wife and father-in-law?

"What do you think about all this, Mecham?" Richard asked.

"I'll tell you what I think: You're a conniving, cheating crook and you've made a mockery of your legal profession. Apparently you've also been very lucky, so far. I'm here because Brooke wanted me here. I'll keep my word and not tell anyone, but I'm not getting involved. One thing concerns me, though: how do you intend to deal with your associates now that Brooke knows about your activities? You don't dare tell them. If you do anything that jeopardizes my daughter, I'll expose you in a heartbeat," Mecham threatened.

"Of course I won't tell them. They'd panic. I think I know the situation, Mecham. Now that you and Brooke know the whole story, you're both at risk. You don't know these people; for this kind of money, they'll do anything. I didn't intend for Brooke to uncover my seedy activities, but now that she has, I'll do anything to protect her," Richard said.

The meeting was over. There was nothing left to say. Richard shook hands with Mecham, kissed Brooke and left. He was ashamed, but mostly he was afraid. He felt alone. Sure, Brooke was in his corner, but he had to deal with Shane and Patton, and she couldn't help him. He couldn't discuss her involvement with either of them. If they knew she had stumbled onto their operation, the danger to both her and Mecham was unthinkable. Richard believed Patton—and maybe Shane—was capable of anything, even murder. Others had been killed for a lot less. Patton's business had been saved through drug trafficking in which he was a partner. Shane's father's bank had been involved in massive money laundering and computer fraud, with an officer of the bank an active participant. His partners still thought that only the players knew any of this. If they learned that they'd been put at risk through his careless behavior, they'd take measures to protect themselves—and that would include Brooke.

MECHAM TEMPLE WAS IRATE. When he left Brooke's home, he drove to his downtown club, hoping no one he knew would be there on a Saturday. Angry that his daughter was involved in Richard's dirty little scheme, he wanted time to think about what he had heard. He'd listened to Brooke's analysis of what would happen to the money, and he suspected that in some ways she was right. He was particularly intrigued with Ray Patton's situation. He still coveted Patton's operation, but there seemed no way to expose Ray's disreputable source of funds without exposing Richard, and maybe Brooke. But he was competing with a man who owed his survival to a drug-trafficking scheme. Here was Richard—if he survived—sitting with $750 million. It was bizarre. He could buy Patton out with that much money. It was obvious now that Patton had given up no equity to bail himself out.

AT THE BANK, SHANE O'CONNOR WAS BUSIER than ever, trying to cover all the bases with secret documentation and computer coding. This, together with his bank duties, left him pretty thin. He worried every moment that some clerk or computer operator, or even Bill Wolford, would stumble onto one of his cover-ups. But he couldn't be everywhere at once. Though he felt he had done all he could to eliminate a damaging paper trail, he worried nonetheless—and it showed. He was terrified when the phone rang, he walked around his car in the parking garage to see if anyone one was watching, kept his shades drawn at home, and rarely went out. What a way to live given the money he had! But his biggest fear was at the bank. There were too many points in the web of deception that were vulnerable to detection, and no way to plug them all.

"Shane, could you come to my office?" Bill Wolford said.

The terror began to grow. What had he discovered? Wolford was a stickler for details. He would discipline an employee for the slightest error. He had internal auditors checking every aspect of the bank's operation. Nothing was left to chance. Shane's father approved of Wolford's overzealous attention to following bank procedures, and Wolford's memory was like nothing Shane had ever seen.

"Shane, remember a few months ago when your father wanted us to check on an account for a Richard Stearns? Well, Brian from offshore transfers brought me this," Wolford said, handing over a sheet of paper.

Shane's eyes glazed. His worst nightmare was coming true. In this overload situation, he knew he'd rushed through some of the cover-up functions, but he also knew he'd covered the most important ones. In his haste, he had inadvertently left a longhand summary of Richard's Swiss account transfers in the transfer area. A clerk, Brian Altman, had found it. It was nothing official but Richard's name was on it. When Brian asked Wolford about it, the lights came on—he truly had a memory like a computer. It wasn't the end of the world but it would take some explanation. Shane was ready.

"This is a summary of Richard's financial plan, prepared by some client of his. He asked me what I thought of it. I must have inadvertently left it in the transfer room. It has nothing to do with bank business," Shane said nonchalantly. He handed the paper back to Wolford, who studied it in some detail. The notations were difficult to read and Wolford finally handed it back to him.

Bill Wolford had been in the banking trade for thirty years. He loved the digital aspects of the business. Everything came out even. Reconciliation was the name of the game. Deposits minus withdrawals minus transfers minus balances always equaled zero. It was a zero sum game. If something didn't add up, he went after it with a vengeance, and there was something about this Richard Stearns issue that didn't add up. First, when Frank O'Connor asked him to check on any Richard Stearns account, past or present, Shane had not been entirely candid with him. Checking further, Wolford found a record of a fund transfer to a bank in Newton, Massachusetts, to the account of Richard Stearns. It wasn't clear where the funds had come from because the computer trail ended there. The amount of the transfer was in excess of $200 million. The paper he and Shane had just looked at wasn't as benign as Shane suggested. In checking transfers to the same bank in Newton, all the entries coincided. Coincidences like that didn't happen in the banking business. And the transfers were adding up—in excess of $750 million to date. Big numbers, even for the International Bank of Boston, larger still for a young attorney. But Wolford couldn't find the error. Everything balanced. He thought he should go to Frank O'Connor, but because Shane was involved, and there was an outside chance it all was legitimate, he decided to go back to Shane.

"I thought you might shed some additional light on some other aspects of the Richard Stearns subject, Shane. Apparently, there is a Richard Stearns account here at the bank and it has been very active of late," Wolford said and explained what he had found.

This was Shane's worst nightmare. It was crippling stuff. How the hell had Wolford traced the deposits to the Newton bank? Shane had covered that trail. He made the transfers every time they made a buy, and he had coded the computer to pull them up only with his own pin number. Something had gone wrong—badly.

He squirmed in his chair. He knew Wolford was looking right through him. He could see the accusatory look in the man's eyes. He needed some time. "That's odd. Did you print out anything I could look at?" Shane asked hopefully.

"No, because the trail ended abruptly. I didn't know what I'd get. I'd like you to look into this before I go to your father. There has to be some logical explanation. See what you can find out," he said, ending the conversation.

It was the beginning of the end, Shane thought. If Wolford were on to something, he wouldn't let go. If the answers Shane gave him weren't satisfactory, he'd dig deeper. Sooner or later, Bill Wolford would know the whole story.

He had to talk to someone. Richard was close, but he'd only panic. Patton was his partner. Maybe he could help.

FOURTEEN

"**H**ow he found out is academic. He did, and I know him well enough to know he'll stop at nothing. This isn't the time to criticize, we need a solution, and now," Shane shouted. "I don't want to talk to anyone else about this. I thought maybe you and I could strategize and come up with a solution."

Patton was livid. Shane had assured him he had every base covered at the bank. Well, he hadn't come this far to lose everything. He told Shane to keep him posted, then called the Taj Mahal in Atlantic City and asked for Doug Simms.

Patton had known Simms, now a security guard at the hotel, for many years. In earlier times he had done many unpleasant chores for Patton.

"Doug, how soon can you get to Boston? I'll be there tomorrow and I have some work for you. Something unexpected has come up and I need you there as soon as possible. Call me here at my office and let me know," Patton barked. When he was angry he expected people to jump when he spoke.

$$\$\$\$$$

Shane knew he should tell Richard. Maybe he'd have some answers. Not likely, but he felt he should know, so he called and told Richard to meet him at the coffee shop.

"Now don't panic, but we have a problem," Shane began. He told Richard of his meeting with Wolford. Richard looked at him in disbelief. They stared at each other. What the hell could they do? Shane told him he had called Patton and was to keep him posted. They seemed paralyzed, unable to do anything.

"Wolford's like a cop: he won't do anything until he has proof and he doesn't have it yet. He doesn't know it, but he needs me to sort out the computer trail, and I can stall on that for a while, "Shane said.

$$\$\$\$$$

Patton arrived in Boston at mid-morning and met Doug Simms at eleven o'clock. They went directly downtown to the Ritz-Carlton hotel. After lunch, Patton outlined what he wanted done. There was no need to tell Simms much more than who the guy was and where he could be found.

"His name is Wolford and he works at the International Bank of Boston, not far from here. I gather he's an older guy so it shouldn't be too difficult. I don't want a mess. An accident would be fine, but there can be no slip-ups. It has to be complete, if you know what I mean," Patton said, "and it has to be no later than day after tomorrow. I'll meet him today so I can identify him for you. That'll give you a day to set him up. When it's complete, go directly back to Atlantic City. Here's $25,000. I'll meet you at the Taj on Friday with the other half."

ON HIS WAY BACK TO ATLANTIC CITY, Patton picked up a copy of the *Boston Globe* at Logan airport. It was front-page news: A prominent banker had been found slain in an affluent area of Boston. The police had no clues and were continuing their investigation. Patton smiled. Simms was dependable. He wondered what kind of message this would send to Shane and Richard. He hoped they would now realize how determined he was to eliminate any potential threat.

Shane was in his father's office when the police arrived. They were polite and asked questions about Wolford's friends and associates. They were gone in thirty minutes.

"It's unbelievable. Here was a man who gave himself to his community. He was totally unselfish, loved his family and was a great asset to the bank. We don't have many like him," Frank said sadly. "It was a strange killing, too. Bill's wallet with $300 was still in his jacket. Who would want to see him dead, and why?"

Shane was sure he knew why, and who. He had known Bill Wolford since before he graduated from high school. He felt a strange sense of relief. He respected Bill, but the events of the last few days had left him angry. Wolford wouldn't let up. His tenacity was overbearing. This was a tragedy, but it did solve a monumental problem. Shane needed to talk to Richard.

"You've heard the news, I'm sure. It's terrible. Meet me in five minutes," Shane said.

"I can't believe it. Patton must have flown in one of his goons to whack him, just like that. He's a dangerous man but I never dreamed he'd do anything like this. It's so cold an act—he never even knew the man. He's solved a major problem for us, but I didn't expect anything like this," Shane said.

"Have you talked to him yet? Boy, it didn't take him long. This is scary,

Shane," Richard said, "he could do the same to us." Thoughts of Brooke's exposure flashed through his mind.

"What could I say to him? It makes me sick. He's an animal, and yes, you're right, he could do something like this to us if anything else goes wrong. It's weird, though. I'm convinced Wolford would have eventually uncovered something that would have exposed us. I took pains to cover every base, but he was persistent beyond belief. Just a little accounting flap set him off. I've since re-coded all that but he would have found it, so in a way, Patton has saved our asses. But at what cost? Also, I'm sure my father will want me to take his place, which further assures us that nothing like this will happen again," Shane said, looking to Richard for some sign of agreement.

Richard knew now that he could never confide in Shane about Brooke's knowledge. If it ever got back to Patton, she was as good as dead. He even wondered if he should tell her what they knew about Wolford's death. While they had nothing to do with it, in a way they were responsible. The whole damn thing was getting messy. He would gladly give up all the money if he could just get himself out—well, maybe not all of it.

He was sitting in his office, agonizing over Wolford's death, when Brooke walked in. She seemed to get more beautiful every day, her long black hair framing that lovely face as she smiled at him.

He knew he had to tell her. He had to tell someone.

"Apparently, you haven't read the papers. Bill Wolford, the president of the bank downstairs, was killed last night. I never knew him, but Shane worked for him," Richard said. He went on to tell her everything Shane had told him. "There's no doubt it was Patton. Now we're involved in murder," he whispered.

This was more than Brooke had bargained for. While Richard had nothing to do with the homicide, his activities had prompted it, but if Wolford posed a threat to Richard and Shane, what was Richard to do?

"You weren't involved. There's nothing you can do now. It doesn't change your situation. You were involved in drug trafficking. You've stopped and you're going to let the chips fall. I don't think I'd let anyone know you've confided in me—Patton might find me a tempting target," Brooke said, smiling.

She was right. There was nothing he could do. Wolford was dead. He'd go on as he had. Shane would be in control now.

FIFTEEN

IN THE WEEKS AFTER PATTON TOOK HIS DRUG profits and paid off all his creditors, including Mecham Temple, his business began to flourish. Much of his success was due to industry growth, but ICC was very aggressive. They slashed prices and worked overtime to meet competitive requirements. They initiated an inventive mail-order division and sales took off.

Mecham watched this with envy and contempt. He was well aware of how Patton had managed to survive—probably the only person in the industry who knew the real secret to Patton's resurgent success. It gnawed at him to have to compete with a company that owed its comeback to drug money. There had to be some way Mecham could discreetly utilize this knowledge to combat Patton without jeopardizing Brooke. What would Patton's suppliers think if they knew they were being paid with laundered drug money? What would his customers think if they knew the computers they bought were built by a company using illicit funds? And what would his employees think if they knew their weekly wages were actually the proceeds from drug trafficking? Patton's whole operation had a stench Mecham could detect all the way to Boston. He was obsessed with destroying him.

His dilemma was how to deal with Richard and Brooke. His promise to Brooke made any attempt to expose Patton impossible, but Patton's continued encroachment on Mecham's market share was damaging his business. In the last quarter alone, his sales were down over 15 percent, all of it attributable to Patton's aggressive pricing. Even if the financial source of Patton's success weren't an issue, Mecham's loss of business was a real concern. In a peripheral way, Richard was just as responsible for this as Patton was, and Shane, too.

"Brooke, this whole thing with Richard, Shane, and Patton is getting out of control," Mecham said, needing to unloaded his problems. "I know I've promised you complete secrecy, but I've got to do something. Patton is killing us. Our sales are suffering because of his crazy pricing. His tainted funds allow him to operate with impunity. He virtually dominates all the markets," Mecham stormed.

This was another turn of events Brooke hadn't anticipated. She suspected her father was overstating the gravity of the situation, but how long could she protect her lover while her father suffered? If she was going to help Richard, and thereby protect his fortune, she couldn't expose Patton. Her loyalties were evenly divided—she was determined to see Richard through to the end, but her father had been the source of all her skills and ambitions. She couldn't allow Patton to destroy him.

RAY PATTON BASKED IN HIS COMPANY'S recent success, strutting through his offices with a renewed sense of power. He was back on top and he intended to stay there. He had never indulged himself much. He lived in a comfortable home, drove luxury cars, and traveled when he wished. He was reasonably faithful to his wife; when he did stray, it was only when he was out of town. He was, however, vulnerable to attractive young women. At forty-seven, he considered himself much more dashing than, in fact, he was.

Brooke Temple could be very persuasive when she wanted to be. As she had grown from a lanky, boyish-looking girl into a beautiful young woman, she was well aware of her looks. In fact, until she met Richard, she thought it great sport to coyly flirt with attractive men, only to dash their hopes with a quick retreat. She had developed the tactic to a high level of skill, and she planned to use it to full advantage.

"Mr. Patton, my name is Brooke Temple. I'm Mecham Temple's daughter. I intend to be in Atlanta next weekend and I would like very much to meet with you to discuss a very personal matter. I'll be staying downtown at the Weston. We could have dinner there on Saturday evening," she said in her most seductive voice.

Patton was both alarmed and flattered. Why in hell would Mecham's daughter want to see him? He and Temple weren't golf buddies. In fact, word on the street had it that ICC was killing CCA. Maybe she wants to explore a merger or buyout. His curiosity wouldn't let him pass.

"I'd be delighted to meet you. I could be there around eight. I'll look forward to it. How will I recognize you?" This was a line she was waiting for. "I don't think you'll have any trouble finding me. Just ask for Miss Temple."

This had to be convincing. Patton must understand that if he continued his predatory pricing and other sales tactics, she could make life very uncomfortable for him. In fact, she could put him out of business altogether. He knew who she was and he would soon know why she was there. She was going to protect her father. Patton knew nothing about her relationship with Richard Stearns or her plans for his fortune. Her mission—to convince Patton to abandon his business tactics or risk exposure—would require superlative finesse. She pondered his options. If he refused, his only alternative would be to silence her. God, was she in over her head? She doubted he would try anything tonight, but getting out of Atlanta could be formidable.

Patton was older than she expected. His suit was expensive and he walked with an air of importance, arrogance almost. He spotted who he hoped was she immediately, standing near the corridor to the seafood restaurant. Holding court might be more accurate: she commanded the attention of everyone in the long hall. In all his years of assessing women, he'd never seen one so beautiful.

"You must be Miss Temple," he said, hopefully. "I'm Ray Patton."

The restaurant was bordered by an outside lagoon and fountain. They sat at a waterside window. Brooke selected a secluded table where their conversation could not be overheard. This might be her only shot at him. After he ordered drinks, she got down to business.

"Mr. Patton, let me get right to the point. I'm here because my father is suffering as a result of your unconscionable sales tactics. He doesn't mind competing on a level field, but you and I both know you've used dirty money to skew the game. I'm here to tell you that if you don't cease your actions, you could have more trouble than you ever dreamed. I know more about you than you can imagine."

Wait a minute, Patton thought. How could this lovely creature possibly know anything about him? She wasn't old enough to know very much about anything. Drug dealers weren't even in her vocabulary. This must be an attempt by Mecham to intimidate him. As he looked into her flashing eyes, he felt a twinge of fear.

"What could you possibly know about me that would convince me to do anything?"

"Mr. Patton, let's not play games. I don't intend to get into all your tawdry behaviors, but maybe this will help you: I know all about your drug trafficking, your partners, how much money you made and where it went. I'm an attorney, Mr. Patton, and a pragmatist. I learned all this from a former lover, Richard Stearns. I'm sure you know who he is. He and I no longer see one another, and I'm determined now to protect my father. I could go the authorities anytime, but I have no reason to hurt Richard, or your other partner, Shane O'Connor, for that matter. What the three of you did is none of my business. As you might imagine, I have taken precautions to protect myself. If anything were to happen to me, . . . but you know how that works," Brooke said.

It was a lie of huge proportions. Neither Mecham nor Richard knew she was here playing a deadly game with Ray Patton on his own turf, but it was worth every frightening minute. And from the pensive look on his face, it was working.

This was outrageous, thought Patton. It was obvious she knew everything. But why, with so much at stake, would Richard confide in this woman? If not to help Mecham, what else could her motive be? It was a pretty gutsy move on her part, coming here alone, negotiating for her father. Patton respected that.

"Why would Richard tell you all this, and how do I know he did?"

"He told me to impress me, I suppose. We were pretty close for a time; even considered marriage. After I learned what he had done, I didn't want any part of him. Drug trafficking isn't me, so we split. But I won't tolerate what you've done to my father. I mean every word, Mr. Patton. Either you stop or I go to the authorities," she said, glaring into his eyes, her jaw set.

BROOKE WENT TO HER ROOM and called Richard. She had told him she was spending the night with her parents. After the usual chitchat she asked him to meet her at her home for lunch the next day. She also cautioned him not to speak with Shane under any circumstances. She'd explain tomorrow. She then called her father to join them for lunch.

She was safe in her hotel room for the rest of the night. Getting to the airport in the morning was beginning to frighten her. The look in Patton's eyes as she left the table was one she'd never forget. Thoughts of Bill Wolford made her throat tighten.

She wouldn't take a commercial flight back to Boston. With Richard's money, she'd charter a jet; the crew could personally pick her up at the hotel, so she wouldn't be alone for a minute.

Flying back to Boston, Brooke was convinced that Patton believed she knew everything. For her plan to work, he had to believe she would expose them all. The stakes couldn't be higher.

PATTON WASN'T GOING TO BE INTIMIDATED by some educated, good-looking, high-class broad. He'd been here before; the game works both ways. Over the years, anyone trying to twist Ray Patton's arm usually ended up wishing they hadn't. There was always a way to deal with people like this. Usually, they were men, but he had no qualms about a woman. Her threats about protecting herself were groundless. If she left a summary of what she knew, they'd all deny it. Proof might be hard to come by. But he was disappointed in Richard; in fact, so disappointed that he would now include Richard in his plans.

SIXTEEN

BROOKE WAS NERVOUSLY PACING THE FLOOR when Mecham and Richard arrived. When they had finished lunch she recited what she had done.

"He was frightened and he believed me. I had to tell him that you and I are through, Richard, so when you talk to Shane, make sure he gets the message. It's crucial he and Patton believe that you and I don't see one another any more," she said, throwing her arms around him, smothering him with a kiss. "I think you'll see some changes in the way he operates, Dad. I told him if he didn't, I'd go to the authorities."

Richard and Mecham looked at her in awe. What kind of woman was this? What she had done was dangerous beyond belief. She had done it for Mecham. Whether it worked or not was academic. She had put herself and Richard in the worst possible position.

"Brooke, my darling, you didn't have to put yourself in that kind of danger. We would have survived somehow," Mecham said, choking back tears.

"Brooke," Richard interrupted, "you don't know this man. He's an animal. You know what he did to Wolford. How could you put yourself in such a vulnerable position? Regardless of whether he thinks you're bluffing, he won't rest until he's silenced you. Do you understand that? What on earth did you think you'd accomplish?"

"Damn it, Richard," Mecham barked, "this is getting out of control. Your thoughtless, demented behavior is beginning to threaten my daughter and my business. I'm not going to continue with this. I'm sorry, Brooke, but I can no longer go along with your insane plan. I'm going to the authorities myself."

Brooke was stunned. This would ruin all her plans. Richard would go to jail, his money would disappear, and her visions of limitless wealth evaporate. She couldn't let him do this.

"You're forgetting a few things, Dad: If you persist, Richard will go to jail, ruined. Also, when Shane O'Connor is implicated, one of your closest friends, Frank O'Connor, will suffer. His bank might fail. And, of course, you'll virtually be throwing away nearly a billion dollars. I admit my trip to

77

Atlanta might have been impulsive, but the outcome could prove invaluable. If Richard is right about Patton's vindictiveness, then let's play into his hand. I don't mind being the target of his wrath, as long as the playing field is level. The three of us can protect me somehow. Let him come after me—we'll be ready."

Mecham was horrified. Use Brooke as bait for Patton and his goons? Impossible! But her analysis was correct: While he had little sympathy for Richard or Shane, the idea of Frank O'Connor and the bank failing was unthinkable. After all, he was a stockholder.

They all agreed that Brooke would have to be protected, but they couldn't come up with a plan. It would have to be soon, probably tonight. Richard agreed to meet Mecham later that evening, then left for home, where he had a message to call Shane. He was sure Patton had contacted him by now. Shane was probably as shocked as he and Mecham had been.

"What the hell did you do?" Shane shouted into the phone. "Why in God's name did you tell Brooke? If what you've done jeopardizes our operation, Richard, I swear I'll kill you myself." Richard had to pretend he had no knowledge of Brooke's visit to Atlanta, and portray their relationship as over.

"What the hell are you talking about?" Richard asked.

"You know damn well what I'm talking about," Shane screamed. He told Richard of Brooke's meeting with Patton. "You're a fool."

Richard gave Shane a hastily contrived reason why he'd been forced to tell Brooke. He couldn't tell him the truth. He also said they were no longer seeing each other.

"Patton doesn't buy any of that. He's in a rage. I wouldn't give you a dime for Brooke's life, or yours either for that matter. How could you have wrecked what we worked so hard for? You're a damn fool, Richard, and I'm not going to let you ruin my life. I've come too far with this setup, and if Patton doesn't stop you, I will."

"Look, Shane, I never dreamed she'd go to Patton, but for your information, I don't think Brooke would ever expose either of us. Apparently all she was trying to do was help her father. When we broke up, I certainly didn't get the idea she was out to get you or me. She wanted nothing to do with the drug thing. I think it's a bold threat to Patton. Hopefully he'll calm down."

"Don't kid yourself, Richard. You haven't a clue what Brooke will do and you sure as hell underestimate Patton. And stop this 'breakup' shit—nobody believes that. You've put us all in a corner. I'd start carrying a gun if I were you," Shane said and hung up.

Richard met Mecham at Brooke's home later that evening. He was happy to have him as an ally. Now was no time to harbor grudges, especially when lives were in danger—including his own. Brooke would have to go to a safe house for the next week or so. Richard was sure Patton would make his move soon.

"Mecham, I know we've had our differences about this whole episode, but the important thing now is to get Brooke to a safe location. I've talked to Shane and obviously he's pissed. He thinks Patton will come after me, too. We don't have much time."

They located a furnished townhouse in a high-rise building near downtown. Its gated garage entrance offered a measure of protection. A phone was installed and all the locks were changed. Brooke took some clothes and a few personal items and made herself as comfortable as she could. At the same time, Richard also moved a few personal things. This should be interesting, he thought. They had talked about living together, but not quite like this.

Under any other circumstances, Richard and Mecham would have gone to the police. Neither had a clue how to ward off armed thugs.

MECHAM TEMPLE HAD, OVER THE YEARS, made many friends. He'd given generously to the causes he believed in. Because he was a Vietnam veteran, his friend Jim Snider had prevailed on him to support a "weekend warrior" effort. Jim and a group of veterans engaged in simulated warfare, in which groups of men were pitted against each other using paint-ball ammunition to identify the "dead and wounded". It was an intense competition, usually lasting all weekend, and they all took it very seriously. In earlier days Mecham had participated, but age and scarcity of time no longer allowed it. Nonetheless, he remained close to Jim and some of the other participants. Now, he thought, he just might have a paying job for Jim and his buddies.

They met early the next morning at Mecham's office. He briefed Jim on the mission: They were to escort Brooke and Richard to and from their offices, and provide around-the-clock coverage at the rented townhouse. They were to be armed, and Mecham instructed Jim to shoot to kill. He didn't go into why he wanted no police involved, but suggested that Jim view it as a personal protection job, like a bodyguard.

RAY PATTON WAS NOT ONLY FRIGHTENED, he was determined to eliminate this latest threat to his financial recovery as soon as possible. Richard Stearns was a fool. Nobody with intact senses would spill his guts about something as important as this to a woman—not even one who looked like Brooke Temple. There was far too much at stake. If he didn't do something immediately, he was sure she would go to the authorities. He phoned Doug Simms.

"Doug, I've got another nuisance in Boston. I need you to meet me there tomorrow noon if possible. You'll be there four or five days. Any problem?"

"No, but I'm not sure I can get away on such short notice. I'll call you back in an hour."

While waiting, Patton pondered calling Shane. If he could take care of Richard and Brooke, that would leave only Shane and himself. Surely Shane could now contain any problems at the bank. This would ensure a seamless transition. There had been too many people involved from the beginning, he thought.

He had to reschedule for one day later to accommodate Simms. They met at the airport and went directly to a hotel.

"This one's a bit more complicated. You'll be taking down two: a guy named Richard Stearns and a knockout broad named Brooke Temple. I think I'll stay here to make sure nothing goes wrong. It's crucial these two go down clean. Both are younger than the old guy, and both are attorneys. I know where Stearns works, and I suspect the woman works at the same place. I'll take you to the office building first thing in the morning and point them out. That'll give you a day or two to stake out their movements. This has to be quick and not messy—maybe a murder-suicide scenario. We'll sort it out when you get the details," Patton explained.

It took Simms much of the next two days, following Richard and Brooke, to map out their pattern of travel to the office and back to the townhouse. It was obvious they had an escort. They were picked up in the morning and driven to work by two men in a black Mercedes. These men accompanied them to the elevator and up to the twenty-fifth floor. They reversed the procedure in the evening when returning the pair to the townhouse. They entered past a guard into the lower-level parking garage. Simms hadn't been able to establish which unit was theirs.

The garage entrance was on a busy, well-lighted street, not convenient for what they had in mind. Maybe the guard could be persuaded to cooperate.

"The only shot I see is in the parking garage. We'll have to either recruit the guard or take him down. It's cleaner to eliminate him," Simms said.

"I agree," Patton said. "Set it up for tomorrow night. I'll be with you. Make sure we have a quick, unobstructed getaway route."

JIM SNIDER UNDERSTOOD HIS MISSION PERFECTLY. In addition to the armed escorts, he had three men stationed in the parking garage and two more across the street in a second-story loft. All were equipped with radiotelephones.

At 5:45 the following evening, the black Mercedes pulled into the parking garage beneath the townhouse. Directly behind it was Ray Patton, driving alone. Doug Simms sat in the guard booth. As soon as the Mercedes cleared the barricade, Simms motioned Patton to follow. When both cars were in the garage, Simms joined Patton in his car. They followed the sedan to the rear, where it parked near the elevator. The escorts opened the rear door and both Richard and Brooke got out. Patton stopped his car and reached for his gun. Simms was already out of the car, his gun drawn. As Patton opened his door he heard gunshots from behind. Simms slumped to the ground. Patton wheeled to face their attackers; four rounds thudded into his chest. He was dead before he hit the concrete floor.

With their escorts, Richard and Brooke scurried to the elevator. In the cavernous garage, the gunshots sounded like cannon. When the elevator arrived, all they could hear was the rumble of Patton's car, still idling.

Within minutes, the sounds in the garage were mingled with the distant high-pitched screeching of sirens, approaching rapidly. Several occupants of the townhouse ventured into the garage, gaping at the bodies on the concrete. A flashing police car eased into view and slowly came to rest at the rear of Patton's car. Two uniformed officers emerged and circled the casualties, bending to assess their condition. Blood seeped from the bodies, trickling aimlessly, staining the cement floor. No one spoke. More police cars arrived.

The two escorts in the black Mercedes leaned against their car, watching the police. They were as shocked as everyone else. Richard and Brooke had left the scene, and the escorts were about to be questioned. They knew very little. They provided the names and destination addresses of their passengers, and related their version of the shootings. The names of the victims were a mystery as was the explanation for their deaths. They were told to wait in their car while the police left to find Richard and Brooke.

Richard answered the ring of the doorbell and ushered two policemen into the townhouse.

Brooke was on the phone with her father. "As soon as we got out of the car I saw this other car stop. The passenger door opened and a man got out with a gun raised and looked right at us. That was when I heard the first shots. Then the driver's side door opened and Patton got out, holding a gun. He started to turn around and then more shots. I didn't see what happened after that—we were running for the elevator."

"I wish I could have been there with you. I'm so relieved you're both all right," Mecham said.

Brooke hung up the phone and sat on the couch with Richard, too shocked to look at the police.

"Could either of you tell us exactly what happened? We spoke with your drivers and they knew nothing about the victims. Who are they and why would they have been after you?" the officer asked.

"The man on the driver's side of the car was Raymond Patton. I have no idea who the other one is," Richard offered. "They were desperate businessmen on a mission of revenge. Patton and this woman's father are fierce competitors in the computer business. He apparently intended to take matters into his own hands for reasons known only to him. We're damn lucky to be alive. The man was a monster, capable of anything."

"I'll need both of you to come to the station to complete a formal summary of what happened here. Your drivers too," the officer said.

Brooke repaired her face and took Richard's arm. Together they followed the police to the elevator and down to the garage, where their escorts were talking to the other policemen. An ambulance had arrived and both bodies were removed. The garage floor remained wet with their blood; the smell of gunfire still thickened the air. Richard and Brooke were ushered into a police car and driven to the station.

"Let me do the talking," Richard whispered. "You can plead distress. This shouldn't take too long."

It took about two hours. The questions were predictable and yielded no surprises. Exhausted, they left, confident that no further problems would arise from this convenient event.

SEVENTEEN

R AY PATTON'S DEATH CAUSED MECHAM TEMPLE NO GRIEF. He'd despised Patton and was glad the man no longer represented the industry. It did, however, offer an enormous opportunity. With Patton gone, there might be a play to acquire his company. ICC was a viable operation; run properly, it could integrate very well with CCA. Together, they could virtually dominate the computer industry.

As Mecham pondered the events of recent weeks, it dawned on him that he might have an asset worth exploring. Brooke had outlined a scenario which, at the time, Mecham had dismissed as outrageous, to say the least. Her premise was that if Richard were to come through all the pitfalls of having been a drug trafficker, and the wealth he had accumulated were still intact, she and Richard would be far better custodians of the money than the Feds. Well, it looked now as though that just might happen. It was down to Richard and Shane, and Richard still had his $750 million safely tucked away. With that kind of money, there was no question in Mecham's mind—he could have Patton's company.

Brooke was happy to be back in her own home. The ordeal with Patton was soon forgotten and she and Richard resumed their romance. Richard was different now, much more relaxed and fun to be with. They talked often about the money and what they might do with it. They traveled on weekends, and Richard talked about marriage. Brooke was beginning to have great confidence in her ability to manipulate him. His fortune seemed just the challenge she needed. Thoughts of all the wonderful things she could do with it consumed a good deal of her time. If they could just get to a time when they no longer had to look over their shoulders, life would hold limitless possibilities.

Richard's life was exactly what he'd hoped it would be when he and Shane had first talked about their drug ventures. With the recent crises over and the demise of Ray Patton, he looked forward to all the great things his money would buy. When Mecham approached him with a business proposition, he was delighted.

"I think if we make them an offer of about $500 million together with stock in my company, they'll jump at it. We've done all the numbers and it works. Your share of the new company would be close to 40 percent. I don't know what your plans are with Don Parker, but I think it would be in everyone's best interests if you joined our company. I'm sure Parker would understand. Money's obviously not an issue with you now. You'd be a major stockholder; maybe even presidential material after some time. What do you think?" Mecham asked.

Richard was flattered. Even with his riches, Mecham was offering him what seemed a great opportunity. He had no interest in staying with Parker and was anxious to get some of his assets invested. He was sure this would please Brooke. Even after investing with Mecham, he would have $250 million left. He couldn't resist calculating the annual interest on that.

"I like it," Richard said. "It sounds exciting and it's something I'd be interested in over the long haul. I do want to recommend one thing, though: I want to handle all the legal work on the purchase. It could get a little dicey with Parker when we write the check. In fact, Brooke can assist me; we'll keep it all in the family."

It was an exciting time for Richard. He left Don Parker's firm and leased a small suite of offices in the financial district. Brooke joined him and together they fashioned the documents necessary to make an offer on ICC. It was fascinating work and the financial preparation intrigued Brooke. She hadn't known just how profitable her father's business really was, and with the addition of Patton's company the numbers grew far faster than she expected. Richard's ownership would assure him an annual dividend income of over $2 million from the combined operations. Mecham had arranged an annual salary of $750,000 as vice president of the new Atlanta operation. Together with interest income from the balance of his funds, Richard's total annual income would begin at around $20 million—over $1.5 million a month! He certainly had become a candidate for marriage with Brooke.

The ICC board of directors quickly approved the sale. Richard, Brooke, and Ryan Tipton worked to get all the papers signed, the money transferred, and the stock issued. They planned for Richard to spend two months in Boston for indoctrination, and then transfer to Atlanta to run the operation there. He would commute to Boston on weekends—more often if necessary.

Marriage was inevitable. Richard talked of little else and Brooke realized that he came with the money. She had no qualms about a commitment but she certainly wasn't about to be relegated to the position of loving wife and mother. No—she had salvaged Richard and his fortune, and now was the time to exploit her success.

She kept the new offices in Boston and continued handling all the legal affairs of the new company. She and Richard had departed Don Parker's law firm under the very best of conditions, and Don understood Mecham's wishes. Married to Richard, and Mecham's only heir, she would someday become a very wealthy woman. Their combined net worth at this moment exceeded $2.5 billion. If it were all hers, she could begin to appear on the Forbes 400!

Her instincts about how to handle Richard had paid off. She was only twenty-four years old and had many years to see that his money grew. And she had one asset no one could ever take from her: she knew where it had all come from. She kept an agreement she'd had Richard sign when she discovered his drug activities and appointed herself as his attorney. The attorney-client relationship survived their marriage. She was under no ethical or legal obligation ever to divulge where Richard's money had originated, neither was she deprived in any way of utilizing this knowledge should need arise. It was privileged information for her to use as she saw fit.

Marriage to Richard was a mixed blessing: Certainly she was a spousal beneficiary should anything happen to him; even divorce would yield half to her. But beyond that, she must impress on him that the control and exploitation of such great wealth was not only her responsibility but also her right. Wasn't it she who had tempted Patton to make his ill-advised attack? Wasn't it her strategy that had allowed Mecham to acquire ICC? Hadn't Richard's prestigious position at CCA resulted from her father's judicious use of Richard's funds? Of course all that was true!

Now her mission would be to use these enormous assets in her quest for recognition. She must discipline herself to think on a scale of colossal proportions. If she became complacent about the existing sums, no matter how gigantic, she'd fail to realize her dreams of unimaginable wealth. She now had every piece in place. It wasn't a matter for Richard to concern himself with. He was safely tucked away at CCA; even better, he was consigned to Atlanta.

One small problem had surfaced, however: soon after their marriage, Richard began to lobby for a family. She had successfully diverted the conversation with subtle suggestions that having children would interfere with their enjoyment of sex, and that life was too complicated right now to even consider it. What she didn't reveal was that she abhorred the very idea. Sharing with Richard was quite enough. In her relentless quest for status, wealth and material gratification, there would never be room for any "little Richards" in her life.

EIGHTEEN

During the next three years, Richard progressed beyond everyone's expectations—his own included. After six months in Atlanta, the operation was running so smoothly that he and Mecham decided he should return to Boston permanently and assume the position of corporate vice president of operations, which included all domestic and offshore facilities. He loved the computer business and found it fascinating. He became adept at predicting industry trends and understood the importance of engineering competitiveness. Two years after returning from Atlanta, he was appointed president of the company. He and Mecham had developed a father-son relationship and greatly respected one another. Richard's rapid spectacular rise in their company and in the industry delighted Mecham, and enabled him to spend more time enjoying his boat and beach house. Richard's adept handling of the company had seen sales increase by 20 percent and net income over 25 percent. Their stock was the darling of Wall Street. At the tender age of twenty-nine he was rapidly becoming an icon in the industry. They never spoke about the nefarious origins of their great success.

Shane O'Connor enjoyed his position at his father's bank. As president, he was afforded prestige in the community and ample time to pursue his other interests, which hadn't changed much since he and Richard had partied together years ago. Women were high on his list of exploitable things, and he had never married. He did, however, spend a great deal of time exploring investment opportunities. When he and Richard ended their drug activities, each had $750 million deposited in United States banks. Now thirty-five years old, Shane had managed to squander most of it. The investments he had indulged in were highly speculative and subject to all the vagaries of global markets. Many were offshore operations brought to his attention through his father's banking connections. He was known in the venture capital centers as "the loser of last resort."

Desperate to recoup his enormous losses, Shane scoured European and Asian publications for word of opportunities. The ad that caught his attention was in the *Asian Wall Street Journal*. Some of his peers in the Chinese and Pacific Rim markets had told him that the shipping business could be a lucrative enterprise in these areas. With the expected development of the Chinese market and the existing level of business in Singapore and Taiwan, it was deemed a growth situation. The ad requested a response to a post office box in Singapore. He quickly composed a flowery letter on bank letterhead, signed by himself as president.

A week later he received a fax from a Mr. Ling Hirosa saying they had received his letter and would send all relevant information immediately. The package arrived two days later.

All the usual *pro forma* information was included together with brochures describing the company. They needed a $15 million investment and were prepared to grant 50 percent ownership of the company. The expected return on the investment was in excess of 25 percent. They also required assistance in obtaining an additional $30 million in bank loans. If he was interested, he was to submit his financial statement together with his banking connections.

It wasn't great but it was better than he had done in some of his recent outings. The next day he prepared all they asked for and expressed it to Singapore. Apparently his response generated some interest; three days later he received a phone call from Mr. Hirosa.

"Mr. O'Connor, we have received your letter and we perhaps have some mutual interest. If you are available, we would like to be in Boston next week to meet with you," Hirosa said, going on to explain additional parameters of the deal. Of course Shane was interested, and would be happy to meet with them.

When Hirosa arrived the next week, he had with him his partner, Mr. Kota Sakamoto. They went over the entire operation and explained that they needed his investment and the bank loans to lease additional ships. Business was good and getting better. They had been in operation for over three years and were projecting phenomenal growth. Shane took the bait.

When they left, he called one of his banking associates in Singapore, and explained what he needed. The banker said he knew of the company and would be happy to lend the money, but only if Shane were an investor for the $15 million. Within a week Shane was in as half owner. They all signed a corporate note for the $30 million and immediately leased two additional ships.

The association was mutually satisfactory until six months later, when Hirosa announced they needed an additional $10 million to keep the company afloat, so to speak. They had been able to find $5 million and needed the rest from Shane. It was a short-term situation and they were sure they would need no more.

God, he thought, no matter what he got into, it went south. He was discouraged by his seeming inability to make profitable investment decisions. As he reflected on this latest loser, he reminded himself of the only positive thing to come out of his venture into the shipping business: a source for small heroin buys for personal use. During one of his few visits to the Boston office of the Far East Shipping Company, he had met a crewmember named Cho Wong, a street-smart Asian who spoke excellent English and made it known almost immediately that he had the goods. Shane had become adept at recognizing the type, and they developed a working relationship. Shane saw him twice a month.

Shane could come up with the $5 million, but it would leave him with minimal operating funds and he wasn't convinced they wouldn't need more in the future. He could refuse, but that would reduce his equity, and if they didn't get the $10 million the enterprise could fail.

$$\text{\$\$\$}$$

SHANE HADN'T TALKED TO RICHARD for nearly a year. He read about him in the newspapers and saw him on television occasionally but they had drifted apart. After he and Brooke were married they had little in common. From all reports Richard Stearns was doing very well. He and his wife were rumored to be among the wealthiest people in the Boston area.

As Shane saw it, Richard owed his start to him, and would still be a struggling attorney if Shane hadn't talked him into the drug operation. And look at him now—one of the most successful young entrepreneurs in the country—probably worth billions. Maybe Richard would like to return the favor.

It wasn't as if Shane were destitute. True, his resources had been substantially reduced and he was making only $500,000 a year as president of the International Bank of Boston. But he feared that if his lousy luck continued he could lose most of it. If he could sell part of his equity in the shipping business, his immediate problem would be solved. Richard should be a natural candidate.

When Shane called, Richard thought he sounded older and more cynical, but it was good to hear from him. When Shane suggested they have lunch he jumped at the chance.

"It's been a long time, Richard, you look great," Shane said.

They talked for an hour, catching up on what each was doing. It took Shane that long to dredge up the courage to make his approach.

"My efforts haven't paid the dividends yours have, Richard. I don't get my name in the papers quite as often as you do, but I've got a deal for you." Shane said, and told Richard about his shipping business investment.

"I put too much money into the damn company. Now they need another $5 million and frankly I'm reluctant to get further involved. They'll probably reduce my equity if I don't come up with it, but I'm afraid the company will fail if they don't get what they say they need. So here's my deal: I'll give you a third of my equity for the $5 million. I've got a few days, why don't you do some research and let me know?"

Richard didn't need to think about it any longer than it took to drive back to his office. But Shane had been a good friend; he'd talk to Brooke about it.

"That's about all he had to say. I can't imagine going through that much money in three years—even the Red Sox have better luck—but I do feel some responsibility to him. As you know, he started all this," Richard said.

Shane had never been one of Brooke's favorite people. She tolerated Richard's friendship with him before she learned about the drug business, but after Patton was killed she saw no reason to keep in touch with him. If there were a problem at the bank, God forbid, he'd let Richard know.

"What kind of shipping business is it?" Brooke asked. "I mean, tankers, cruise lines, cargo, what?"

"I didn't ask. It was of no interest to me. If he came to me for a $5 million loan, I'd be more receptive."

Brooke had become one of Boston's most astute investment advisors. She managed Richard's entire, very considerable, portfolio, and invested excess funds for the company. She also wrote a weekly financial column for the *Boston Globe* that gave her the visibility she so coveted.

"Why don't you call in the morning and get the name of the company? Maybe he'll tell you a little about what they do. Some shipping deals, particularly in the Asian markets, are about to explode," she said, casually.

After talking to Shane the next morning, Richard called Brooke. "As usual, you're way ahead of us all. It's an Asian operation named Far East Shipping Company. Shane doesn't know much about the day-to-day; maybe that's why he continues to watch his investments evaporate."

Brooke had access to a computer database on just about any investment. She had contacts at all the major brokerage houses, and real-time reports on all the stock markets came across her screen. Because the Far East Shipping Company was private, she had to tap her personal sources. It was one of a few companies operating in the Chinese/Singapore corridor. It had been in business for nearly four years and, except for some short-term cash flow difficulties, it was a mover, showing all the positive signs of growth. Maybe Shane had finally stumbled onto a winner. This was a situation Brooke loved.

"Hello, darling. I've got some news for you, and some advice. Shane might have inadvertently picked a winner. Call and tell him you're not interested in buying a third of his equity; tell him you'll buy it all. If he needs money as badly as it sounds, offer him what he paid for it. Tell him he can have our check in a day."

Shane jumped at the offer. It had been ages since he'd had a break-even situation. He'd never liked his relationship with the Asians, except for his heroin source, Cho Wong. As Shane watched his fortune shrinking, his mind occasionally drifted back to the days of easy money in the drug business. Except for Wolford and Patton, there had been no problems.

In casual conversation he had questioned Wong about his source of heroin. When Shane was an owner of the shipping company, Wong had felt compelled to be cautious: he liked his job and enjoyed his trips to America. But when Shane told him he was no longer involved, Wong opened up. They had long conversations about his connections in Hong Kong and the potential for large heroin buys there. It was intriguing, and visions of recovering his declining wealth raced through Shane's mind. The numbers for heroin were far better than for cocaine. Wong had told him he could buy a kilo of heroin in Hong Kong for $25,000. When Shane checked with Marty Stinson, he was told that the price to the distributors in the United States was $75,000. The margin was almost double that of cocaine!

If he invested $10 million with Wong he could buy four hundred kilos and sell them for $30 million. If he parlayed that two or three times he'd be right back on top.

As the conversation grew more serious, Wong told him how he was able to spirit heroin aboard one of the ships and transport it to America undetected. The quantities were small but Wong insisted he knew how to handle larger amounts.

"Let's say we wanted to ship four hundred kilos, almost half a ton. Could you handle that?" Shane asked.

Wong thought for a moment. "I'd need some help for that much. I have a friend on the ships. Between us, I think we could arrange it," Cho said.

"How about your suppliers? Can they get us that much in Hong Kong?" Shane asked.

"Oh, sure, no problem. They ask me all time how much I can take. That would be easy," Cho said, grinning.

During the next two weeks, Cho Wong made a trip to Hong Kong and verified what he had told Shane. The material definitely would be available.

It would be delivered to the docks. Wong would be responsible for getting it on board, and cash payment was to be made in American dollars.

Shane called his friend at the Imperial Bank in Hong Kong and arranged to wire-transfer $10 million of his own funds, to be picked up when he arrived the following week. Wong had contacted his supplier and they would meet them on the docks on Friday of that week. It was all so simple if you had the contacts, the money, and the guts, Shane thought—it was simple supply and demand.

Shane flew to Hong Kong to await the arrival of Cho's ship. On Friday he went to the Imperial Bank and picked up the $10 million in cash. Shortly before the bank closed, he put it in two large attaché cases and left for his hotel. He was to meet Cho in three hours.

He took a cab to the docks, keeping the attaché cases on the floor. It was dangerous to attempt this without some protection, but Cho had assured him it was safe. As they approached pier thirty-nine, he told the driver to stop. No one was there.

He waited ten minutes before he saw a large gray van pull up 100 feet from his cab. He watched Cho emerge from the passenger side and walk toward him. Telling the driver to wait, Shane stepped outside. Just as he moved to greet Cho, the van sped toward them. Cho rolled to the ground as Shane tried to get back in the cab. He immediately knew how foolish he had been. He froze as two men holding guns emerged from the van. He glanced at the attaché cases in the cab, confused. The men were only thirty feet away. Nowhere to run. Before he could devise any sort of escape, three shots caught him in the back. He staggered toward the cab, clutching his chest, knees buckling. As he stumbled, trying to reach the cab, he fell to the ground. He could hear the two men running toward him. They grabbed the attaché cases, threw them inside the van and sped off. The last thing Shane Taylor O'Connor heard was the screech of tires as the van careened away. Cho scrambled to get out of the way but was caught under its wheels. Broken and bleeding, he struggled to the edge of the pier and collapsed.

An investigation by the Hong Kong police yielded no information on the drug dealers. Recovering, Cho told them he was a crewmember of the Malaysia Princess and knew nothing. When the cab driver confirmed that he'd had nothing to do with the killing, Cho was released.

NINETEEN

THE AMERICAN EMBASSY WAS NOTIFIED of Shane's death. The cab driver told them he had picked up Shane at the Princess Hotel and that Shane had carried two large attaché cases that were stolen by the men in the van. When the story broke in the local newspapers, the president of the Imperial Bank of Hong Kong came forward with the news that the American, Shane O'Connor, had picked up $10 million in American dollars that same day. The embassy called the International Bank of Boston.

"Mr. O'Connor, this is Nathan Statton of the American embassy in Hong Kong. I'm afraid I have tragic news." He told Frank of the killing and of the circumstances surrounding it. Did he know a Shane T. O'Connor? He told him Shane had been killed in an apparent drug transaction in the company of another man named Cho Wong, a crewmember of the Malaysian Princess. The ship was leased to the Far Eastern Shipping Company, owned in part by an American couple named Richard Stearns and Brooke Temple-Stearns. The embassy would be shipping the body to the United States along with Shane's personal effects.

Frank was overwhelmed. There must be some mistake. Shane had been away from the bank for over a week, but Frank thought he was in the Caribbean. Shane had no business in Hong Kong. Was Statton sure? There was no mistake. Shane, his beloved only son, whom he had so carefully groomed to take his place at the bank, was dead. The son he had nurtured from birth. Sobbing, Frank dropped his head to the desk. As the awful truth sank in, his shoulders racked and he cried uncontrollably.

Frank called his wife and said he'd be home in an hour. He wanted to be with her when she heard the terrible news. She had been as close to Shane as he had. How would they endure the days ahead?

Shane's body arrived the next day and Frank made burial arrangements. Because he knew many people at the *Globe,* no mention of drugs was included in the front-page article. He had never known such despair.

Teary-eyed and on the verge of breakdown, Frank sat through the funeral service. He stayed away from the bank all the next week. He needed time to sort out his life. As he continued his grieving, thoughts of his conversation with Statton churned in his mind. A drug transaction? Shane knew nothing about drugs, he thought. And in the company of someone from a shipping company owned by a Richard Stearns?

When Frank returned to the bank he was somewhat refreshed. He had spent the entire week at his beach house on Martha's Vineyard. As the reality of Shane's death seized hold of his consciousness, he became obsessed with finding out what had happened. His son was no drug dealer, and whatever he'd been doing in Hong Kong had nothing to do with drugs.

One of the first things Frank did when he returned was spend a morning in Shane's office. He went through every piece of paper and every drawer. One was locked; he had to have the maintenance people open it. Inside he found a series of file folders with the names "Ray Patton" and "Richard Stearns" on the tabs. There were also files bearing Shane's name. Each contained information in Shane's longhand: a dozen or so sheets of paper with what appeared to be account numbers, dates and amounts of money. In Ray Patton's file there were a number of promissory notes stamped "CANCELED." The signature on every note appeared to be his own—Frank O'Connor! But he hadn't signed them. Who had?

There was no indication of the source of the funds, just deposit dates and running balances. There was no mention of where these balances were kept, and the account numbers meant nothing to Frank. The dates went back nearly three years—about the time Bill Wolford was killed—and the amounts were unbelievable: hundreds of millions. In Shane's file were numerous receipts from foreign companies. The amounts were in the millions. Included was one receipt from the Far Eastern Shipping Company. Frank went through each file again and again, trying to make some sense of the entries.

Ray Patton had been dead nearly three years. His ending balance was only a couple million dollars. When the entries ended, both Shane and Richard showed balances over $750 million. Astounding, Frank thought. But where did it come from? Except for receipts in Shane's file, none of it appeared to be from any official source. These were just longhand entries of large amounts of money. They were hard to dismiss as some great good fortune. It began to look as though Shane might have been involved in activities that had nothing to do with the bank's business, and it appeared that whatever he'd been up to, Richard Stearns was involved.

He reread all the papers in Shane's file, looking for bits of information to confirm his suspicions. Finally, he concluded that Shane, Richard, and Ray Patton had engaged in a massive drug operation. Beyond what he read in the newspapers, Frank knew little about drug trafficking, but it was the only enterprise he could think of that could generate so much money so quickly. This was not the Shane he knew.

No, someone had pushed Shane into this activity. Richard was his best friend when all this started and they were together constantly. In fact it was at about this time that Mecham Temple had asked Frank to look into some account Richard was supposed to have had in the bank; the amount in seven figures. It was obvious to Frank that Richard had gotten Shane involved, and the strange events surrounding Shane's death pointed directly to Richard Stearns.

As Frank pondered a strategy, it became clear to him that Shane's role must have involved circumventing bank regulations. He hoped no bank funds were involved—Bill Wolford would have discovered that. But moving so much money through and around all the bank procedures must have been a computer monstrosity. It would also have required extensive correspondence with cooperating banks, yet none of that was in the files.

It wouldn't be appropriate to get other bank employees involved in a search for additional documents or computer printouts. He'd have to keep this quiet until he had a better handle on the entire operation. God, there could be serious repercussions if any of this were discovered. He locked all the papers in his file cabinet.

Frank required a more detailed analysis of the papers he had found. He needed someone to systematically go through the entire group of files and come up with an underlying methodology. It would take more time and computer skill than he had, so he called an accountant who had done some internal audits for him several years ago.

James Digby was a skilled CPA who had a good banking background and knew his way around computers. Frank outlined what he had and what he wanted Digby to do.

"I don't have to tell you how important it is for you to keep what you're doing completely secret. I've arranged an office for you next to mine. I don't know exactly what you'll come up with, but I do know it could be a problem for the bank. I don't think any bank funds were involved but you might find evidence of improper or illegal transfers. Take your time and keep me fully informed."

It took Jim Digby a week to summarize and analyze all the entries. He created hundreds of "what-if" scenarios on his computer. Because the files lacked any official bank entries, he had to make assumptions about how the money had been moved through the bank's computers. After another week a pattern began to develop. All the activity had been made through the ICC account. Consistently larger and larger amounts passed through the account.

Where these went was a mystery, but it was fairly obvious they ended up in accounts controlled by Shane, Richard, and Ray Patton. The amounts grew weekly but they led nowhere.

Digby showed Frank the summary sheets. "I've summarized the files at least fifty different ways. I've used what little additional information is available here at the bank, and come up with this." Dates were printed across the top, amounts and individuals listed down the left side. The entire sheet summarized only about two months. The ending balances were astounding.

As Frank studied the sheets, he began to recollect some of the things that had happened during that time period. He marked the dates when Bill Wolford and Ray Patton had been killed. He pondered what had happened in the months following the end of the operation, all the while looking for some event relating to Richard.

"It looks like Shane and Richard each had around $750 million when it ended," Frank mused. He stared through Digby and got up from his desk.

Bingo! Four months after the operation ceased, Mecham Temple had acquired ICC. Of course! Ray Patton was dead and his company went on the block. Richard Stearns's money was used for the deal. It didn't sound like something Mecham Temple would do, but that's how Frank put it together. It also accounted for Richard's prominent position at CCA.

TWENTY

FRANK O'CONNOR WAS NOT FLAMBOYANT but he lived an elegant life. Happily married for nearly forty years, he wanted for very little. Beautiful homes, lengthy vacations, seagoing yachts, and luxury automobiles—all were his. Over the years he had amassed a ten-figure fortune. The bank's major stock-holder, he owned the bank building outright and other prime real estate as well. He was known throughout the city as a prime mover in downtown development, financing numerous major projects.

It was so sad. He had done it all for his only child. The void created by Shane's death was immeasurable. He was sure that without Richard Stearns's depraved behavior, Shane would be alive today. Frank could not allow this to go unpunished. He would see to it that Richard, and Mecham too, paid for their outrageous illegal acts.

His loathing for Richard went to his very soul. He couldn't rest until he found suitable revenge. The police would have been his first choice but he wasn't sure how deeply the bank might be involved.

He was beginning to formulate a plan. The first phase would be to create a scenario that would drain Richard's and Mecham's resources to the point where their empire could collapse. He thought he knew how to accomplish this. The second phase would take more planning.

DON PARKER KNEW ALL THE LEGAL PEOPLE at the old ICC operation in Atlanta. Even though Richard and Brooke had handled the legal aspects of the acquisition, Ryan Tipton kept in touch with Parker. They had both been amazed some years ago when Ray Patton was able to settle the litigation with CCA. There had been some minor correspondence following the settlement and in the wake of Ray Patton's death and CCA's purchase of ICC.

When Frank O'Connor called to inquire about the CCA-ICC acquisition, Don was puzzled but agreed to meet with him.

"That was over two years ago. Quite a coup for Mecham; looks like it must have been a success. What did you want to know, Frank?"

When Frank explained that he wished to talk with their legal people, Parker was more than puzzled. "What's this all about?"

"How long have I known you—almost fifteen years, right? This is confidential for the moment, but I promise, when the time is right you'll be the first to know. In fact, you'll be one of very few who'll know. I don't like to play these games, but trust me; you'll understand when I do tell you. And please keep this meeting confidential."

Frank called Ryan Tipton the next morning and told him he would like to meet him in Atlanta as soon as was convenient. No, he didn't want to go into details on the phone. Tipton agreed to meet later in the week. It was already Wednesday. He'd have to hurry.

On arrival in Atlanta, Frank went directly to his hotel and called Tipton. It would be impossible to meet him in his office. He wanted no one to know he was here. For his plan to succeed, it must appear that Tipton was the instigator, at least for now. They met downtown at the Ritz-Carlton.

"First," Frank began, "I want to thank you for seeing me on such short notice. Second, anything we discuss must be kept in strictest confidence. I know that as an attorney this is routine for you, but I need that assurance. Now, Mr. Tipton, I know you were involved in the CCA acquisition of ICC some years ago. Don Parker, a very good friend of mine, was kind enough to give me your name. You don't know me, but please be assured I can give the very best references. Before we start, would you please tell me a little about ICC before the acquisition?"

Tipton told of the precarious fortunes of ICC for most of the time he had known Ray Patton. ICC had had some very good years and some very bad ones. Ray Patton was a man of motion, driven by ambition and prone to many frailties. His people were devoutly loyal, and deeply saddened by his death. They had been equally distressed when CCA, a major competitor, acquired their company. Most stayed on, but were circumspect about the future.

This was good news. Apparently, the staff was, for the most part, still intact. Frank assumed that Tipton was part of that group.

"If this cadre of people were given the chance to leave and embark on a startup operation to replicate pretty much what they had at ICC, would there be any interest?"

Tipton would be among the first. While now a stockholder in CCA, his legal duties had been reduced to few more than those of a clerk. Brooke Temple-Stearns handled all the major dealings from Boston. He wistfully remembered the wild rides with Ray Patton. It was always a little frightening but never boring.

"Are you suggesting a revolt, a mutiny, a divorce from CCA? If it's any of the above, I'd like to hear more."

"It's all of the above and a lot more, but there are a number of things I need to flesh out before I get into my proposal to you. I've been in banking for thirty years and I know a little about running a business. What I need from you is a complete business plan prepared as if you were starting from scratch to produce and sell computers. I'm a great believer in these products and have the resources to do what I'm suggesting. Why don't you talk to some of the financial and operational people and see how soon we could have something? But remember, this must be treated with the utmost confidentiality."

Tipton was perplexed. Why would anyone want to risk starting a company in a competitive market like the computer business? Even in a high-growth situation it could be suicidal: prices were falling and margins were razor thin. But if he could dissect the critical group of personnel out of the Atlanta division of CCA and use them for the startup, he could accomplish two very important goals: create a foundation of seasoned professionals and, more importantly, cripple half of CCA's production and sales. It would be exciting—shades of Ray Patton!

Back in his office, Tipton called the Atlanta chief engineer, Craig Hess, a longtime employee and one of the best. He had been with Patton since ICC started. Hess had designed the latest CD-ROM platforms and had begun the introduction of voice recognition features. He was highly regarded in the industry.

"We've been asked to come up with a rather bizarre plan. When I explain, I'm sure you'll have many questions, but the most important—I repeat—the most important issue is secrecy." He explained what Frank had proposed. "I suggest you select suitable candidates from finance, sales, marketing, and manufacturing. Take them to dinner or some discreet venue so you can all talk candidly. If you think you have a consensus, get back to me."

Craig Hess knew the computer business as well as anyone in the industry. A Stanford graduate, he had devoted his entire professional career to development, and had patented many innovative features. He had been with Ray Patton through many pitfalls, but admired his gutsy approach to the business. During the time that Richard Stearns ran the operation in Atlanta, Hess found him arrogant and difficult to work with. Stearns's obsession with pleasing Mecham Temple diminished his ability to effect a seamless transition; there was still some hostility among many of the senior staff.

After a lengthy meeting at a secluded resort near Atlanta, it was obvious to Hess that what Tipton was suggesting was very doable. The management people he assembled were enthusiastic and immediately began compiling the necessary information.

Frank O'Connor called Tipton. "Ryan, I want you to include in your business plan the cost of moving the entire operation to the Boston area. I've been in touch with some of my friends at MIT; they've convinced me that with the excellent high-tech labor pool available here, we might be able to accelerate the startup. Let me know if you need any extra help."

This would be an enormous undertaking. Tipton called in additional consultants to help with the logistics. He hoped Frank O'Connor had all the pieces in place. What with overtime and outside vendors, Tipton had his neck out a mile. If Richard Stearns at CCA's Boston headquarters ever got wind of what he was doing, he could be sued, maybe even disbarred.

His fears were greatly allayed when he received Frank O'Connor's check for $100,000. He was to deposit the money in an escrow account and submit weekly summaries of his expenditures, keeping all business plan costs out of any CCA accounts. Tipton was still wary: any leak from the group working on the plan could have grave consequences.

Tipton's office was in downtown Atlanta, some distance from the CCA Atlanta operation. He was a partner in a medium-sized firm specializing in corporate finance and litigation. He had called Craig Hess to his office a number of times during the preparation of the business plan. Today, he intended to find out how much longer the procedure would take. He got right to the point.

"You've been at this for ten days now. Every day we continue, the danger of a leak grows. I don't have to tell you how calamitous that would be. Are you comfortable with your progress?"

Hess had handpicked his staff and was confident there was no danger of compromise. They all had too much to gain if the plan was implemented. Each one talked of the enormous opportunities the cabal offered.

"You can relax. I'd bet my life we're safe. The relocation to Boston has created some delays, but we should have the entire plan complete sometime next week. Do you have any idea how much this could cost?"

"Not a clue. We've done a lot of IPOs and some municipal bond work, but nothing like this. What's your guess?"

"Our early estimates are in the range of $50 million; that doesn't include the move to Boston, nor does it take into account the minimum of a year until the operation breaks even. Your man had better have at least $100 million. Are we in his ballpark?"

God, could Frank O'Connor even have guessed at this amount? He's a banker; all he knows is balances and overdrafts. Tipton was worried. Even if they could contain any leaks, was this a mere exercise in business plan preparation? It had gone long past "what-ifs."

"Frank, this is Ryan Tipton. When we first talked about the operation you suggested, did you have any numbers in mind? I mean, do you have any notion what it might cost?"

Of course Frank had some idea. He had discussed the entire plan, in confidence, with Bruno Davidson—Dean of Computer Sciences at MIT and a recognized icon in the computer and software industry. Bruno had delivered many papers and written extensively on the future of the Internet. He also wanted out of the academic end of the business. He was tenured and secure, but longed for the seven-figure income he saw in industry. He was an ideal candidate for Frank.

Together with Bruno, Frank enlisted the help of Jack Evers, one of the premier venture capitalists in the Boston area. Evers was on the board of the International Bank of Boston and had contacts nationwide for acquiring startup capital.

"Yes, I have a ballpark assessment of what the costs could be, but I need your people's estimates before we get down to specifics. When you've completed your work we'll get together and see where we are. How soon do you think that might be?"

"Craig Hess believes he can finalize the entire plan in another ten days. I'll call you when it's complete."

"Fine. I want you and Hess—and anyone else you believe can contribute to a final meeting—here in Boston. Let me know when you're ready."

TWENTY-ONE

IT WAS SNOWING IN BOSTON when they all arrived. They met in Jack Evers's office in the International Bank of Boston building. Frank hadn't invited Don Parker: it wasn't quite yet time to apprise his old friend of what he had in mind. The group from Atlanta included Tipton, Hess, and Jill Overton, head of sales and marketing, an attractive woman in her early thirties. The Boston contingent consisted of Frank, Bruno, and Evers. Tipton, Hess, and Overton began their presentation. It was lengthy and the Boston group had many questions. After four hours it was pretty well established that the plan was feasible.

"It appears that we could have another computer operation here in Boston," Frank said. "I'd like Ryan, Craig, and Jill to take a break. Get settled in your hotel rooms, get a bite to eat. Bruno, Jack, and I have some cleaning up to do. Be back here at 9:00 A.M."

Frank's enthusiasm struck Jack Evers as eccentric. Both were investment experts, familiar with risk and reward, but Frank appeared determined to proceed at any cost. Bruno Davidson's assessment assuaged his fears somewhat.

"I'm impressed," Bruno said. "These people have done their homework. Any undertaking of this magnitude has some potential pitfalls, but I'm comfortable with how they intend to mitigate them. The market is in an expansion mode and will be for the foreseeable future. In fact, I believe they've underestimated it."

"As I understand it, they estimate that $105 million will accomplish six major objectives: Carve out fifty key people as the core of the new operation; relocate them and their families to Boston; acquire and equip the new facility here; design and manufacture the new products; set up a sales and marketing team; and provide enough reserves for the year before the operation reaches break-even. Is that about it?" Jack Evers questioned.

"That's right, and it pretty well agrees with what Bruno and I have independently come up with. But to allow for a little more room to move, I want to come up with $125 million. My bank will secure the first fifty, which means we'll look to you, Jack, to raise the other seventy-five. See any problems?" Frank asked.

101

Jack Evers had been in the venture capital business for twenty-five years. He had seen what devastation cyclical businesses could inflict. Even the computer industry had suffered its share in the short time it had been around, but high-tech spurred the current economy and greed drove him and his associates. He could place this before the end of the week.

"I assume Bruno will be active in the new operation. His reputation in the industry will be a great asset in selling the issue. I'll need résumés on all the other key people. Who'll be drawing up all the legalese?" Evers asked.

"Don Parker will take care of all that. I'll meet with him tomorrow."

Frank was elated. All his planning was beginning to pay off. He could envision CCA's dismay when they began to piece together what was happening. It could destroy them. A company whose success and growth was all based on illicit drug money was about to see some tough times. Shane wouldn't be here to delight in their demise, but Frank O'Connor certainly would. It would be the beginning of the revenge he craved. As he began to see the end of Richard Stearns, Brooke Temple-Stearns and, yes, Mecham Temple, the closure he yearned for was nearly in sight. Even phase two was beginning to take shape. They'd all pay for what they'd done to Shane O'Connor. It was time to visit Don Parker.

PARKER, OF COURSE, KNEW NOTHING of Frank's research into Shane's files, or what he had found, or about his vengeful obsession. They had been friends for years, and both had known Mecham Temple nearly as long; now he needed Don Parker to complete the destruction.

"What I have to tell you, Don, isn't easy or pretty, but it's all true. When I finish, if you want proof I'll provide it," Frank said, and related the entire sordid story about Shane, Richard, Brooke, and Mecham. It was exhausting and uncomfortable, but he omitted nothing.

"It should be obvious to you why I didn't go the authorities. I'm not going to get the bank involved in this, at least not now. I demand a price for what they did to Shane, and here's what it is." He described his plan with the Atlanta group.

Don Parker was stunned. He knew all of these people and couldn't believe what he was hearing. Certainly not Mecham Temple, or Richard and Brooke either, for that matter.

"You're talking about some of most successful, wealthy, and well thought of people in Boston, maybe the country. This just can't be true, Frank." But it was, and Frank had the proof. It was almost more than Parker could comprehend. "What do you want from me?"

"A number of things: First, we'll need you to draw up all the necessary papers for the offering. Second—and I don't need this right away—I want your assessment of any exposure for the bank based on what Shane evidently did. Third, we'll need all the usual documents for the new corporation. Bruno will be president and CEO; he'll get you all the other information. We'll need to move on this immediately. We expect to be in operation within six months." Frank was beginning to feel the rapture of revenge. He wondered if Don could detect his excitement as he unfolded the plan. "The name of the new company will be Boston Technology Corporation. I want a local flavor to enhance acceptance of what we're about to do," he announced, looking directly at Don.

WITH THE ACQUISITION OF ICC, CCA was rapidly becoming the leading computer manufacturer in the Western Hemisphere. Sales were soaring and profits were at an all-time high. Richard Stearns's net worth now ranked him among the *nouveau riche* elite. Brooke reveled in their ostentatious lifestyle. Her need to be recognized and envied propelled her into binges of buying, acquiring designer clothing, luxury automobiles, and high-end jewelry. They now maintained homes in Boston, New York and Vail. By staffing her downtown office with competent professionals, Brooke allowed herself extensive time for travel and speaking engagements. She saw less and less of Richard. They were both busy with their success.

The news struck at the very heart of their existence; everything was threatened.

"I don't know how it was put together or who's responsible, but our Atlanta operation is virtually shut down. People are leaving by the score—and these are key people, the best we have. It's astounding. Where have all these high-priced professionals found work? It makes no sense," Richard screamed at Mecham.

"When the hell did all this happen?"

"Must have been yesterday. I got a call this morning from some underling in accounting saying all the executive staff in engineering, finance, manufacturing, and sales had resigned. The whole damn operation is without any management. This could be disastrous, Mecham."

"Good God, Atlanta ships over half our products! What could have happened? We pay our people the best in the industry. Who ever heard of a mass exodus in an economy like this?" Mecham lamented.

They arrived in Atlanta late that night and were at the plant early the next morning. They met first with Ross England, second-in-command in engineering. Ross had been with ICC since before CCA took over. He was an able technician but not management material. "What the hell happened? Where do you think they all went, and why?" Richard asked.

England was not used to dealing with corporate executives, certainly not the ones he worked for, but he did have a good idea what had happened: There had been too many late-night meetings; too many hushed conferences in Craig Hess' office; too many Saturday work days for selected personnel. It had annoyed England that he wasn't included, so he had begun snooping. Boxes of drawings and specifications, lists of suppliers, costs, customer lists, flowcharts of production layout and quality control—all had disappeared with Craig Hess and his friends. It was obvious they intended to replicate what they'd taken. He told Richard and Mecham what he had seen.

"It's a conspiracy, dammit! They've taken proprietary data to use for God-knows-what. But who's behind all this? You can't just walk out with this kind of information and hope to use it without colossal amounts of money." Richard said. "Any ideas, Ross?"

"I really don't know. Craig wasn't very forthcoming with me, but I do know he saw a lot of an attorney who came here a few times during the past month or so. I know he was an attorney because he was here when Mr. Patton was killed some years ago."

They both knew immediately who he was: they had come to know Ryan Tipton quite well. What was his role in all this? They called his office. When they announced who they were, Tipton was unavailable. They spent the rest of the day organizing what was left of their staff. It would be months before they could hope to replace the lost personnel. Mecham feared they might never recover. Richard was enraged.

"I'll find out who's behind this if it's the last thing I do. This is outrageous, and probably illegal. I don't think Tipton has the balls to pull this off by himself. I'm not sure what they intend to do, but if what I suspect is true it would literally take tens of millions of dollars. Some deep-pocket people are behind this. What's your take on it?"

Mecham was too dazed to answer. It was all too bizarre. This just didn't happen in his structured world. But Richard was right; they'd get to the bottom of it. They had to. He placed a call to Don Parker.

Parker's secretary had Mecham on hold, and told him who was on the line. He had been expecting the call. In fact, he was surprised it'd taken this long. Although he dreaded confronting Mecham, there was no alternative. Frank O'Connor had convinced him he'd have to sever his decades-old relationship with a dear friend.

"Hello Mecham," he said curtly. He had sided with Frank because Frank was obviously in the defensible legal position. He probably should have met with Mecham and explained his position. But the more he thought about what Frank O'Connor had told him, the more he realized that any dealings with Mecham could be hazardous.

"I have a problem here in Atlanta, Don, and I need some advice. We've had a virtual mutiny and I think I know at least one person who's behind it. How soon can you get down here?"

The dirty deed was at hand. It was a tactless way to end a longstanding relationship but it had to happen.

"Mecham, I must tell you that I don't intend to get involved in any further legal matters with you—or Richard or Brooke either. For reasons I won't get into, our business relationship is over," Parker said and hung up. It was crude and unprofessional and Parker felt sick. No one should be treated like that, but to continue with Mecham Temple meant collusion with a corrupted man.

Mecham was speechless. He had known Don Parker for almost fifteen years and held him in the highest esteem. This was beginning to have all the elements of well-orchestrated conspiracy. It was truly alarming. Parker wouldn't behave this way unless something awful had happened. All the soul-searching he had done three years before began to reoccur; the consequences of what they had done flashed through his mind. Utter ruin might be at hand.

He turned to Richard and told him of his short conversation with Don Parker. "Something has happened. This isn't like Parker. I'm concerned, Richard. My fear is that someone has uncovered the truth about our resources—about your resources. It could have come from only one source."

They left for Boston that night. This would take drastic action. Richard knew he should get Brooke involved but she would go ballistic. They didn't need that right now. They needed cool reason and a well-planned offense.

TWENTY-TWO

Brooke Temple-Stearns had come to view her wealth as a preordained right. She accepted the accolades as evidence of her arrival as one of Boston's upper crust. Her marriage to Richard, on the surface one of tranquillity and devotion, was hollow. Brooke had successfully diverted the issue of children—there was no room in her life for anyone but herself and, occasionally, Richard. Her selfish, arrogant demeanor demanded total attention from those around her. She flaunted her beauty with a confident ease. Boston was in love with her.

When Richard announced the problem in Atlanta, she calmly told him that she wouldn't allow anyone, not even Frank O'Connor, to deprive them of what was rightfully theirs. They had worked too hard and endured too much to be intimidated now. "What in hell do you think he's up to? Our departed employees haven't just disappeared—they must be working somewhere. Have you heard anything from other manufacturers?" Brooke demanded.

"No. I haven't had time. This is a clandestine operation orchestrated by O'Connor. He must have most of the pieces in place for replicating a complete operation somewhere. Good God, the money that would take is inconceivable!"

"For Christ's sake, Richard, you've got to stop it now! Where in hell would he locate an operation like that? We've got to find out. We'll deal with what to do then," Brooke screamed.

It was about what Richard expected: maybe a little low-key for Brooke, but the message was in her usual demanding tone. She was knowledgeable in many fields, but the day-to-day running of a business was not her long suit. She didn't have the tenacity to develop close relationships with those around her. She was used to telling people what she wanted and requiring results. Effort was fine, but results were what counted.

"I don't think you have a clue what this means. If our early assessment is correct, it could destroy CCA. We've lost almost half our ability to meet customer orders, at least in the short term. Atlanta shipped most of our newer products, certainly those with the highest margins. Our cash flow will be affected for months. Profits will be a fraction of our projections, and the markets will go wild. Our losses could be astronomical—we could be facing a crisis in six months!"

This got Brooke's attention. Financial crisis was an embarrassment she could not, would not, endure. Why had Richard allowed this to happen? Certainly there must have been some indication of what was going on in Atlanta. She refused to accept what he was telling her. "How far are you willing to go to stop this? I mean, there are ways, you know. Maybe not completely kosher, but effective. Our friends in Atlantic City might be willing to help. They're not averse to bending the rules; I hear it happens all the time," she announced, lighting a cigarette, head thrown back, smoke escaping her lips.

THROUGHOUT THE TIME THAT BROOKE had been overseeing the growth of Richard's fortune, she had been careful not to leave much of a paper trail. It was difficult and sometimes required "creativity," but she believed she had run the gauntlet successfully. In recent years it had become increasingly onerous: the vast amounts of money and the Byzantine nature of their investments made it challenging. Brooke became immune to all the normal signs of danger. The power and prestige of their wealth had clouded her vision of life in the real world. Over the years, she had insulated herself with layers of people who performed the mundane tasks of everyday life. While most of their holdings and investments were long-term, some were transient, requiring periodic reassessment. The latter amounted to at least a hundred million dollars.

She had invested in a series of gaming stocks recommended by friends in the entertainment world. They were highly speculative and she knew little about the business. What she had learned was that most of the gaming businesses were controlled by less-than-upstanding citizens. While Brooke wasn't involved on a daily basis, what she was learning was not encouraging.

She received an ominous-sounding call from a casino operator in Atlantic City; he wanted to meet with her as soon as possible. His name was Stan Miller; he would be in Boston the following day. She was reluctant to meet with him and told him so. "I think it would be in your best interest, Ms. Stearns, to at least listen to my proposal. You have a considerable investment in our operation and I believe you'll find what I have to tell you very interesting."

"I can't imagine what that might be, Mr. Miller, but if you insist, I have a few minutes around 4:30 tomorrow afternoon. I can meet with you briefly then."

Stan Miller was a manager with Primus, a major player in the gaming industry and owner of one of Atlantic City's most prestigious casinos, the La Samanna. For years Primus had done very well. During the past year, however, Miller had embarked on a major acquisition effort. With the proliferation of gambling in many areas, he had also invested in a number of startups. The net result was a drain on Primus' cash flow. They needed nearly $20 million to sustain day-to-day operations. His board of directors had authorized him to borrow up to that amount on a short-term basis.

"It's kind of you to meet me on such short notice. I'll get right to the point." He outlined the problem and what their needs were, then went on to suggest a remedy. "We're prepared to offer you over half of Primus in return for $20 million in cash. You currently own about a third of all outstanding stock. At the current price, that amounts to nearly $50 million. If you agree to our request, you would own about 80 percent—enough to control the entire company."

Brooke looked at him in amusement. Twenty million dollars was about what she spent on clothes, jewelry, and travel each year—virtually chump-change. She had made the investment some years ago on the premise that the company would grow. Her strategy was to set a benchmark to sell, or hang in for the longer term. This, she thought, could be a different situation. "How soon can you get me audited financial statements? If I like what I see, I might have a counter-offer for you."

Miller tried not to show his impatience. It would take more time to prepare the necessary documents, but her offer was intriguing.

Brooke saw the casino as a great opportunity to flaunt their wealth and entertain friends. The glitzy ambiance suited her continual need for adoration and provided a setting for exploiting her seductive beauty.

It had taken longer than Stan Miller expected, but when she called he left for Boston immediately. "Sorry it took so long, but we've completed our examination of your financials and it looks like we might be able to do business" Miller was ecstatic! He'd almost given up on her. Their position had deteriorated and he had depleted other sources. He mustn't appear too anxious. He had prepared all the necessary papers for the transaction. All they had to do was enter the proper amounts. "I'm delighted you were able to be here." Brooke got down to business.

"We're prepared to purchase all of the outstanding stock for $35 million—that's $4.5 million over book—and we'll assume all the debt. We've gone over your financial statements carefully, and while we see some short-term problems, on balance we think we can turn things around," she announced. "Of course, part of our offer includes your staying on as manager. I hope this is something you want to do." Her firm, authoritative manner gave

Miller to believe this was the best and only offer he'd get from her. And he still had a job!

They closed the deal before Miller left for Atlantic City. Thirty-five million dollars clear would give all the shareholders a substantial return on investment, and he was left with a very generous employment contract. But why would a gorgeous creature like this want control of a gambling casino? It could be very lucrative but it was fraught with dangers. Maybe she knew something he didn't.

RICHARD THOUGHT BACK TO BROOKE'S PURCHASE of the La Samanna. At the time, he'd concluded it was folly—it meant total management responsibility in a business they knew nothing about. But his concerns proved unfounded: Stan Miller had done a masterful job, not only turning the operation around but even showing impressive growth. They had spent many weekends in the opulent accommodations afforded the owners of such establishments, but the casino held little interest for Richard. He didn't gamble, and the pretentious behavior of most patrons depressed him. He preferred spending his weekends on Martha's Vineyard, enjoying their beach house and his boat. Brooke reveled in the attention. "What on earth are you talking about?" he asked her. "You want to involve your seamy friends in our business problems? Not on your life! We'll deal with this in our own way. I want you to stay away from them. Any connection with that crowd will only complicate our situation. I hope you understand me."

She was furious. How dare he talk to her that way? Brooke thought. Doesn't he remember who parlayed his fortune into one of the largest in the country?

"Well, Richard, what do *you* suggest? We probably don't have much time. If what you say is true, we could be hemorrhaging cash in a month. Don't you see the immediate need for drastic action?"

"Yes, but I don't see any way the people in Atlantic City could possibly help. You aren't suggesting some sort of violence are you?"

Brooke wasn't sure what she was suggesting. She did know that some of her friends could be very persuasive, so why not nip this in the bud at once?

"Let's not fight. Lean on your friends in the business; see what they can tell you. Meanwhile, I'll find out what I can about Frank O'Connor. My contacts in financial circles might know something. We know why he hasn't gone to the authorities, but there could be some other skeletons around, OK?" Brooke could be very conciliatory.

TWENTY-THREE

BRUNO DAVIDSON WAS A WORKAHOLIC. He loved the technical aspect of what he
was about to do, and he was adept at sorting out who could best handle
the other chores of the enormous task at hand. The first challenge was to
locate and reconfigure suitable quarters. Of the many properties available,
the one that caught his attention was the vacant 200,000-square-foot former
headquarters of Rainier Electronics. Rainier had moved to Seattle eight
months ago and the buildings had stood empty since. The site consisted of
twenty acres with a campus setting of four buildings. It was ideal: it had
the opulence Bruno so desired after years of stodgy existence in the academic world, and it fit his conception of where he ought to be. He knew he
was obsessed with image, but he was willing to work to make Boston Technology succeed. Of course, they would need security—lots of it. Who knew
what CCA might do? When CCA employees began leaving, anything could
happen. He called his friends at Pinkerton.

DURING THE NEXT TEN DAYS, CRAIG HESS and the other members of the transition
team arrived in Boston with their families. Implementation of the new facility began to take shape, and within two months production had begun. It
went smoother than anyone expected. Jill Overton put together a sales staff
that blanketed the country, and orders poured in from everywhere. Hess
and his engineers developed innovative new features that were far ahead of
others in the industry. The short-term startup of BTC was a huge success.

WHEN BROOKE MOVED FROM DON PARKER'S law firm into Richard's downtown
offices, she spent most of her time investing Richard's huge fortune. It was
fascinating, and with the funds she had available every brokerage firm in
the city wanted her business. She soon became adept at trading and hedg-
ing, at arbitrage, derivatives, and straddles. Her ability to track and foresee
market trends was uncanny. Her office was filled with the newest state-of-
the-art market electronics. As she became more comfortable with her system,

she hired others to do the database management, reserving her own time for weightier pursuits and for social diversions. While she was, so far, rigidly faithful to Richard, many of the rich and famous downtown crowd missed no opportunity to seek her company. Through this network she came to know most of the socially powerful and establishment-savvy mavens.

Robert Sands was on the editorial staff of the *Boston Globe*. He was a thirty-year veteran and active in financial circles. He was also one of Brooke's closest friends.

"Robert, you've been around here for decades. Tell me what you know about Frank O' Connor. He appears to be one of the city's senior goodwill guys—active in downtown development, good for lots of bucks at charity events, successful international banker. Where'd he come from?"

Robert, who adored her, watched and had difficulty concentrating. He gave her a complete chronology on Frank O'Connor and his banking empire.

"He's been a member of the power group for years. Comes from an old, wealthy Boston family. Respected, visible, and above reproach—a solid guy. Word around town is he might be involved in BTC, the new computer company. But you probably knew that."

"That's what I wanted to talk to you about. What he's done is clever. It could hurt us. Who are his financial backers? This had to cost tens of millions. And he's private, difficult to get at ownership. It would help if we knew a little more about his patrons. See what you can find out."

It was a long shot and a little dangerous to use Robert Sands for clandestine help. He knew everyone in town and was known to protect his sources. But if Mecham and Richard knew how the BTC deal was put together, it might help them strategize any weaknesses. CCA's sales were beginning to suffer the effects of BTC's aggressive marketing tactics. In fact, current quarter financials showed a substantial loss. And it was getting worse: Atlanta had been slow to recover from the disastrous loss of key personnel; shipments would be below projections for months; losses would mount.

Mecham Temple found Frank O'Connor's behavior contemptible. It could have devastating consequences for everyone; it could bring down the company. Apparently Frank had stumbled onto something at the bank that implicated Richard or Mecham or both. Until now Mecham had never been happier. The company he had put together with the acquisition of ICC was the nation's leading computer company. Sales were at $4 billion and profits soared. He and Don Parker had taken the company public at the beginning of the year, and their stock was now trading at five times its opening price. It just kept getting better. Mecham was wealthy beyond anything he had ever dreamed. He owed much of his success to Richard's investment three years ago, without which it never would have been possible.

As time passed, the stigma surrounding the source of Richard's wealth disappeared in the euphoria of their success. In the years immediately following the acquisition, Mecham worried constantly about the repercussions of exposure. Brooke assured him that if Richard were ever caught, Mecham could plead ignorance. At the time he'd felt implicated, but that had passed; now he rarely thought about it, but Frank O'Connor's actions had begun to change all that. Apparently, Frank knew more than anyone suspected. If they didn't do something soon, they could lose everything.

"We've got to stop this, Richard. We could be out of business in six months. I didn't build this company with sweat, risk, and a hell of a lot of hard work just to let it slip out of existence overnight. We've lost Don Parker, but you and Brooke are bright attorneys. I want the two of you to find a way to stop him. There's got to be some legal approach to all this," Mecham shouted.

"Brooke and I have talked about it at length. There are some avenues we could research but they all take too much time," Richard replied, throwing his arms in the air. He was at his wits' end. This wasn't the type of crisis he excelled at. "Brooke suggests we get her friends in Atlantic City involved. I want nothing to do with that, though I suspect it could be very effective, at least in the short term."

"What the hell could they do?"

"Do you really want to discuss it? That crew specializes in arm-twisting, and they aren't subtle about it. They have the resources to change the course of events overnight: thugs who have no regard for law and order, or life and limb for that matter. They're capable of anything. Is this something you want to be involved in?"

"If we can't devise a legal strategy and we can't compete with them soon enough to avoid what looks like disaster, what would we have to lose?"

"A hell of a lot. If whatever we allowed them to do backfired, someone could get killed and we could be implicated. We'd be in worse shape than we are now—if that's possible."

"I vote we talk with Brooke and see what she has in mind. Just talk. See what the options are, what avenues are available. We don't have to come to any finite decisions immediately. It may be the only course of action we have, Richard. I don't suggest anything illegal, but maybe we could intimidate them."

This wasn't like Mecham at all. What was he thinking? They were already living on the edge, and had been for three years. Any association with Atlantic City would only intensify their exposure. These people played for keeps—once in, you never got out. It was unthinkable that Mecham would even talk about such a solution. But what other options did they have? CCA would disappear without some sort of herculean intervention. They'd talk to Brooke.

The three of them met at Richard and Brooke's estate in Weston. It was tense and none of them really wanted to broach the subject they were there to discuss. Even for Brooke it was somewhat awkward. What was it they wanted Atlantic City to do? How many options were there? Who would approach them? What would it cost? How would they be paid? Too many unknowns for people who never ventured into the arena of the underworld.

Brooke began. "Let's put on the table what we think we know: Frank O'Connor has apparently sorted through records at his bank and concluded that the three of you conspired to make a fortune dealing in drugs. He also concluded that his bank might have been used to launder hundreds of millions of dollars. His son was killed in a drug-related transaction with someone from a shipping company we had an interest in. He's pissed about his son, can't go to the authorities, and blames Richard for Shane's death. He also figured out where you, Dad, got the funds to buy out Ray Patton three years ago. So he put together a consortium to reestablish ICC and put us out of business—that's his vengeance for Shane's death. Don Parker has to know about all this; that's why he cut you off when you asked for his help.

"Okay, let's assume he knows just about all there is to know. But he's stymied: big problems at the bank; laundering money is a federal offense. The Fed could close him down and he'd lose everything. So, to assuage his need to retaliate, he resurrects ICC—or BTC—hoping to destroy us, and he knows we know. It's a standoff. And it had to cost him a fortune. Of course if BTC prevails, he'll make it all back and plenty more. Either of you have a problem with any of that?"

Mecham and Richard knew she was right. What else could it be? It all fit. But it was academic—they had to do something, and now! "You've probably sorted it out correctly," Richard began, "so tell us what you think your friends can do for us."

Brooke didn't have a clue. What she thought she knew was that certain people she had met could persuade others to "cooperate." How they accomplished this was none of her concern—only results were. Stan Miller was her contact. He had successfully managed their interests in Atlantic City and given her the impression he was well connected in all sorts of activities. He could probably be in Boston tomorrow.

"Our best source is Stan Miller. I suggest we get him up here as soon as possible, discreetly explain our problem, and see what he has to say. He knows his way around the clandestine side of Atlantic City. What we tell him will be minimal; he obviously doesn't need to know the whole story. Could be interesting."

STAN MILLER WAS A MAN OF MANY TALENTS. He'd grown up in Colorado and had attended Colorado School of Mines. His father was associated with the mining business in the Telluride area, and was successful enough to send his son to one of the best technical schools in the country. Stan graduated near the top of his class when he was only twenty-three. The mining trade had never interested him much, but a fascination with numerical statistics consumed him. He spent endless hours calculating the odds of each casino game and how he could beat it: roulette, dice, blackjack, pia gow, poker, baccarat, even the slots. He drove from Denver to Las Vegas on weekends to test his theories. His rugged good looks afforded him ample diversion when he was away from the tables.

After Stan graduated, he moved permanently to Las Vegas and took a job with a video poker machine supplier. This gave him a modest income that allowed him to cruise the casinos at night. His uncanny ability to beat the tables eventually made him unwelcome at most places, but he was able to establish rapport with some of the management, which led to a permanent position with one of the largest casinos in Vegas. His affable demeanor and instinctive knowledge of the gaming industry made him an ideal candidate for rapid advancement. Five years after arriving there, he was one of the city's most sought-after managers.

Stan also acquired a penchant for the stunningly beautiful showgirls and the intriguing activities of the sinister elements associated with the gaming industry. The girls were merely a diversion, but the disreputable underworld players offered opportunities beyond his day-to-day management activities. And their turf was not limited to Las Vegas.

On one of his infrequent vacations he went to Atlantic City with one of his many female friends. The trip was not entirely for pleasure: he had been asked by a local syndicate kingpin to contact an Atlantic City drug baron for help setting up an operation in Las Vegas. His contact was a man named Fred Marcus, whom he was to meet at the La Samanna, one of Atlantic City's most elegant casinos.

He and Fred Marcus hit it off immediately. Marcus was loud and gregarious, and flirted with every woman in the restaurant, but Stan liked him. As conversation moved to the business at hand, it struck Stan that he

Clark Shannon

might make a permanent move to Atlantic City. Marcus informed him that opportunities abounded in the corrupt side of the town. Stan's abilities as a casino manager could be a perfect fit; Marcus agreed to introduce him to the owners of the La Samanna.

The casino was owned by Primus, a group of shadowy men from Jersey City who were involved in a variety of unsavory activities. After an hour's conversation, during which it was established that Stan was not only a well-placed casino manager but a capable after-hours entrepreneur, he was hired.

His talents as a raconteur were in great contrast to the owners' crude demeanor. They welcomed his conspicuous sophistication and he was quickly accepted into their crooked world. He learned their methods and cultivated their friends. He also introduced the very latest in computer-assisted management. He hired a staff of bright young computer geeks to implement what he thought necessary, and in less than two years had one of the city's best-run operations.

Unlike the odds on the casino floor, nothing was left to chance. Stan loved the digital nature of computers: everything was black or white; no gray. The talented staff he put together shared his enthusiasm, and spent many hours with him figuring how best to use the considerable electronic strength they had created. He also spent time with his new superiors, listening to the dangerous and nefarious aspects of their operation, which ran the gamut from drugs to prostitution to barbaric behaviors he had no need to know about.

As the proliferation of gaming spread across the country, he convinced his associates to expand. He encouraged them to go for acquisitions and startups because these were in the most gambling-prone areas—Indian reservations and riverboat operations. All went well until growth stalled and debt nearly brought it all down. Enter Brooke Temple-Stearns. Her rescue had been a godsend for Stan Miller. He would have faced a hazardous future with his employers had the losses continued, but with Brooke the sole owner and himself the CEO, everything was in good order. Even his former associates held him in high esteem, having salvaged a hefty price for their business. He envisioned himself as one of Atlantic City's premier operators. Brooke seldom interfered with the day-to-day administration, and only occasionally visited. Her phone call was surprising.

"Good evening, Stan, Brooke here," she casually announced. The usual banter over, she went on. "We have a situation here in Boston; I believe you might be able to contribute to a solution. I'd like for you to be here tomorrow, as early as you can arrange it. I'll set up accommodations for you. Try to make it before noon."

He was at loose ends. What possible situation in Boston could he contribute to? He barely knew where Boston was. Had never been there—too cold—but Brooke sounded impatient and this worried him. It meant pressure to perform. While he was good at that in familiar arenas, nothing in Boston was remotely connected with what he did for a living. This could be a long week.

Stan was thirty-four years old and secure in his job—as secure as one could be in this business. He hadn't thought much about the future. Day to day was his style, not because the future wasn't important to him but because he knew he had the moxie to survive almost anything. That's what he loved about his business. Every day was different and the money was fantastic. He cavorted with some of the world's most beautiful women and was cozy with some of the most influential people in the gaming industry. The law was his ally when it pleased him. In the meantime he just wanted to be left alone.

While all this was at odds with his conservative upbringing and rigid education, it suited his renegade personality perfectly. He was an opportunist who performed best when he knew the players. Brooke Temple-Stearns was not someone he knew well, and he trusted her even less.

Stan arrived at eleven the next morning and went directly to Brooke's office. He met Richard and Mecham for the first time and was impressed with their professionalism. Money certainly enhanced breeding, he thought. They met in her spectacular conference room and settled into casual conversation. Brooke explained their connection with CCA and gave him some background on Richard and Mecham. She finally got to the situation with BTC.

"Without getting into all the players or how BTC came to Boston, suffice it to say that they represent an overwhelming problem: They've pirated virtually all our Atlanta personnel and have succeeded in developing new products that will be difficult to compete against. In a word, it would be convenient if they were to evaporate, so to speak. I don't mean to be whimsical, but we must stop them—at any cost. We thought you or your friends might have some ideas. We're open to almost any suggestion."

This wasn't exactly Stan Miller's long suit. He wasn't sure he wanted to get involved, but she had said "at any cost." "I suppose there are the usual ways of disposing of unwanted associates. I don't get involved in that sort of thing but I know some people that do. It's so messy, though, and often has unexpected consequences. Maybe you should think in terms of some sort of industrial sabotage. I have contacts who specialize in that kind of thing; it could be a lot more cost effective and also be a lot more permanent. Unending glitches in vital areas can be disastrous and very expensive."

Richard listened with amusement. In some bizarre way this guy made sense, considering what they were about to embark upon. Sabotage and the subsequent damage made a hell of a lot more sense than crude force.

Mecham took it all in despairingly. What had his life become? Was all the success worth this? He had assured himself that he was safe with all that Richard's wealth had bought. Brooke had convinced him and greed had possessed him. The opportunity to capitalize on Ray Patton's death had driven him. It violated everything he believed in. As he listened, he wondered if he would do it all again.

ROBERT SANDS HAD LIVED IN BOSTON most of his life. A graduate of the University of Pennsylvania and the Wharton School of Business, he was well regarded in the Boston establishment. Frank O'Connor was one of his oldest and most trusted friends. While Brooke Temple-Stearns was the darling of the fast market set, and Robert was enamored of her spectacular beauty, he had been around long enough to know the ephemeral nature of new technology.

He had also known Mecham Temple for many years, and greatly admired the man. After CCA had acquired ICC three years earlier, Robert had spent considerable time interviewing Mecham and writing about his great entrepreneurial spirit and how beneficial his new company would be for Boston. When CCA went public, he wrote glowing narratives on their expected growth.

But the arrival of BTC and the resources of Frank O'Connor made the outlook for CCA less attractive, particularly with the addition of Bruno Davidson. That combination could spell trouble for CCA and Mecham Temple. Sands was betting on Frank O'Connor.

"As you know, my beat is the area's financial goings-on. Word on the street is that you're behind the BTC move and the appointment of Bruno Davidson. We've known each other a long time, Frank. I'd like your comments." This was Robert Sands's standard entrée and worked very well. He'd get to the Brook Temple-Stearns angle later. He'd also get to the Jack Evers connection—when he felt it would enhance his story. He loved his work, and little tidbits of financial information helped his own portfolio. If BTC became a force in the computer industry again, he wanted to be in on the ground floor.

"Word gets around, doesn't it? It's no secret we've been active in the high technology segment for some time. This looked like an attractive opportunity and Bruno was ready for a change. It's about as simple as that," Frank reasoned.

"Word also has it that Jack Evers was involved in the placement of a lot of the venture capital required for the deal. Any comment?"

"Yes, Jack was involved, but he works with a lot of startups. BTC isn't exactly a startup, but many people viewed it that way; that's why we went that route. We'll get to an IPO as soon as the first year's results are available, and from early returns, it should be a slam-dunk. We've got some awfully good people. Whom else have you talked to?"

"Off the record—and I know you'll keep this confidential—Brooke Temple-Stearns has shown more than casual curiosity about what you're up to. Obviously, BTC will have a negative impact on CCA. Her specific questions about you, personally, were visceral, even hostile. I didn't respond because I have no knowledge of much of what she asked. Beyond that, I've talked to no one."

This was no surprise to Frank. It didn't take a Ph.D. to judge what was happening, nor did it take great intelligence to conclude what the consequences for CCA would be if BTC succeeded. The great unknown for Frank and his people was how CCA would respond. He and Bruno had conjectured endlessly without resolution, but no doubt, there would be a response.

Robert Sands went to Jack Evers next. Evers had been in the Boston area for as long as Robert could remember. He put together some of the largest deals in New England, and operated in diverse circles. He was just as comfortable with the computer business as he was with the medical, real estate, and gaming businesses. He found financing for all of them, becoming one of the wealthiest men in Massachusetts in the process. There were few deals consummated from Washington to Boston that Jack Evers didn't know about.

"Thought I'd check to get your take on the BTC deal," Sands began. "Got any numbers you'd care to share with me? We know the International Bank was involved but we don't know the split."

Jack Evers came from the old school: He never divulged anything; name, rank and serial number was his credo. Sands knew this but hoped Evers might make an exception. After all, it was one of the most publicized operations to move to Boston in years.

"How long have you known me, Robert, maybe twenty-five years? Your paper has been very kind to us over the years and I don't want anything to change that, but I'd rather not comment. If we get involved in an IPO with BTC, we might have something to say, but not now. I'm sure Frank would want it that way. I'll keep you posted if anything changes."

It was what Sands had expected. Evers's business demanded axiomatic confidentiality, and in the past he had never strayed from it. As the confrontation between BTC and CCA unfolded, Sands would keep in close touch with Jack Evers.

TWENTY-FOUR

S TAN MILLER RETURNED TO ATLANTIC CITY in a state of cautious euphoria. He was excited about the prospect of implementing his vandalizing efforts and about the associated reward, but the risks were huge. It would involve a number of people, require extended absences from his duties at the casino, and entailed an omnipresent fear of exposure. If anything went wrong he would lose all he'd worked so diligently to accumulate. Greed, however, is a pervasive emotion, and in Stan Miller's business it always prevailed.

He and Brooke had not arrived at a fee for his services before he left Boston. On the flight home he prepared a list of all the expenses. It would cost Brooke $2 million, and it should take no more than two months to accomplish what he thought she wanted. A quarter of the fee would be his.

He would need a few technicians who were knowledgeable about the myriad chips, CPUs and motherboards integral to the manufacture of computers. He would also need an expert in the peculiarities of the latest software. Viruses and glitches could be introduced that would take forever to uncover. It took him a week to assemble his small team. They flew to Boston the following Monday and checked into a hotel. It took less than a week to gain employment at BTC.

FRANK O'CONNOR AND JACK EVERS met frequently to discuss BTC's progress and to contemplate the issue of an IPO. At the rate the company was proceeding, it might happen sooner than they had anticipated.

"That's what he does for a living. I thought he was a little pushy in his search for information. We'll need him and his newspaper when we do go for the IPO," Evers commented.

"He's okay. At least he's knowledgeable about what we're doing. By the way, Bruno has invited us to the new plant this afternoon. Channel 7 and the *Globe* will be there for more coverage on our arrival in the area. He wants us to be there after lunch."

When they arrived, the television crews were setting up their equipment, and two reporters from the *Boston Globe* loitered in the lobby. Bruno was basking in the glare of the lights, loving every minute. Evers and O'Connor walked past them to Bruno's office—an elaborate affair with mementos and diplomas covering two entire walls. When Bruno arrived, they all left to tour the facility.

They went first to the security department, where he showed them brand-new state-of-the-art surveillance equipment designed to make the entire plant impenetrable. Next they went through the immense production area, where robot-like machines flailed unerringly, inserting components into printed circuit boards.

As they were returning to Bruno's office, Evers eyed a familiar face standing at an inspection table. He couldn't place where he'd seen the guy, but he knew he had seen him someplace before. He almost went and spoke to him but thought better of it. The name would come to him. Interesting how events and faces came together.

As they drove back to the city, Evers pondered where he had met that guy. In the course of business he met hundreds of people and remembered most of them, particularly if they were clients.

Like an epiphany it came to him! Two swarthy-looking men had come to him some years ago looking for capital for a gaming operation. Only because they had most of the cash themselves did he agree to help find the rest. The amount was relatively small—under $10 million, he recalled—and even more unusual, just last year they'd been able to pay it all off. And at that closing had been this guy in the plant. He'd check his files, maybe the name would be there. What was a gaming executive doing working at a computer manufacturing plant?

"Frank, something mighty strange is going on. During our tour of the plant, I noticed a guy I know working there in the production area." Evers then took Frank through his recollection. "This guy is a half-million-a-year casino executive. What's he doing in a twelve-dollar-an-hour production job? Get me back to my office, I want to check my files on that closing."

Frank went with him. As he pulled the file, Jack knew who the guy was. He had been introduced to him, along with the two principals, as the new CEO of a company called Primus. He couldn't remember the guy's name. He'd found an investor to buy the whole thing. The buyer was never identified and the deal was closed with certified funds. Evers was out of it with a tidy profit. They called Bruno.

"We've got a problem, Bruno. At your plant today I recognized a guy in the production area from a transaction some time ago. He's a heavy-duty executive with a casino in Atlantic City, making six figures. I don't know his name but I'll stop by tomorrow and point him out to you. I'll be there when you open."

Bruno was appalled. As of this morning, there were 1800 people work-ing two shifts, and more being hired every day. Their hiring procedures were conventional, no extraordinary provisions for weeding out undesir-ables. All prospective employees were tested, and their references carefully checked. What with the frantic hiring they were doing, oversights were certainly possible, but surely they'd spot a six-figure casino executive. What would he know about computer assembly anyway?

He called his production manager, George Agar, to his office, together with Craig Hess and their human resources manager, Charles Winston. This would have to be handled with great care. He'd just ask questions about procedures and security, and wait until Jack Evers identified the man in question. It made no sense to make a move on the guy until they knew who he was and how to deal with him. They'd decide that tomorrow.

Jack Evers and Frank O'Connor arrived at the plant promptly at nine the next morning. George Agar and Evers casually wandered through the production area. Stan Miller was at the same inspection table and Evers pointed him out. They both returned to Bruno's office where Agar identi-fied the employee as Sheldon Mason. Hired three weeks ago, he was considered an able employee, and was paid thirteen dollars an hour. George Agar was excused.

"I don't think we should spill what we know about him just yet," Bruno said. "Let's confirm our suspicions first. It would be helpful if we could get a positive ID on him directly from Primus. We'll keep an eye on him—he probably has other associates here in our facility."

"Our bank has connections in Atlantic City. Let me see whom I can get to help us," Frank said. "If I can find a contact, we'll discreetly confront someone in the casino with his badge photo. At least we'll know for sure who he is."

It didn't take long for Frank's contact in Atlantic City to confirm that the picture on the badge was Stan Miller, CEO of Primus and headman at the La Samanna. He also informed Frank that the sole stockholders of Primus were Richard and Brooke Stearns. It didn't surprise Frank: it was common knowledge that he was heavily invested in BTC and, from all indications, CCA was suffering financially. Mecham, Richard, and Brooke were at the heart of Stan Miller's treachery, whatever it was.

"I doubt he's here alone. Put full-time surveillance on him. Ferret out his associates. Once we know who they are we can form a plan to oust them. I don't want them loose on the floor any longer than necessary," Bruno announced.

Frank thought there might be an alternative strategy. Stan Miller was a malleable subordinate of the Temples. If he was willing to imperil himself for payment from them, maybe he could be useful as a Judas. It would play into his hand; he could work both sides of the street.

"Before you scare him off—and with a tail on him that's likely—try this. He's obviously doing whatever he's up to for money. What if we approach him with an offer to fake doing what he's here to do? He gets money from both of us and the plot fails. It would be well worth paying him rather than dealing with whatever mischief he makes. My guess is they'll abandon the conspiracy if they get no results."

Bruno was impressed. "What do you think it'll take to sway him?"

"No idea. We'll approach him and negotiate," Frank said. "Bruno, have your people bring him to your office. Give me thirty minutes alone with him. I think I can convince him. He might even have some ideas of his own."

Stan Miller was brought in. He looked puzzled. They had been in Boston for less than a month, certainly not long enough for anything to have gone wrong. They hadn't even begun their chicanery. Frank O'Connor sat in Bruno's chair, Miller opposite him. Sizing him up, Frank thought he saw enough fear to make Miller vulnerable. "Your badge says your name is Sheldon Mason. Is that right?" Dummy up for now, Miller thought. What could this guy possibly know? "Yes, that's correct. What's this all about?"

"It's all about why you're here, Mr. Miller. We know more about you than you've been able to discover about us. Let's not waste each other's time. Your name is Stan Miller and you have a very responsible, well-paid position with Primus in Atlantic City. Further, it's obvious who sent you here. Am I right?"

So much for stonewalling: dammit, this guy knew everything about him, even who hired him. Was there more to why he was here than Brooke had told him? He didn't need this. He was in way over his head. The crew he'd brought with him knew all the soft spots in the manufacturing process. He was here to oversee the operation, but now it was over before it had begun.

"You obviously do know more about me than I do about you. What do want from me?"

"I want the whole story: why you're here and what the people from CCA have told you. Once I understand that, we might have more to talk about."

Miller was through. The scam with Brooke and CCA was over. How they were able to discover him so quickly was academic. He quickly described the meeting with Brooke, Richard, and Mecham Temple, and what he was expected to do.

"How many people are here with you and how much were you to be paid?"

"Counting myself, there are five of us. The entire fee for me, my crew, and all expenses was $2 million. I've been paid a retainer and the rest was to be paid when our expected results were evident. How I happen to know Brooke Temple-Stearns is a long story and I won't bore you with it. She's my employer and she approached me with this scheme to damage BTC. Her reasons are obvious. I knew the risks when I started. I should have followed my instincts. What do you intend to do?"

"What do you want to do now that you've been discovered?"

"I'd prefer to forget the whole thing and go back doing what I do best, but I'm afraid that's in jeopardy now."

"Let me make a suggestion." Frank started. He had the guy now and intended to press. "Suppose we let you continue with your little escapade, but now you're working with us. We see to it that you do no damage, the people at CCA assume all is going as planned, at least for a while, and your position at Primus remains secure."

Frank gazed at Miller, trying to assess his reaction. "Before you give me your answer, tell me more about your activities in Atlantic City. If we can come to an accommodation, we might do more business in the future."

Miller outlined, in generalities, his Atlantic City activities. Gambling and the associated vices were part of the daily life he loved. Sure, some of the people he did business with were a bit unsavory, but that was part of the business. It was why he was involved with Brooke. That, plus the fact that she was his employer.

"I knew this was chancy but I didn't expect to be discovered. Also, there was no physical danger to me or my people. We were to cripple your operation by sabotage. I knew it was illegal but I felt the risk was worth the reward. You take your chances." He paused, wondering if he had said too much. "Your offer is tempting. Now that we've been exposed, it solves a number of problems. How would you want to proceed?"

"You've been pretty well paid so far, and if we allow you to stay you'll apparently get at least some of the balance of what Brooke agreed to pay you, right? Let's assume you and I can arrange a situation whereby you act as a sort of counterspy. Let us know what they're up to, how badly we're hurting them financially, what their next move will be. This won't take long, maybe a month or so. If it appears to be working, we'll pay you fifty thousand a week as long as you're here. You can send your crew home."

This was going too well, Frank reflected. How could Miller stay here for an extended period?

"I never intended to stay here for the duration. The plan was for me to set up the operation and put one of my men in charge when I left. I was to be in daily contact with him to check on our progress." God, Miller thought, this really could be his way out. "If I agree to go along with what you're suggesting, that would still work. I think we should leave at least three of my people here just for a show of activity. I don't know how closely Brooke and Richard intend to monitor what I was supposed to do. They live here. It wouldn't be that difficult to check on our comings and goings, particularly if what I'm supposed to be doing isn't getting the desired results. They'll know that within a week or two."

"That's exactly the point," Frank replied. "When the results aren't what they expect, trust me, they'll devise something else, and this time it won't be as benign as industrial sabotage. That's what I need you for. In the meantime, you and I might develop a plan of our own. Your connection with Brooke is a big advantage. Apparently she trusts you, and we've got to keep it that way."

TWENTY-FIVE

MECHAM READ THE LATEST QUARTERLY FINANCIAL REPORT. Richard was standing in his office as he grimaced at the numbers. "This is getting worse every day," Mecham snorted. "It's going to ruin us, Richard. We're down 10 percent from last week. What a hell of way to run a business: sabotaging the competition. I don't know how much longer I can deal with it. At this rate we'll have to close the doors in six months."

"Mecham, you and I hold an enviable position in the industry. As of today we're number one. That might not last, but we can survive longer than you think. I know our actions at BTC are unconventional, but what Frank O'Connor is trying to do to us isn't exactly by the book either. We'll survive and we'll do whatever it takes," Richard responded, scarcely convinced.

"Why don't you take a few days off? Take Hanna out to Martha's Vineyard and spend some time on your boat. It'll do you good. When you come back things will look a lot different."

Mecham thought it might be just the thing to get his mind off what was happening. He knew Hanna would enjoy it. They really didn't need him here all the time. Richard pretty much handled the day-to-day, and he hadn't had a vacation for over six months. God, he had to get away from this madness!

"I really shouldn't be away right now, with everything that's going on, but you've got my number out there, I guess, my boat too. Maybe a few days wouldn't hurt. I'll make plans and let you know when I'll be leaving."

Over dinner that night, Richard remarked to Brooke that Mecham would be taking a few days off. "He looks awful. This BTC thing is really getting to him. I sometimes wonder how long he can continue. The mess with BTC, Don Parker, Frank O'Connor, and the money weighs heavier on him than on you and me. He's what, almost sixty? A little old for playing these games."

Brooke was worried. She'd never heard Richard speak of her father that way. Ever since the acquisition of ICC, Mecham had had the enthusiasm of a forty-year-old, but she had seen the apprehension in his face since BTC moved to Boston. She knew the alienation of Parker and O'Connor troubled him more than he ever spoke of.

She also knew that he took great pride in CCA's successes since the acquisition of ICC. He rarely mentioned Richard's money and seemed to relish the enormous sums he was accumulating. He should—it was now in the two-billion-dollar range. At that moment she remembered that it would all be hers someday. They'd just have to work their way through all this. It would soon be over. Stan Miller should have begun the dirty deed by now, and the results would soon begin to show. For what she was paying him, he'd better perform. He was due to call her tomorrow.

"He's pretty resilient," she replied. "The BTC issue should be resolved in a month and he'll just have to deal with the Don Parker thing. As for Frank O'Connor, I don't think he feels any sense of friendship lost. Look what he's doing to us. And the money is a closed issue. He's had to deal with that for three years; he'd better get used to it. We've got to get on with other things in our lives," Brooke said, and added, "I should hear from Stan Miller this week. The news had better be good."

IN THE WORLD OF COMPUTER GEEKS, Jim Ahern was about as good as they get. Stan Miller had planned to leave him in charge of the BTC operation on his return to Atlantic City. Now that the situation had changed, Stan had to drastically alter his instructions. "We came here to wreak havoc. Are you sure you know what the hell you're doing?" Ahearn asked.

"I know it sounds wacky, Jim, but trust me, this is the only course. You'll make a lot more money and it's a hell of a lot safer. Actually, this guy O'Connor seems like a straight shooter. I feel a lot more comfortable with him than the others," Miller said. He knew it was tough for Ahern to shift his mindset a hundred and eighty degrees, but the sooner they started, the quicker he could get back to Atlantic City. Today he had to meet with Brooke.

"I think I've got things set up as well as can be," Miller told her. "This is delicate work and has to be done carefully. I've got the best men I could find and we should see results within a week or two. As I told you before we started, it's not fail-safe; anything could go wrong. If that begins to happen we'll have to leave quickly—I'm not going to expose those men to criminal charges. But we'll know soon. I'll keep you posted," he said, hoping Brooke caught the implication of possible failure. "Have you given any thought to an alternative plan in the event this doesn't work?"

Brooke didn't like what she was hearing. Miller had given her every assurance that his plan would yield the desired results. Yes, he had offered the expected caveats, but today he sounded less optimistic. Dammit, they didn't have time to deal with surprises.

"I don't want to speculate," she said. "Get on with what we agreed to and let me know how it's progressing. I'll deal with alternatives if that becomes necessary. I want a complete update in three days."

It went much as he'd anticipated, maybe better. At least she was prepared for bad news. There was a nuance of suspicion in Brooke's demeanor that annoyed Miller. He didn't trust her, which made his arrangement with O'Connor even more acceptable. An element of retaliation was beginning to develop in his relationship with Brooke. Her motives began to appear foreboding and he was relieved to have found a way out. He also wondered why her husband was never included in their conversations, her father either, for that matter. There was more to Brooke Temple-Stearns than Stan Miller wanted to know.

Miller departed for Atlantic City that night, leaving Jim Ahern and two other members of his crew at BTC. It was all show; none of them did anything "unproductive." Stan would return in a week and report to Brooke that their efforts had failed. Then the fun would start, Ahern thought.

$$$

MECHAM TEMPLE WAS AMBIVALENT about a holiday at his beach house with Hanna. The problems at CCA and the other difficulties in his business world worried him more than he told anyone. He needed some time to sort out his life. He was fifty-eight years old; he should be able to enjoy his remaining years without this growing turmoil. CCA's mounting losses and the disintegration of his relationship with his two closest friends was devastating. His only remaining joy was the knowledge that he had built one of the nation's most successful computer operations, but even that was clouded by the shady methods he had employed. It all came down to that fateful day he'd agreed to knowingly use Richard's ill-gotten drug money. It would never go away, not ever, and now Frank O'Connor's relentless efforts to destroy him made all his earlier achievements feel hollow. Would it never end?

Mecham and Hanna arrived at the beach house late in the afternoon and started the usual ritual of grocery shopping and meal planning—things they enjoyed doing together and that set the stage for their stay. The boat was not one of Hanna's favorite pastimes. It represented too much work for very little reward. She hated the wind, and preparing food on board was a chore she abhorred. This left the seafaring recreation to Mecham by himself. He loved the sea and the solitude, particularly today. He could collect his thoughts and maybe find some resolutions to the uncertainties in his life.

His fifty-five-foot sloop, Mehanna, was in pristine condition and well stocked. Onboard he had a small library, a bar and some personal items, among them a laptop computer, his Colt .45 revolver, and plentiful fishing gear. He cast off the lines and slowly motored out of the marina. His despondent mood suppressed any desire for a lengthy bout with the sea. A mile or so out, he throttled the engine down to an idle and let the craft wallow in the calm water. He went to the bar and poured a large Johnny Walker Black over ice, then another. It was to be a long, dark day for Mecham Winston Temple.

TWENTY-SIX

THE SLEEK BOAT WASHED ASHORE NEAR EEL POND, just off Beach Road. The body of Mecham Temple was slumped over a small desk in the main cabin, the Colt .45 still gripped in his hand. A note lay on the desk, scribbled in a barely legible hand and sealed in an envelope. It was addressed to his wife, who was notified immediately.

Richard and Brooke rushed to her parents' beach home on Martha's Vineyard. The shock had left Hanna bedridden, prostrate with grief. She and Mecham had been married for over thirty-five years. He was the only man she had ever loved. She had always been a frail woman, having nearly died at Brooke's birth. Mecham had been her sustenance throughout their marriage. "Why would he do this to me?" she howled at Brooke. "He was all I had, all I wanted. I can't go on without him," she sobbed. Unable to contain her own emotions, Brooke buried her head in her mother's bosom. She had been close to Mecham but her thoughts now were with her mother—and the enormous estate she would now inherit. Hanna knew nothing of the source of their great wealth. She had been a mother, a wife, and a great social asset to Mecham. Their lavish entertaining enabled them to mix with the cream of Boston's elite. Because the business held little interest for Hanna, Mecham never confided in her, intentionally withholding any bad news. The BTC issue was never discussed; certainly not Richard's initial investment in ICC. In her view, her husband's great success was all due to Mecham alone.

The envelope the authorities had brought from the boat lay unopened on the nightstand next to Hanna's bed. Brooke noticed it and asked her mother what it was. The scribbled name was barely readable and she didn't recognize the handwriting.

"I don't know. The police left it when they told me about Mecham. Said they found it on the boat. Let me see it."

Hanna looked at the writing and knew it was from Mecham. Closing her eyes and sobbing, she handed it to Brooke, who opened the letter and began to make sense of the scrawled writing. She read with astonishment. It was a confession, pouring out his heart in contrition for all the vile things he had done. He lamented the loss of his friends and apologized to his wife for leaving her. This was something no one should see—certainly not Hanna. She crumpled it in her hand with a dismissive gesture, implying triviality: nothing Hanna would be interested in. "What is it? Let me see it," Hanna insisted.

"It's nothing. Must have been left in the boat for some time. Don't trouble yourself."

"No. If it was on the boat it must have come from Mecham. I want to see it."

Brooke had no choice but to hand over the note. As she watched her mother squint to decipher the scribbling, her heart sank. The look on Hanna's face told it all. She dropped the note on the bed and buried her face in her hands, crying uncontrollably. She wailed about how unnecessary his death was, how he never would have done the things he wrote about. "This can't be true, Brooke. He wasn't capable of such things. Were you aware of any of this?" Brooke knew her mother. Hanna's total disengagement from anything connected with the business made the revelations in the note irrelevant. She knew nothing, and Brooke would keep it that way.

"Of course not, Mother. Dad was not old but he was approaching a time in his life when things might not have been as he would have liked. I have no idea what he was trying to say. I think for your sake we'll just forget this." She took the note from the bed and put it in her purse, hoping Hanna would agree. A frail woman, her mother now looked dreadful. Burying her husband would be devastating. Brooke would make the arrangements.

Mecham Temple was buried in the family plot where his own father and mother were interred. It was a simple ceremony attended by only the closest of friends and business associates. Hanna collapsed near the end of the service, and Brooke rushed her home. She and Richard arranged for 'round-the-clock nursing care. They met with her doctor, who confirmed their worst fears: Hanna might not survive the shock of losing Mecham—she simply had no will to live. Two days later, at the age of fifty-seven, she died in her sleep.

BROOKE HANDLED THE LOSS OF HER PARENTS with her usual cool self-assurance. She missed Mecham terribly and longed for his firm, thoughtful guidance. She had seen his collapse approaching but dismissed her role in his demise and continued her relentless pursuit of riches and notoriety. Her inheritance now made her a major stockholder in CCA, and made the need to destroy BTC paramount. Stan Miller was now more important than ever.

Brooke and Richard returned to their home and began the task of catching up. There were several calls from Stan Miller, one rather urgent. Richard would return to his office at CCA to assess what damage the past several days had brought.

"He's had almost three weeks to do the deed. He'd better have some news for us," Brooke fumed. "You should have the latest financials at your office. Why don't you call?"

Richard was beginning to see an unmistakable change. Brooke's increasingly authoritarian behavior since her father's death alarmed him. They had briefly discussed her role in the company as a major shareholder, and Richard assumed her involvement would be as passive as Mecham's had been. On the drive home from the funeral she'd announced her intentions: She would attend the next stockholders meeting and would lobby for a seat on the board of directors. That would be a slam-dunk, given the size of her holdings. She seemed determined to upstage him. Although Richard's holdings in CCA were slightly less than Mecham's had been, he was president and CEO and ran the company. Mecham, as chairman of the board, had been largely a ceremonial figure. The composition of the board would now include both Brooke and Richard, with Brooke a likely candidate for chairman.

This was ominous for Richard. While it wouldn't change day-to-day management, it could drastically alter the company's long-term objectives. Most of the other members of the board were solidly with him and had been ever since they had acquired ICC and begun to enjoy unparalleled success. Recent developments regarding BTC hadn't been discussed in detail, but the latest financial reports would surely change that.

"Last week's sales were off 15 percent and the weekly P&L shows a loss of nearly $10 million. You'd better get Miller on the phone." Having allowed Brooke to handle the Miller thing by herself annoyed him. "I want to meet with him when he gets here. I've been out of that loop too long; I need to know how it's going."

Brooke was shocked. She was perfectly capable of handling Stan Miller and his undercover activities, but now didn't seem an appropriate time to confront Richard. Her power in the company could manifest itself later.

Miller was delighted to hear from her. He had pretended to undermine BTC as long he cared to. If he was to do anything for Frank O'Connor it had to be soon.

"Sorry to hear about your parents. It must be difficult for you. You have my sympathies." He paused. "I'm afraid I don't have any good news." He explained the problem at BTC. "They've implemented some very effective quality control procedures that virtually preclude sabotage. We've tried, and only been reprimanded for sloppy work. It's not working, Brooke, and

I think we should abandon it before we become suspect. Our people have been accepted in the organization, which could be an asset in the future."

For the money she was paying Miller, this was unacceptable. He had essentially promised results, but if the plan was ineffective it made no sense to continue. She and Richard would have to devise a new strategy. Their losses were mounting and time was running out.

"That's not what I wanted to hear. You assured us your plan would work. How do we know a new strategy would be any more effective?"

"I can't answer that. I do know that they're very well organized and are producing at an impressive level. I have no other suggestions for thwarting their efforts. If you have any ideas, let me know," he said, not knowing what to expect. He suspected she was capable of almost anything.

"I'll get back to you tonight. We'll devise another approach and let you know."

TWENTY-SEVEN

MILLER'S FAILURE DIDN'T SURPRISE RICHARD. He knew that modern manufacturing processes were virtually immune to assault. He should have discouraged Brooke when he listened to what Miller had suggested. They'd wasted valuable time, and losses were multiplying. If they were going to put a stop to BTC's encroachment on their markets, it would require drastic measures, and damn soon.

"BTC must vanish. Disappear. Cease to exist. If we don't do something immediately, Mecham's prediction might turn out correct. Our financial people told me yesterday that our losses are now projected at $230 million for the quarter. Our stock has dropped almost 45 percent and no one sees an end to it. We might be unable to meet our obligations for payroll, materials, and overhead. If we were to sell our combined stock today, Brooke, our total loss would be well over $2 billion. CCA is hemorrhaging, and if we don't stop it within the next two weeks we could face bankruptcy or worse. Wall Street tolerates just so much," Richard shouted.

"What do you have in mind? We could arrange to annihilate their facility but that seems rather primitive. There has to be some permanent way to remove them as a competitor. Do you suppose Frank O'Connor would be willing to negotiate some sort of truce? Maybe we could convince him it would be better than a traumatic 'accident' to him or his plant," Brooke suggested.

"I like the idea of a truce. How would we approach him—an alliance? Shared technology? Maybe he'd like to acquire us."

"I don't think so. His mission all along has been to destroy us financially, and buying us out wouldn't accomplish that. We could try selling to some third party, but with our stock depressed we'd take a bath. It appears he's accomplishing what he set out to do. We just can't let this happen, Richard. I'm prepared to do whatever it takes to stop him," Brooke said.

"So am I, but we've got to be realistic. The sabotage thing was deniable but it didn't work—not surprising, everything considered. We know that he's basically a banker; BTC is a sideline for him. True, Bruno Davidson is a huge asset and well respected in the industry, but O'Connor is dabbling in a business he knows very little about. He's apparently made a colossal investment. If BTC were to fail, his losses would be immeasurable. So, where's he vulnerable? I don't know enough about the banking business to see any areas of weakness, but they must exist somewhere.

"Part of our problem stems from our unfamiliarity with the sordid ways some people deal with these issues. If we were determined to destroy his operation, we could arrange to have it eliminated, I guess. Stan Miller suggested that he has people who do this sort of thing, but it's got to be our last resort."

The very thought of literally eradicating BTC was repulsive to Richard. He knew there had to be a realistic alternative. Instead of a truce, which he knew Frank O'Connor would never accept, maybe there was one option: they could purchase BTC, integrate it into CCA and permanently close Atlanta. Even if O'Connor were receptive to an offer, the cost of such an acquisition could be enormous. But if they continued as things were? He didn't want to ponder that.

THEY HADN'T BEEN IN THE INTERNATIONAL BANK building since leaving Don Parker's law firm three years ago. Their appointment with O'Connor was for two that afternoon and Brooke was nervous. They had pored over financial spreadsheets with CCA's financial people for a week, concluding that the BTC operation was worth between $600 million and $900 million. They'd start at $500 million, which was nearly half their current net worth and would leave them critically short of cash.

Frank O'Connor was delighted to meet with them. It was the beginning of the end. He could guess why they were coming. What else could it be? And he had his own number; they needed him more than he needed to sell. No, it would cost them dearly, and forcing them to pay an outrageous price could mean trouble downstream. If they wanted BTC it would cost them $750 million. He'd take some stock but most would have to be in cash. He also wanted a lifetime contract for Bruno at $2 million a year, and guaranteed termination benefits for all the employees who came from Atlanta. He was sure they'd buy it all.

"That's outrageous! No startup company is worth that much," Richard screamed. "Our best offer is $500 million, all in stock."

"Well, if that's your best offer we have nothing further to discuss. If you'll excuse me, I have another meeting scheduled. Nice to see you both."

If revenge were something one could hold and touch, this moment would be the epitome of tactile joy. He could see their desperation, feel their panic.

He knew they would respond—they had no other choice.

They agreed to every demand: $50 million in stock and $700 million cash; the deal closed in a week. Bruno was delighted, and Craig Hess, Jill Overton, and the other employees from Atlanta were ecstatic—job security was a benefit few enjoyed these days. Ray Tipton was paid a handsome fee for his services. Jack Evers netted a profit of almost $6 million. CCA and the Stearnses had paid for all of it.

When it was over, Brooke and Richard sat for days with their financial people, sorting out the soaking they had just taken. The total loss, including the drop in their stock and the continuing losses at CCA, totaled over $2.5 billion—nearly eighty percent of their net worth. The *Boston Globe* carried alarming stories about the imminent demise of CCA.

Brooke was in a daze. How would they face their friends? The embarrassment alone was more than she could bear, and if the trend continued, they could lose everything. It wasn't fair, she thought. Her lifestyle was threatened, and that she could not abide. Her every fiber demanded recovery of the assets that she could not live without. Somehow she would find a way.

TWENTY-EIGHT

F RANK O'CONNOR WASN'T CONTENT to let the Stearnses agonize over their current plight. He had structured the buyout to allow them what he thought were sufficient funds to continue an uphill battle to resuscitate CCA. After their contractual obligations to Bruno and the other employees, they would have under $700 million available. It would be a tough recovery. But they did have enough funds to pursue what Frank had in mind. He called Stan Miller.

Stan had resettled into the daily routine of managing the La Samanna. He loved the work and was glad Brooke had abandoned her foolish attacks on BTC. CCA's buyout left him uncertain about his future at the casino, particularly if what he read in the trade journals was true. While the Stearnses owned the immensely profitable casino free and clear, any financial reversals in Boston could have disastrous consequences here at the casino.

The call from Frank O'Connor left him wondering if his demise was at hand. O'Connor would be in Atlantic City at the end of the week to discuss a matter he thought would interest Miller. He was a little unstrung about these crazy people from Boston. What insane activity did O'Connor want him for now? He made arrangements to house Frank in their finest suite.

Frank O'Connor knew what he wanted Miller to do but was a little unsure of how to go about it. He was not at all comfortable with this sort of thing. It wandered into the realm of the unsavory, but he wouldn't be involved directly. Only Miller would know the sordid details. It would be the consummate undoing of Richard and Brooke Stearns. His revenge would be complete.

He arrived late in the afternoon and was met by a limousine from the casino. This ostentatious display of wealth made Frank uneasy. The last time he was in a limo had been at the grand opening of his bank. He disliked it—too flashy—but if he was to persuade Miller to assist in his plan, why not? They met later that night for dinner in a private dining room.

"You really roll out the red carpet for your friends, Stan, I'm impressed. Must be serious money in the casino business." Getting familiar with Stan Miller was unsettling. "I do appreciate your indulgence in my bizarre requests. Someday all this will be over and we can enjoy a civilized outing together. In the meantime let me outline what I have in mind."

Miller looked apprehensive and toyed with the buttons on his jacket. He wasn't sure he wanted to hear this.

"I won't bore you with all the background surrounding my obsession with what I need done—my reasons are sufficient. Nor do I intend to disclose to you how I know what I know." This was alien territory for Frank. Why bare his soul to this cretin? Tell him just enough to gain his confidence.

"Let me begin with this: My only son was killed about a year ago in a vicious drug-related incident. Richard Stearns, who was deeply involved and made hundreds of millions of dollars in drug trafficking, duped him into a dangerous situation. I want Stearns back in that business.

"Without casting aspersions on your character or your reputation, Stan, I'm assuming you might know people who could assist us in this regard. It shouldn't be too difficult to entice him; he has a calamitous need for large amounts of money. We'll give him every opportunity to replenish his shortfall. My guess is he's laboring to untangle his financial nightmare as we speak. His wife, Brooke, was not involved in the original drug dealing but has since become the keeper of the wealth. She's probably the driving force behind their obsessive need to recover their lost fortune."

The hard part was just ahead. Miller had to take the bait.

"Now here's what I'm suggesting. Using your connections, select an individual you think can gain Richard's confidence. The entrée will be that Richard has large amounts of cash available to make huge drug purchases. He probably has sources offshore; he might even know people who can get it into the country. I don't know if he's still connected with the same group he used some years ago, but I do know, with his dilemma, he'll find a way."

Miller was astounded. Here was a wealthy, respected banker soliciting him to find a big-time drug dealer. What would these clowns from Boston think of next? Of course he'd do it; the way O'Connor described it, there was absolutely no risk to him.

"I can probably find someone, but I want it understood that I'll have nothing to do with drug dealing. I put the guy in touch with Richard and I'm out of it. I don't want to know what your plans are for Richard after you get him back in the business. One more thing: If you're successful, they could lose this casino and I could lose my job. I've worked damn hard here for the past couple of years getting this operation back on its feet, and I'd hate to lose it."

"I've thought about that. My associates have assured me that in such an event we will arrange to buy them out and guarantee your employment. I can't put that in writing, but here's half your fee for what I'm asking now. As soon as Richard is set up you'll get the other half. Any other questions?" Frank handed Stan $125,000 in cash.

Hell no, he didn't have any other questions! These people threw away more money in a week than he made in a year. And his risk was zero. He knew exactly whom to call. Fred Marcus was the best connected and least visible drug king in the area. His exploits were legend and he had never been arrested. The trafficking group had dubbed him "The Untouchable." Miller, of course, knew Marcus and had, in fact, entertained him and one of his lady friends recently; he stopped by the casino frequently. Stan told O'Connor he had no idea how to reach Marcus, and would have to wait for him to show up.

TWENTY-NINE

RICHARD AND BROOKE WERE AT THEIR WITS' END. CCA stock was falling almost two and a half points a day. The losses were beginning to level out, however. In the two months since they acquired BTC, Bruno had performed brilliantly. If they could stem the tide, maybe they could survive. But surviving wasn't what Brooke was all about—she wanted back on top, back in the sanctity of the social set she so desperately needed, with her four-billion-dollar fortune intact. It was so embarrassing to attend the few parties they were invited to, and the incessant depletion of their assets made entertaining awkward. They were home alone nearly every evening.

When Stan Miller called to invite them to Atlantic City for the weekend, they were delighted. "How did he know we needed some R&R?" Brooke asked as she unpacked in their sumptuous suite. "After our false start in Boston, I'm surprised he still wants to see us."

Stan Miller arranged a lavish meal for them in the main dinning room and invited Fred Marcus to join them for after-dinner drinks. He came with a stunning beauty, dressed to kill, her ample bosom barely concealed. Richard was charmed; Brooke pouted. Marcus was an amiable man in his late forties, with black hair and a chiseled face. Miller had spent the morning with him, detailing what he hoped would be the proper setup. He characterized Richard as a freewheeling big spender, wise in the ways of the drug business.

He seemed like a natural to Fred, but he'd have to approach him cautiously.

They talked for an hour, then Miller suggested they retire to the baccarat tables. It was just what Brooke needed—she'd competed with Marcus' lady long enough. Richard, however, detested the game, opting for the bar, where Miller and Fred Marcus soon joined him. The conversation finally came around to why they were there. Casually, and with some humor, Miller announced that Fred could get them some first-class heroin. Would Richard be interested? It had been years since Richard had indulged in any drugs, and had rarely used heroin. "We don't see much of that in Boston. Is it hard to get here?" he asked, more than a little interested.

"Not if you know where to look, and a look is all you'll get if you ask the wrong guy. This is touchy stuff. You into dealing?" Marcus asked.

"No. I use a little, but not much. Stan must have told you, we're in the computer business."

"He did. With your money you could hit a home run in no time. Our ballpark is ready for a new player, if you get my drift," Fred said, eyes wide, head back.

God, Richard hadn't thought about that in years! He shuddered as he recalled the fear he had carried so long. Even now the notion struck terror in his throat, but the money . . . the money was extraordinary.

"I guess I'd better get back to my wife, see how much she's lost. Baccarat isn't her long suit. Nice to meet you, Fred, maybe we'll see you again before we leave. Good night, Stan."

In silence, Richard walked Brooke to the elevator, his thoughts returning to those nights with Shane, flying to Florida: the cases filled with millions in cash, the near-exponential growth of his account. God, the money had just kept piling up, and it was so easy! Of course, Shane had put all the pieces in place, and his position at the bank made it happen. But that was long ago.

"What'd you think of Mr. Marcus? His lady looked like a hooker."

"I thought they both were trash. Her vocabulary consisted of two-syllable words. God, I detest cretins like that. Why did Stan want us to meet them?" Brooke asked.

"I don't know, but I do know the guy's into dealing drugs. Stan knows what we've been through; maybe he thought we needed a hit. In fact, I got the impression Marcus wanted me to make a buy with him. Pretty tempting considering the problems we've got. Could get us back on top damn quick," Richard mused.

"Are you serious? You forget the dread you lived with during your heyday. What makes you think Marcus was hitting on you?"

"He's apparently into heroin. Twice the margins compared to cocaine. Easier to transport and it's where the demand is. Some knowledge I picked up from Shane. He thinks we command big bucks. Probably learned that from Stan. Call the desk and ask them to send up a laptop."

Through most of the night Richard punched numbers into the little computer and watched the amounts grow across the screen. It was the same old game: make a buy, unload and reinvest; keep doing it, say, five times and the money reached eleven figures. God, it was like a disease.

"Look at this," Richard said to a barely awake Brooke. "It's amazing! With just five buys we'd have over $10 billion! We'd be back in business, recover all our losses and have $6 billion in the bank. It's infinitely better than my deal with Shane—we were sharing everything with too many people, and it was cocaine—heroin is much more profitable."

"You're crazy. You don't have the contacts Shane had. That was three years ago and the buyer, whatever his name, is probably in jail. And if you really are talking that much cash, how would you possibly get it deposited in a bank?"

"This guy Marcus knows the ropes. He's the buyer; he must know how to contact any number of sources. Our role would be to supply the money and transportation. As to depositing the cash, we could try either the Cayman Islands, Antigua in Barbuda, or a Swiss contact."

In what remained of the night, Richard convinced Brooke this was their salvation. It was quick and nearly flawless. They would be back in the center of Boston's elite, admired and exalted. Richard would assume his rightful position as head of the most successful computer maker in the free world. Brooke would once again reign as the princess of conspicuous consumption. It was really all they had ever wanted.

FRED MARCUS WASN'T ACCUSTOMED to being awakened before mid-afternoon. His late-night escapades with a succession of women left him exhausted. When one of his lieutenants rang to announce that Stan Miller was looking for him, he said Miller could wait till he arrived at his casino, later that night. It was four in the afternoon—Marcus needed breakfast.

Richard had called Stan Miller at noon and announced he'd like to meet with Fred Marcus. How much did Miller know about this man? Could he handle the quantities Richard envisioned? Did he have the money? Who and where were his sources? Did he have distributors lined up? Richard expected that working with Marcus would be similar to the way he and Shane had operated with Marty Stinson. They would buy from the source and transport it into the United States, where Marcus would take delivery and make payment. The huge amounts of cash could be a problem. He didn't have Shane to slide it through the banking system. He'd need help with this; maybe Marcus would have some ideas.

He was waiting in the elaborate cocktail lounge when he spotted Marcus sauntering in alone, wearing Bermuda shorts and a frightful-looking tropical shirt. He looked more like a tourist than like a drug king. Maybe that was what he had in mind.

"Good evening, Richard. What brings you out so early?"

Smart-ass, Richard thought. It was 9:00 P.M. and he'd been waiting an hour.

"Hello, Fred, nice to see you again. We're leaving tomorrow and I thought we might get a little more specific about the conversation we had last night. I might be interested in establishing a working relationship, but I need some questions answered."

Marcus looked puzzled. What possible questions could this guy have? He bought drugs and sold to distributors. Pretty simple operation, no paperwork, just cash. Marcus liked it that way. If it got complicated, he passed.

"I'm not too good at questions. Sometimes the answers require talking. That could lead to unpleasant things, and I hate unpleasant things, if you get my drift."

Richard wasn't sure he got the drift. Brooke was right: a certifiable cretin, not at all like Marty Stinson. But what the hell, he wasn't going to entertain Marcus and his bimbos, it was just a business deal.

"You suggested last night I might be able to hit a home run and that your ballpark was ready for a new player. Tell me more."

God, they're all alike, Marcus thought. Greed does strange things to people. He suspected Richard had all the money he could ever want, and yet here he was offering his credentials as a drug trafficker. "In a nutshell," he began, "I can unload all the heroin I can get. Problem is, it's tough to line up a reliable supply. I need a steady stream of the stuff. If you've got sources and a way to get it here, we can do business. My price is $75,000 a kilo in cash, delivered into the States. I can take it any time you can deliver."

"Do you currently have a source? I mean, who are you getting your supply from now?"

"I do, but it's sporadic; can't depend on them. With demand the way it is I need my pipeline full all the time. I can't tell you who my suppliers are— you should know that."

Richard would need help. There were too many things he wasn't current on. His only friend in the business was Marty Stinson, and it had been years since he had even thought about Marty. He remembered the bar where he and Shane had met him.

"We're leaving in a few hours. I'll set up my end and get back to you. How do I get in touch?"

Marcus handed him a phony business card with the name and phone number of a plumbing company. How original! "You can get a message to me any time at this number. How do I reach you?"

Richard gave him his home and office numbers. "Not a good idea. Get a new number in someone else's name. We don't want the DEA snooping." The wheels were turning. This was dangerous beyond belief. His whole world could fall apart, but it was falling apart anyway. He so desperately needed the cash he could almost smell it. And so quick—he'd be back in business in two months, with more money than he'd ever dreamed. If Fred Marcus could take that much heroin, maybe Marty Stinson could take a similar amount. My God, the possibilities were limitless!

On the flight back to Boston, Richard and Brooke talked endlessly about how the plan would work. If they could get Marty Stinson on board, it would require delivering in both Boston and New York. With their shipping company, that should be no problem.

"I'll contact the guy Shane was working with. The report from the embassy in Hong Kong should have that information. If he's still a player, we can make him rich beyond his wildest dreams; if he's still on our payroll it'll be that much easier. This might require your involvement in the dirty end of the business, Brooke. I hope you're up to it," Richard announced.

"What on earth are you talking about? There's not one thing about drug trafficking I know or want to know. Explain what you mean."

"Relax. All I meant was, I might have to rely on you to act as the agent at the point of collection if I'm tied up elsewhere. It's nothing we can't work out; I just wanted you to be aware of the possibility. We'll be spread pretty thin between receiving the merchandise, making the transfers to Marty or Fred Marcus, and hauling the cash to some far-off banking establishment. You can't hire people to handle that end of the business—it's all cash, and tons of it. The only people we'll hire will be some muscle; Stan Miller can help us with that."

Brooke was torn between the excitement of being back in the race and the tawdry activity it would require. This was all beneath her. She'd do what she thought was appropriate and no more, but with their net worth in a death spiral, what would that entail? She certainly wasn't going to deal directly with the human dregs she suspected ran the drug business—she'd had all she could handle with Fred Marcus. But the thought of a bank balance in the billions obliterated any trepidation. She'd do what she had to.

RICHARD BEGAN THE SEARCH FOR MARTY STINSON in the bar where he and Shane had first met him. He assigned Brooke the task of running down Cho Wong. The Embassy in Hong Kong confirmed that name, and it was a simple matter to have their shipping company check whether he was still employed. When she called Richard on his cell phone to announce that Mr. Wong was still an active employee of the Far East Shipping Company, Richard answered from the seedy bar where he was awaiting Marty Stinson's arrival.

"Great! Set up a meeting with him as soon as possible, in a nondescript area of town. I should know sometime this afternoon whether Marty is still available. I'll see you at home."

Marty Stinson arrived at the bar at just the time the bartender had said he would. He was dressed in a cheap suit, wore no tie, and looked like he hadn't slept for days. His face was unshaven, his eyes wide and unseeing. He perched on a stool near Richard. It wasn't until the bartender announced that Richard was there to see him that Marty showed any sign of lucidity. He looked at Richard with suspicion, then slowly indicated recognition. "Well, look who's here. Haven't seen you in years. What brings you to this mangy hellhole?" He turned on his stool and faced Richard. "Got a deal for me?"

Richard wasn't sure he wanted anything to do with Marty, who had aged badly and was plainly hung over. This was certainly not the picture of the affluent trafficker.

"Glad you remember me. What have you been up to since I last saw you?"

Marty stared into space and began a sordid tale of bad luck and poor judgment. He had associated with greedy dealers and unreliable sources who had managed to separate him from a sizable amount of money. Yes, he was still in the drug business, but recent events had left him with no resources and few contacts. Those he still had were reluctant to deal with him because of the quality and paucity of product. He needed a drink. Richard obliged and began to ferret out what, if anything, Marty could contribute to his grand plan.

"If I could get you top quality heroin in virtually unlimited quantities, are you still in touch with reliable dealers? I mean, could you cut deals with American dealers who could pay on delivery and take all we could supply?" He looked at Marty, who appeared to finally come alive. He straightened his jacket and brushed his hair with a comic flair. Smiling, he ordered another drink.

"I haven't dealt in 'H' for some time but I have contacts who say they can move carloads. And these are big-time movers, well known in the trade. Money? No problem, they just want a steady source. What've you got in mind? Are you and the other guy back in the game?"

"'The other guy' is dead, killed in a blown deal in Hong Kong some time ago. My interest is immediate and I need reliable dealers now. How soon could you set up a meeting?" Richard knew he sounded impatient, but was relying on Marty's obvious need for a resurgence of his business.

"Let me check around. I should know in a couple days."

"OK, set it up. Meet with them and get a reply. You'll have to sell them on quantity and quality. Tell them we can deliver right here in Boston. They'll need $75,000 a kilo, cash. You'll handle all the transfer details and I'll pro-vide you with a group of very persuasive gentlemen. Here's a number where you can reach me. How do I get hold of you?"

Marty gave him a phone number and promised to be in touch before the end of the week. So far, so good: relying on Marty was a little dicey, he thought, but he knew of no other course. He'd been dependable in their earlier dealings so, until there was a problem, Marty was his man.

As he drove to his home in Weston, Richard thought again of Shane and the trips from Florida with tons of cash. It was so easy letting Shane take care of all the laundering and the intricate paper and computer trails. He and Brooke would have to improvise a system to deal with all that, but how? Twelve billion in cash would fill a freight car and weigh tons. Getting it to some far-off Caribbean bank could be a logistic nightmare. It would take dozens of trips by both Brooke and him; they couldn't trust this part of the plan to anyone else. And if Marty performed, they would be transport-ing the currency from both Boston and New York. This was no job for a plane—they'd need transportation by sea.

THIRTY

BRUNO DAVIDSON WAS THRIVING in his new position as executive vice president of CCA. The acquisition of BTC had necessitated numerous changes. First and most dramatic was the closure of the Atlanta plant—with all the key people having moved to Boston, it had become a dinosaur. With the consolidation of all CCA operations in Boston, the stock price began to climb and the balance sheet was beginning to show a profit. In fact, the outlook for CCA was better now than it had been in months. With Richard gone a good deal of the time, Bruno took over more of the day-to-day operations. He was the technical guru of the company. Richard had always been at the helm in his capacity as CEO, and excelled in sales and marketing. Bruno longed to control the entire company, and spent many hours with Jill Overton, head of sales, a seasoned marketer who understood the vagaries of the computer business. Richard's absences allowed Bruno to partake in most of the strategies required for CCA to remain competitive. He also spent time with the financial people to acquaint himself with the unending task of bottom-line improvement. He felt he was becoming a well-rounded executive, as did Frank O'Connor.

With CCA's purchase of BTC, Frank insisted, as part of the deal, that he sit on the board. While he held substantial stock shares, Richard and Brooke could still outvote him. But with cumulative voting, Frank prevailed on most issues. It was touchy at best. Richard and Brooke had difficulty coming to terms with the man who had tried to destroy them, but with things progressing as they were, they should soon be over it.

Frank also demanded that Bruno have access to all the monthly financial and marketing data the company generated. He was positioning Bruno for the time when Richard might be unable to continue. His strategy with Stan Miller could render Richard too extended to oversee the corporation, he thought, but that was downstream; the immediate objective was to get CCA back in the black. As Frank saw it, with Richard gone, he could gain control of CCA, put Bruno in charge, and watch the operation grow. And he was sure Richard would soon be gone.

FRANK GOT AN OVERVIEW FROM STAN MILLER as to the current relationship between Richard and Fred Marcus. Not much was happening since the two had met, but Stan was confident that would change. Richard called nearly every day to inquire about Marcus' credibility in the woeful world Miller thrived in. How would he pay the enormous sums due when the heroin showed up? Did he have the staying power to continue? Were there others supplying him? Was he bulletproof with regard to the authorities? Miller was able to quell Richard's concerns and assure him the relationship would yield the desired results.

With the money Frank was paying him, all he wanted to do was watch from the sidelines. He might even negotiate a fee from Richard.

RICHARD ARRIVED HOME AFTER HIS MEETING with Marty Stinson, convinced the plan would go as intended. It was difficult to make long-term assumptions when dealing with the likes of Stinson and Fred Marcus, but with the magnitude of the money involved, risk was part of the game.

As his desperation grew, his need for the money became obsessive. Even though CCA was beginning to show a modest profit after months of staggering losses, his net worth had shrunk alarmingly. If Bruno Davidson hadn't been able stop the bleeding, he would have been forced to consider bankruptcy. Brooke was another matter: her despondency over their financial condition was unbearable; her constant harping about their loss of prestige and their inability to run with the movers and shakers was beginning to wear on him. For a woman with inordinate depth of intellect, her shallow need for personal approval was appalling to Richard, but he needed her now, and her pernicious behavior could work to his advantage. Certainly the endeavor they were about to embark upon required the mind of a predator.

Brooke was able to get Cho Wong's schedule from the Far East Shipping Company. She arranged with the local manager to have Wong call her on the pretense of her need for minor boat repairs at the marina on Martha's Vineyard. The ruse was successful; Cho called her the next day.

"Mr. Wong, we have need of your services, and would like to meet with you at your earliest convenience. There's an excellent Chinese restaurant near our shipping offices neighboring the docks. Three this afternoon would be convenient for us if it works for you."

Wong arrived early, apprehensive as to why the owner had singled him out for some obscure repair work. He remembered having met another owner some years ago, which resulted in a most unpleasant incident that had damn near cost him his life! These Americans were so deceptive and superficial, particularly when dealing with Asians. He didn't trust any of them and was determined not to be intimidated—unless there was money involved.

"We appreciate your meeting with us on such short notice," Richard began. He looked at Wong with curious interest. He was in his mid-thirties, reasonably well dressed and with a certain Asian air of authority. His black hair was slicked back on his diminutive head, making him appear smaller than he was.

"We have a mutual friend, or did have. You probably recall Shane O'Connor. He was a close friend of ours. His death was unfortunate and untimely. I'm sure you remember it well. Reports have it you were badly injured," Richard continued.

"Yes, it was a terrifying experience. I hope I never have to go through anything like it again. Shane was good to me. I'm sorry for what happened to him," Wong answered nervously. He wanted to get on with why they were here.

"I'll get to the point, Mr. Wong. We have a proposal for you, which, if you agree to cooperate, could make you a very rich man. I'll get to the specifics shortly. Right now I want you to know that if you have a problem with what I'm about to suggest, we'll call it a day—this meeting never happened." Richard looked for any sign of distrust. If Wong was edgy, he wanted to know it now. If he was cool, not rattled, he felt he could work with him.

"What is it you want from me?" Wong asked in perfect English, with just a touch of arrogance.

"I know you had a bad experience with Shane O'Connor but what I have to offer you in no way resembles the ill-conceived arrangement Shane apparently got you into. It does involve drugs, however—heroin, as a matter of fact, and lots of it. Tell me about your contacts in Hong Kong."

Wong was intrigued but skeptical. His experience with Shane O'Connor had left him wary of all Americans. Since that painful day, he had engaged only in small transactions with local street-corner distributors in Boston's poorer sections, without incident and without much cash reward. He often thought of a larger operation but his lack of contacts and funds prevented such transactions. It also struck him as most unusual that the owner of a successful shipping company would take such risks. On the other hand, it was the shipping operation that made the whole thing possible.

"Before I do that, why don't you tell me how much you want and how often? There are a number of sources available but their ability to deliver in quantity varies."

"We'll take all you can get. The quality has to be the best; we won't take it unless it passes our tests. We have distributors lined up in Boston and New York. Your job is to acquire the stuff from your sources, get it safely aboard our ships and get it to the United States. We'll assist in offloading once it arrives. We'll also provide you solid protection in Hong Kong to handle the purchase. We'll pay your people $25,000 a kilo in Hong Kong and pay you $30 a kilo delivered You'll have to make arrangements aboard ship to avoid detection en route. In that regard we can give you a free hand to do what you think is necessary.

"We require ten thousand kilos a month in both New York and Boston. Within six months, that will go up to more than thirty thousand kilos a month for each. You can do the math—that's over $600,000 a month for you to begin with and three times as much later on. One thing you should understand: if anything goes wrong, we will deny ever having met you."

In his few years trying to make a buck dealing drugs, Wong had never dreamed of this kind of money. His best year netted him nearly $20,000 and it was hit-or-miss at best. Now his boss would not only pay him to deliver but would supply the transportation.

"You're right, I can do the math. For the first shipments of ten thousand kilos each to Boston and New York you'll show up in Hong Kong with $500 million dollars? You do know these people would kill their families for a fraction of a fraction of that. The transfer would have to be in a Brinks truck."

"You underestimate us, Cho, that's all been arranged. We'll provide cartage from the transfer point to the dock and then aboard. Your job is to stow it on the ship. With our instructions to the captain, you'll have no problems. Just keep it under wraps until it arrives in the States. Your primary function is to locate sources who can deliver the quantities and the quality we want."

It sounded too good. They'd need an army at the transfer point. He wasn't going to get caught in a crossfire again for any amount of money.

"How do you intend to secure the transfer? I'm not going to risk exposure to what I went through before. It could be a battlefield."

"Simply stated, we'll have them covered the instant they arrive at the transfer point. Our Asian partners in the Far East Shipping Company have assured us that 'sensitive' material shipped from Hong Kong will be protected with all the resources necessary. If we ask for fifty or even a hundred armed guards, they'll be there. We wouldn't have it any other way—it's our $500 million."

In fact, it was Richard's last $500 million. He and Brooke would have to borrow against most of their assets, including all their stock in CCA. It was coming down to all or nothing at all. If this failed he'd be right back at Don Parker's law firm or one like it. And Brooke? He wasn't sure how she'd cope. He remembered agonizing over how he would provide for her on his meager salary from Parker, and how she had so quickly accommodated his rapid rise to wealth. He thought of Mecham and how hard he had worked to build success at CCA. Now they could lose it all. He wondered if Cho Wong could detect the urgency in his plan.

My God, it was foolproof, Wong thought. He'd be an idiot not to go along. In less than a year he could quit the whole thing, job and all. He'd have millions. No more traveling around the world in cramped crew quarters, no more greasy food and no more meager paydays.

THIRTY-ONE

FRANK O'CONNOR WAS BECOMING RESTIVE. It was unlike him to exhibit impatience; he was far too mature and methodical to blunder into the trap of poor judgment. He could feel the jaws of devastation closing around Richard and Brooke Stearns. The satisfaction of complete and absolute annihilation drove him, but he wondered if he would luxuriate in this euphoria when it was all over. What if it weren't enough? He called Stan Miller and announced he would be in Atlantic City the next day.

Miller had some news: He knew that Marcus and Richard had come to an accommodation, but wasn't privy to the details. All he could tell Frank was that Richard had called and wanted him to arrange for a contingent of musclemen to be in Hong Kong in a week. Richard hadn't said how long they'd be there, but said he'd give them their marching orders when they arrived.

They had dinner the next evening in the casino's private dining room. Frank was unusually friendly and gushed with excitement when he was told about Hong Kong. Miller was suspicious. He was in as deeply as he wanted to be, and hoped Frank wouldn't prevail on him for yet more clandestine chores.

"This is about what I expected. With Fred Marcus lined up as a distributor, Richard has arranged an Asian source, but it's risky transporting large amounts of cash, especially in that part of the world. I know—that's where my son came to his early death. How ironic, Richard Stearns back in the business and in the same locale," Frank said wistfully. Miller couldn't tell if he was stricken with anger, grief, or delight.

"What I want you to do now is get everything you can from Richard's files," Frank said, handing Miller a sophisticated-looking camera.

What the hell does he want now? I'm not getting close enough to anyone to snap a picture. "What's this? I can screw up an Instamatic. What do you expect me to do with this?"

"Just listen. This is the very latest in digital photographic technology. I want you to locate the absolutely best clandestine photographer and computer geek in the area, and bring them to Boston when I give you the go-ahead. We'll get them into Richard's office, where I want them to photograph every scrap of paper and every file. In addition, I want diskettes of everything on every hard drive in every computer in his office.

"Further, Richard and Brooke travel a good deal these days, which takes them away from their home in Weston. We'll schedule your people into their home to coincide with one of their trips. Again, I want every fragment of paper photographed and every computer covered. Timing will be important, so get your people lined up and on standby."

God, they must think I'm an employment agency, Miller thought. This time he might strike out. He didn't have a clue where to find the photographer, though the computer geek would be a piece of cake.

"Am I supposed to keep this camera? It might help to break the ice with a prospective candidate, though I must tell you I know of no such person. But I'll have my scouts see what they can find."

"Yes, keep the camera for now. When you've found our subject, he'll know how to use it. I'll let you know when to move in."

Frank was beginning to see the end of Richard and Brooke. All had gone according to plan. If Richard was as adept as history would suggest at spiriting drugs into America, he should soon have enormous amounts of money stashed somewhere. Richard didn't have the banking ally he'd had in Shane, so he'd have to get creative in this regard. Frank was sure Richard would solve the problem.

SINCE SHANE'S DEATH, FRANK HAD BECOME a different man. He had hired Rob Myers as his new president and was pleased with Rob's performance: he was knowledgeable and respected in the banking community, and hiring him allowed Frank time to pursue his obsession with destroying Richard. It also allowed Frank time to explore other latent passions.

He was virtually alone now and confided little in Martha. At sixty-one, he'd become acutely aware that his life was slipping away. Concern lingered that the grave deceptions Shane had conducted at the bank could be uncovered. Don Parker assured him the possibility was remote. He certainly had no reason to be troubled about his personal or business resources. He had managed to accumulate a net worth of nearly $2 billion. His stake in CCA alone was now worth over $500 million.

Nonetheless, events in the banking industry over the past few years had left him feeling abandoned. The International Bank of Boston was among the largest in the state, but he had no national presence. His global connections assured him his share of small- and little-margin action, but he longed for the clout of a Chase Manhattan or a CITIBANK, which would require billions in assets to buy or acquire by merger. With the end in sight for Richard Stearns, he began to ponder, deep in his soul, how he might accomplish such a coup. Two years ago he never would have dreamed of such deceit. His life had been exemplary: he valued the trust and respect his associates bestowed upon him; his word was his bond; every aspect of his being reflected honesty.

This began changing soon after Shane's death. He'd lost his compass, his priorities shifted, banking became mundane. Without an heir to all the success his family had attained, he needed a loftier calling. Recognition and clout were now his mantra. It surprised him how easy the transition was, from jewel of virtue to rock of corruption. He even found it comfortable consorting with the likes of Stan Miller.

Getting massive amounts of money into his bank would be challenging. He'd have to rely heavily on Rob Myers. He'd also need the artful legal mind of Don Parker. He didn't want to corrupt either of them but he couldn't pull it off by himself—there were too many pitfalls. Rob could assist in the complex movement of funds, and Don could create the wide-ranging transactions that would validate the need for such substantial amounts. He would pay both men very well.

Stan Miller, for his part, was ecstatic. The disdainful Brooke was out of his hair, busy conducting drug activities with Richard. Richard needed his assistance with muscle in Hong Kong, and Frank his expertise in photography and computers. And the pay was outrageous: with his salary from the casino plus the perks from all his extracurricular deceptions, he'd gross nearly two million this year. While it was more than he'd ever dreamed of, he'd acclimated quickly. At age thirty-one years, he lived in a lightning-fast milieu, consorted with the world's most beautiful women, and enjoyed a following of the most scandalous clan in Atlantic City.

During his years at the La Samanna, a lust for his own casino had blossomed. He knew exactly how he would manage and staff it, how he would arrange the appointments to enhance the gambling experience. But it was only a dream. The money required was light-years out of his reach, so he resigned himself to enjoying what he had. Which was considerable.

THIRTY-TWO

Cho Wong left for Hong Kong before the end of the week. Upon arriving he went directly to his sources and became an overnight sensation. Was he serious? Did his new associates really want thousands of kilos? The heroin trade had always been lucrative but sporadic. With this turn of events they could count on a sustained cash flow in the millions.

"And don't try any strong-arm stuff," Wong cautioned them. "This group has resources to deal with any disorder. It would be suicide to attempt to disrupt the transfer. You should have the first shipment ready in three weeks. I'll let you know where."

Cho was ecstatic. He must now arrange to stow the material aboard. The shipping schedule he was given showed one of the larger ships leaving for Boston to accommodate the first shipment. Twenty-two tons of heroin would consume an enormous amount of space; he would need the cooperation of at least three of the crewmen and that could be dangerous. He reasoned that if he could buy the support of men he trusted, they would also be very useful on the delivery end in Boston. He'd implement the same plan for the shipment to New York, scheduled to arrive a week later. The cost would be minuscule compared to his fee, and he'd gain great respect from these subordinates. What a turn of events for a mere roustabout! A week ago he was a common deck hand; now he was a wealthy drug trafficker.

He called Richard's private number. "Everything is set. You should arrange to be in Hong Kong on the fifteenth with the money. My sources can assure you top quality at the price we discussed. I've made arrangements for the onboard stowing. We should arrive in Boston no later than the twenty-ninth."

Richard could hardly contain his excitement. Marty's people would pay him nearly $1 billion for this shipment, and Fred Marcus would equal that amount a week later. In a month it would double. A month after that he'd be out of it with $10 billion, back on top and no one to stop him. He would repurchase the CCA stock he'd hocked. Brooke could reinvest in all those trendy issues she so loved talking about. His life would get back to normal, the nightmare over at last.

The first shipment arrived on schedule and Marty's people paid Richard in cash as agreed—$750 million. The volume was staggering: eleven tons of heroin converted into nearly ten tons of hundred-dollar bills! The logistics required heavy equipment unsuited to air transport. The money had been packaged in ten large metal containers weighing a ton apiece. Under the eyes of an armed contingent supplied by Stan Miller, these were moved by forklift aboard a chartered boat Richard had arranged, for shipment to Antigua. He and Brooke would accompany the money and make the deposit. Once safely in the offshore bank, they could disperse the funds to American banks through dummy corporations.

Before the whole operation was over—Richard vowed it would end in under three months—it would take at least half a dozen trips to the Caribbean, each lasting a week or more. It was a cumbersome process that couldn't be assigned to others. They both resigned themselves to the arduous task. The risk was minimal, though they had to avoid encounters with the United States Coast Guard.

At the end of the first month the bank in Antigua held over $6 billion, and Richard, together with Brooke, had made four trips to the lush island. It consumed imprudent amounts of time and kept Richard away from CCA at length, which allowed Stan Miller and his professionals to enter Richard's home and office to snap photographs and tinker with the computers as Frank had demanded. Holding nearly 400 photos and fifty diskettes, Frank called to terminate the effort. He had what he needed.

By THE END OF THE SECOND MONTH after Richard began this operation, both Marty and Fred Marcus had purchased over $10 billion worth of heroin. All the money was safely in the Caribbean bank. Richard was contemplating his next move. It was reminiscent of the days with Ray Patton and Shane O'Connor. They'd known that if they continued, the risk of capture was tremendous. It was no different now. Even though things had gone smoothly, to continue held dangers beyond calculation. Richard was loath to stop, the same rationale prevailing: all the pieces were in place and nothing had gone wrong, so why quit?

Brooke was eager to transfer the money back to the States. It represented her passport to the life she so missed. She, too, was reluctant to abandon the source of their financial rebirth. It was a delicious dilemma. They decided to put it on hold for another week while they basked in the glow of retribution. They knew they had defeated Frank O'Connor and would prevail at CCA.

DESPITE RICHARD'S EXTENDED ABSENCES during recent months, CCA was returning to profitability. The stock had climbed back to pre-BTC levels. Bruno

Davidson had done an outstanding job during the transition, earning Richard's respect and admiration. He integrated BTC operations into a seamless flow of new products and improvements to old ones. He was solely responsible for the renaissance of CCA. The only problem Richard had with Bruno was his persistent allegiance to Frank O'Connor—a vocal board member and partisan crusader for whatever agenda Bruno put forth. This left Richard, as CEO, in a somewhat crippled position. Frank's argumentative behavior infuriated Brooke, who pulled no punches with her jabbing invectives in heated discussions at board meetings. It was becoming subtly evident that Frank O'Connor had plans for CCA that did not include Richard Stearns.

Between Richard and Brooke, they held considerably more stock than Frank and could easily outvote him, but the cumulative votes of the other six board members could carry the day. It had not come down to a show of force, but it was obvious that day was not far off.

THIRTY-THREE

Slowly and methodically, using a large magnifying glass, Frank O'Connor sorted through the stack of photographs. They were of excellent quality and showed even the smallest detail. He made a number of separate piles of the pictures he wanted to keep, and discarded the rest. He then inserted each diskette into his computer and printed what information he wanted. When he was done, there were only two small stacks containing less than ten photos and twelve sheets of hard copy. He took the photos to a photography shop and had them all enlarged, and then returned to his office where he carefully noted the information he was after.

Frank was now more determined than ever to complete his plan. He had what he needed and nothing would deter him. His dreams of a greater International Bank of Boston were about to come true, and he knew he had destroyed Richard and Brooke Stearns in the process. Revenge was sweet.

Though he had graduated from the Harvard School of Business and had made generous grants to the school, Frank had no enduring affinity for the institution. Some had approached him over the years to contribute to a new business school that would be named after him, but he had no interest in such frippery. His mission now was to make the International Bank of Boston the envy of the entire national financial community.

After a week of vacillation, torn between the enormous risks and their insidious greed, Richard and Brooke made a seminal decision. Bowing to incessant calls from Marcus and Marty Stinson, they agreed to make one more buy. It would be the largest they had ever done, maybe the largest anyone had ever done. It would require the utmost cooperation from their sources, and the continuation of their amazing luck.

To satisfy the voracious needs of both distributors, the transaction would involve eighty thousand kilos of heroin, at a cost of $2 billion. The logistics would be monumental, involving over one hundred and fifty people in both Hong Kong and the States. When it was all over, it would add $6 billion to their Caribbean account. From the time they made their needs known to their sources, the entire operation would take less than three weeks.

Cho Wong was astounded. He wasn't sure the suppliers could deliver. To safely stow eighty-eight tons of heroin onboard would be extremely dangerous. His three associates had been indispensable throughout, covering for any disturbing or suspicious activity. What Wong was paying them had a lot to do with that—five dollars a kilo. On each trip they made over $150,000; this one would net them $400,000. Wong's take would be $2 million. Since the beginning, Cho Wong had made over $7 million. The suppliers had better come through.

STAN MILLER HADN'T SEEN FRED MARCUS for nearly two weeks. When he walked into the casino one Friday evening, Marcus was beaming, a stunning blonde on either arm. He went directly to the desk and registered in the most expensive penthouse suite, a lavish two-story layout with spa, wet bar and oversized king beds. As the clerk handed him the key, he turned to see Miller smiling.

"Haven't seen you for some time. Business must be booming. How are you and Richard hitting it off?"

"Couldn't be better. Richard's quite a guy," Marcus announced proudly, pulling Stan to one side. Lowering his voice to a whisper he said, "Biggest shipment ever arrives in two weeks. The best quality I've ever seen, and I can move it all in under ten days." Turning to his companions he said loudly, "Let's hit the tables, girls," and swaggered off.

Frank O'Connor should know about this, Miller thought. He had called just that day for any new information, sounding more excited than Stan had ever observed. His questions were more searching, his language more urgent. Miller had a sense of impending doom for Richard Stearns. It could also mean the end of the substantial fees both were paying him.

This was the best news Frank had heard since embarking on his haunting scheme for revenge; precisely what he needed to exact the ultimate payback. He was looking forward to the end. His supreme weapon, money, had secured it all.

THIRTY-FOUR

THE OFFICES OF THE DEA WERE LOCATED two blocks from Frank O'Connor's bank. To create the best possible setting, he invited Tom Romer, the local agent-in-charge, to come to his luxurious office for what he described as a very important meeting. It was crucial that Romer view him and the essence of this meeting as substantial. What he had to say—and how Romer reacted—would either cement the plan or create an irreversible impasse.

Tom Romer was in his early fifties, balding, and slender as a rail. He had no idea why this dignified-looking banker had invited him to his opulent workplace. The receptionist ushered him to Frank's ground-floor office and offered him coffee.

Frank cleared his throat and began. "Mr. Romer, I appreciate your seeing me. This could take awhile, so please bear with me. I don't usually get involved in such things, but when you hear my story I think you'll agree it warrants your immediate attention." How he proceeded to say what he was about to reveal was crucial.

"A few weeks ago, I was advised by a reliable and unassailable business associate that large quantities of illicit drugs were arriving here by means of a shipping company with offices and dock facilities in Boston. At first it was of little concern to me—I know nothing about that business or about anyone involved in it—but a few weeks later I received a call from a banking associate of mine in Singapore." *God, I hope this isn't getting too complicated.*

"I really don't know him personally, but apparently my son, Shane O'Connor, had dealings with him some time ago involving the purchase of that very same shipping company. At the time, Shane was president of our bank. Last year he was killed in a grievous accident." He paused, hoping Romer detected a suitable degree of grief.

"Before he died, he disposed of his interest in the company—I'll get into that later. One of the original owners, a Mr. Hirosa, contacted the banker in Singapore to announce that his new partners, now located here in Boston, had defaulted on payments due on loans his bank had made while my son owned shares in the company. Shane had sold his interest in the company to the Boston partners, who were now responsible for payment on those

159

loans. He wanted to ask whether I knew anything about these people."

He stopped. The tale was running longer than he'd planned and he was just getting started. He wasn't nervous, but the convoluted story had to be unraveled carefully.

"This is a rather complicated narrative so please be patient. I'll do my best to keep it understandable."

Tom Romer had said nothing after greeting him. He sat stoically, gazing at O'Connor. It was difficult for Frank to determine what he was thinking. "Mr. O'Connor, I'm here to listen and I've got all afternoon. Please continue."

"The people the Singapore banker was referring to are Richard and Brooke Stearns. I'm sure you know who they are, very well known, successful people here in Boston. He heads the CCA computer company, and she is a well-known financial analyst and business writer. They're quite wealthy, but, as you might have read, they found themselves in serious financial difficulty some time ago.

"At any rate, the connection between the shipping company and the Stearnses rang a bell with me. Here are people who have accumulated great wealth, have had recent disastrous financial problems, and who own part of a shipping company reported to be bringing enormous amounts of drugs into the area.

"My interest in this whole affair has nothing to do with drugs. The Stearnses used my bank to purchase their share in the shipping company. We acted as an intermediary for the Singapore bank when my son transferred his stock to the Stearnses and assisted the Singapore bank with the additional funds the Stearnses needed for their new partners. My son handled all this without my knowledge, which wasn't unusual.

"This brings me to the crux of the story. The Stearnses are still in arrears to the Singapore bank. Because my bank acted as a fiduciary in the original transaction, we are now liable for the defaulted loan, which as of today amounts to about $30 million. We'll sue and probably collect, but that's not why I'm here. If what I was told about illicit drugs and the shipping company is true, and I'm convinced that it is, I want them put out of business. I can offer you information I've since gathered from a source that I cannot and will not disclose. If this interests you, I can help. I believe it to be a much larger operation than anyone suspects"

Romer studied Frank. Not a week went by that he didn't hear some convoluted tale about large amounts of drugs finding their way into the greater Boston area. Most were anonymous and probably from disgruntled drug dealers. This information from one of the most visible and highly respected men in the state was unprecedented—singularly remarkable, actually. He would have to proceed carefully: how he responded could either greatly enhance his career or utterly destroy him.

"Mr. O'Connor, your story is intriguing and I suspect we might be interested in learning more. Before we go any further, I'd like you to arrange for a stenographer to come to your office and take down exactly what it is you have. We'll need everything: names; locations; dates, and whatever else there is. The more detail you provide, the better able we'll be to establish the reliability of the information."

Frank knew most of the players from the data pilfered from Richard's home and office. He had committed them to memory. The shipping company was easily identifiable, as was the name of the charter boat used in the Caribbean. He chose to omit the latter, and generalized the dates as having been during the past three months. The locations—Boston and New York—were obvious. He began with the names.

"Richard Stearns is the man behind it all. Even with his recent financial reversals, he has access to significant sources of capital. His wife, Brooke, has been instrumental in all the transactions and signs many of the checks. His local distributor is a man named Marty Stinson, and the crewmember who apparently has contacts in Asia is a man named Cho Wong. I have no information as to the Hong Kong source. Wong evidently was responsible for getting the material onto the ships and subsequently into the States. He probably had help from Richard Stearns in his role as an owner of the shipping company. Also, there's a distributor in Atlantic City named Fred Marcus.

"Now, here's the part I hope will allow you not only to confirm what I've told you, but also to intercept them. Sometime within the next two to three weeks, the largest shipment to date will arrive in Boston. Again, I can't disclose how I know this, but believe me, my sources are unimpeachable." Frank paused. This was at the very heart of his strategy. He must convince Romer to proceed exactly as he was about to suggest.

"One more thing: We have reason to believe the Stearnses have stashed vast amounts of money somewhere in the Caribbean, a large expanse to search. I strongly suggest that you allow them to leave Boston harbor and track them. This will enable you to establish the location of the funds. Such a seizure would certainly add to the DEA's coffers."

Tom Romer was impressed. Rarely did informants have such depth of information, and never had there been one of such stature—O'Connor was a man of unquestioned integrity. While he would prefer to know the source of the information, that could wait. The idea of allowing the Stearnses to leave the area wasn't entirely within DEA doctrine, but the massive amount of money that could become available to the DEA could certainly accelerate promotions.

"Quite a story. You seem to have spent a good deal of time assembling your facts. We'll get right on this. I assume we can reach you on short notice if we need additional information. If you're right about the timing, we'll need to act immediately. One other thing: You mentioned this next shipment would be the largest they've done. How do you know this and just how large is it?"

Frank had no idea. All he knew was what Stan Miller had told him, and there'd been no mention of the quantity. He did know the dollar value of most of the shipments, however. Maybe Romer could translate that into quantity.

"All I can tell you is that the most recent shipment involved a payment from the distributors to Richard Stearns of over $4.5 billion. I don't know the value of drugs, and, as I told you, I won't disclose my source."

Good God, Romer thought, it must be heroin, and in vast quantities. It would be difficult for even the most seasoned dealer to bring that much into the United States; more importantly, it would take an army of pushers to dispose of it on the street. And it would have to be stored somewhere. This could be one of the largest interceptions in DEA history; something Tom Romer would handle with flawless attention. This was a career-maker.

THIRTY-FIVE

RICHARD ASSEMBLED HIS USUAL CONTINGENT of Asian strong-arm men and the smaller group sent by Stan Miller to handle the transaction. All appeared to be progressing as planned. Cho called to tell him the entire load had arrived in Hong Kong. Tests proved the quality superior. Richard took extra precautions to assure safe stowage of this immense mass of heroin. It consumed half the forward hold, and required diligent camouflage efforts from Cho and his men. Once underway it would have to be constantly monitored. Cho was nervous about the size of his small force. Three men, with other duties to perform, would have their hands full. It would be an around-the-clock effort.

TOM ROMER MOVED QUICKLY, sending three of his best men to Hong Kong to work with their drug enforcement people. The plan was to identify the source of the heroin but not interdict those responsible before the shipment arrived in the States. He also sent four of his best surveillance men to accompany the ship. They would identify any onboard collaborators and assist with the destination activities. Each was equipped with his own satellite communications gear, and the ship was under continuous observation by satellite from the moment it left Hong Kong. Two navy destroyers shadowed at a safe distance throughout the long journey.

MARTY STINSON AND FRED MARCUS were alerted to expect the large shipment within the next week and to have their money ready. The entire transfer would be made in Boston. The exact hour of arrival would be established as the ship neared the mainland. Richard and Brooke made the usual arrangements with the charter boat for passage to Barbuda. It would be the last trip for all of them, Brooke thought. She looked forward to the time when it was finally over. It was the most stressful time of her life, but thoughts of the immeasurable amount of money they were accumulating assuaged her anxiety. When they arrived in Antigua and made the final deposit, they would have $16 billion safely in the bank—all tax-free. That, together with the residual value of assets they hadn't had to borrow against or liquidate, would put their net worth at nearly $17 billion. Yes, she thought, it was worth it.

AS THE SHIP APPROACHED THE UNITED STATES mainland, the four surveillance men contacted Tom Romer's headquarters. They identified Cho Wong and the other three crewmembers as participants, and announced that the ship would dock in Boston at eleven the next morning. Romer assembled a contingent of thirty men to pounce on the dealers and seize the heroin. The plan was to allow Richard and Brooke to leave with the cash and follow them. They would know nothing of the seizure. Cho Wong and his men would be apprehended, along with Marty and Marcus.

The ship docked on time in Boston harbor. Romer was in a position to observe the entire scene. The dock had been cleared of all activities except those relating to this ship.

Two large tractor-trailers pulled into position alongside the water. Fifteen men milled about the trucks, waiting for the action to begin. Other typical dock trucks waited to handle the normal cargo. When the ship was secured, the booms began to swing material onto the waiting trucks. The standard freight was offloaded first, as Romer had instructed. As the containers holding the heroin were hoisted over the side, the tractor-trailers moved into position. In all his years with the DEA, Romer had never seen so much dope. It was astonishing; he could only imagine what it was worth.

As the last container found its way to the trailers, Romer saw two more trucks moving slowly toward the water. Everything seemed to be happening in slow motion and with great momentum. Squads of men, obviously armed, prowled among the trucks. As the second two trucks came to a halt, a long limousine arrived. A man from one of the squads opened the door, and out stepped a younger man, impeccably dressed, ushering a beautiful young woman. They spoke for some time with two men from the trucks carrying the heroin, then quickly went to the far end of the dock. The second set of trucks followed them to a smaller boat resembling a tanker, with a flat deck and a small cabin protruding from its stern. The man and woman boarded. Immediately, a mobile crane began loading the containers. They were lashed to the deck. Six or seven men, all armed, accompanied the shipment on board and the ship left the harbor. The entire operation took less than two hours.

As soon as the tanker-like craft had cleared the harbor, Tom Romer and his colleagues made their move. The group that accompanied the trucks carrying the heroin, together with the squads of armed thugs, probably totaled twenty-five men. It was obvious none of them suspected what was about to transpire. The trucks slowly departed the dock and the squads dispersed into three nondescript cars. Romer dispatched ten of his men to intercept them; the rest followed the trucks as they made their way toward the end of the pier. As they turned to enter a line of light traffic, six Humvees blocked their path. Armed DEA agents jumped from the wide-track vehicles and surrounded the two trucks—Marty Stinson in one, Fred Marcus in the other. Neither offered resistance as they were cuffed and chained to the rear seats of the Hummers.

Romer arrived to see the stunned traffickers sullenly wondering what the hell had gone wrong. He instructed the drivers to take them to the detention center and ordered his other men to drive the heroin-laden trucks to the central garage. Frank O'Connor had been right: it would turn out to be the largest heroin bust in the nation's history; eighty thousand kilos—eighty-eight tons!

WHEN RICHARD AND BROOKE STEARNS were allowed to leave the Boston area by boat, as O'Connor had suggested, Romer arranged with the Coast Guard to deploy a cutter with the latest radar and satellite tracking equipment to follow them. They would never be more than five miles distant from the Stearnses. It could take some time, but it was more efficient than scouring the entire Caribbean.

Onboard, in fifteen steel receptacles, was $6 billion in hundred-dollar bills, weighing seventy-five tons!

THIRTY-SIX

PRIOR TO THE SEIZURE, TOM ROMER had briefed Frank O'Connor, vaguely outlining their overall strategy. In deference to O'Connor's suggestion, Romer not only allowed the Stearnses to leave, he assured Frank they would be under constant surveillance until they arrived at their unknown destination.

Immediately after Romer's briefing, Frank was on the phone to Stan Miller. They had arranged to have one of Miller's minions at the dock, observing everything when the heroin arrived. When Richard and Brooke boarded their money-laden boat, Miller's man was to call Stan, who was to alert Frank.

"They're on their way, with $6 billion in hundred-dollar bills lashed to the deck. Hope they don't hit any rough seas—the fish wouldn't know what to do with all that money," Stan joked. It reminded him of the era of the Spanish galleons, laden with gold, many still on the bottom of the Caribbean.

The joke was wasted on Frank. He needed one more effort from Stan. This would be the last. He'd never have to rely on the dregs of the underworld again. He outlined his needs. Miller's ability to enlist the skills of so many charlatans amazed him. The outrageous fees he was collecting probably engendered his success.

This time Stan contacted another pernicious friend of his, an old acquaintance who had been successful in the gunrunning business during the Nicaraguan uprising. Miguel Espinoza had the latest in sleek, ultra-fast boats armed with radar-guided missiles. After all, Frank had insisted he hire only the very best.

Espinoza was to follow the Stearns's boat and the Coast Guard cutter at a safe distance from both. Detection could terminate their mission. Once in the open sea, a hundred miles or so from Miami, he was to destroy the cutter, preferably at night, causing as little turmoil as possible. The Stearnses must be allowed to proceed to their destination unhindered.

Three days out of Boston, the Coast Guard lost radio contact with its escort cutter. No messages had been received for four hours, and all attempts to reach them had failed. Search-and-rescue helicopters sent to their last known location found nothing.

Two days later, Richard and Brooke, oblivious to what had happened in Boston, docked the chartered boat in Antigua and arranged to have their bank pick up their deposit. Barbuda made things so easy—few questions, no endless holdups at the antiquated customs desk, and armed guards to assure safe passage to the bank—all done in less than two hours. They met briefly with the bank president to confirm the amount of the deposit and verify their latest balance: $16 billion! They'd done it, safe, secure, nontaxable and all theirs. True, it wasn't in the United States, but they'd deal with that later. Right now they wanted to celebrate with a whirlpool bath, a superb dinner and a stiff drink. Maybe more than one. They planned to stay a few days before flying back to Boston.

Tom Romer was frantic, his decision to allow the Stearnses to flee was unraveling. With no word from the cutter, they assumed it had gone down at sea. But that was extraordinary—those ships were designed to withstand the worst—few if any had ever been lost. There were too many unanswered questions. Why had he let O'Connor convince him this was a prudent course of action? Now that the Stearnses were temporarily free, where in the Caribbean were they? Had he lost the immense fortune he assumed was destined for the DEA? With great bravado he had announced this to his superiors. It was imperative that he recover the initiative. Richard and Brooke Stearns would return to the States; he would be ready. He called his friends at Customs.

Customs alerted every major port of entry. Two days later, Richard and Brooke were apprehended in Miami. Irate, arrogant and uncooperative, they demanded to see their attorney. When advised that their associates had been arrested in Boston, they stared in utter disbelief. How? Why? Who had allowed them to escape? What the hell was going on? They had all been together on the dock in Boston, and if Fred and Marty were seized, why not they? The money! The Feds followed them and the money. But it was safe in their Caribbean bank, wasn't it? During the four-day trip to Barbuda there was no evidence they were being followed, but with satellite tracking, anything was possible. It was a tumult of incomprehensible events, more than either of them could handle. If their money was safe they could buy their way out. Brooke Temple-Stearns simply would not allow her story to end this way. Being detained like this was an egregious act of irresponsible interference with their ordained way of life. Richard panicked and asked to be allowed to go the men's room, nauseated.

Their incarceration became more unbearable: At a preliminary hearing, they were denied bail: they were to be transported to Boston and formally charged with drug trafficking. How would they face their friends?

Upon arrival in Boston, Richard and Brooke were housed in the Federal Detention Center to await further legal proceedings. The *Boston Globe* carried detailed accounts of their escapades and the names of their associates. It was a scandal of colossal dimensions, involving two of the most highly visible, socially prominent Bostonians. The national press had a field day. Frank O'Connor was elated. Tom Romer was relieved, but nonetheless determined to retrieve the cash.

FRANK O'CONNOR'S METAMORPHOSIS was complete. During the months since Shane's death, and during the exhilarating annihilation of Richard and Brooke Stearns, he'd become obsessively convinced of his invincibility. He couldn't explain it, but it didn't trouble him, nor did the clandestine activities in which he had been involved concern him. Certainly he had not corrupted Stan Miller, who did those sorts of things routinely, and he had paid him damn well. With Richard gone, he would control CCA, and Bruno would restore the company to the lofty heights it once commanded.

His entire plan had gone exceedingly well. There hadn't been a significant glitch. He had thought about little else. Thank God he had competent people at the bank. He'd spent little time there during the past three months, but now he could pursue his other obsession.

The banking business in the nineties required global access to a host of financial services his bank did not provide. With deregulation, interstate banking, and the imminent entry of banks into the sale and trading of equities, expansion was an absolute necessity. He now had the requisite financial resources to do just that.

With the information he'd surreptitiously extracted from Richard's files, access to the funds parked in the bank in Barbuda was assured. With the latest deposit, it probably would exceed $15 billion—maybe insufficient to acquire the prestigious competitors he so coveted, but certainly enough to make an interesting merger.

He began outlining the plan: intricate movements of funds; dummy corporations; wire transfers; and the final deposit in his own bank. He would do it all from his own office, virtually untraceable, except for the bulge—as yet unaccounted for—in the bank's balance sheet. He'd have to alert his new president, Rob Meyers. He viewed Meyers as a useful cohort, and would soon know how cooperative he would be. The banking business required imaginative endeavors from time to time. With some creative bookkeeping, the funds would be buried in a real estate venture that Don Parker would invent. He could now begin the aggressive pursuit of suitable merger candidates.

THIRTY-SEVEN

T HE CAPTURE OF RICHARD AND BROOKE STEARNS was a great relief. The recovery of the money, however, topped Tom Romer's list. He was also puzzled about the mysterious loss of the Coast Guard cutter. Aside from the DEA and the Coast Guard, the only person who had known anything about the tracking ship was Frank O'Connor. It was outrageous to think he might have had anything to do with it. A respected banker who had, after all, been the sole source of vital information that allowed the seizure to occur almost flawlessly.

Almost. The money had escaped them, its location a mystery. To search the vast Caribbean would require inordinate amounts of time and expense. Maybe Frank O'Connor could help. His international banking connections and experience certainly would better their chances of a speedy recovery.

"I can't tell you how helpful your information was in pulling off the entire seizure," Romer started, "and the capture of the Stearnses was brilliant. But as you might have read, the cutter following the Stearns's boat disappeared without a trace. This, of course, allowed the Stearnses to continue to their Caribbean destination undetected. We'll have to locate the money to wrap up the case. I was wondering if you'd have time to strategize with me just how we might go about that. With your banking experience and connections you might be able to expedite things. I'd appreciate it." He hung up and hurried to Frank's office.

Frank knew better than to deny Romer a meeting. These guys could be tenacious. A little misleading information, together with some tedious banking verbiage, and he'd move on. Besides, it might be helpful to glean what he knew.

Romer entered Frank's office nearly out of breath. "Thanks for seeing me. This won't take long, just some insight from you, and a few minor questions. By the way, we've completed interviewing Marty Stinson and the guy from Atlantic City. This Fred Marcus is a real character—full of wisecracks, thinks he's hilarious. If he knew how much time he was facing, he'd change his attitude. He did mention a guy who's an executive with a casino there, a Stan Miller. We've got one of our men interviewing him. He might know something. We're also talking to the Stearnses, but they're too concerned about their own situation to tell us much."

He took a deep breath. "If you could just give me an overview of how you would begin to screen the myriad places the Stearnses might have stashed the money. You know—places where the banking laws are a bit lax and few questions are asked when huge amounts of cash are deposited— places known to accommodate the drug business. Anything you could tell me would be very helpful."

Frank knew that once the heroin seizure was complete and the Stearnses, together with the rest, were in custody, the questioning would begin. Stan Miller had no reason to tell them anything. He wasn't the problem. But if the Stearnses, in an effort to save themselves, revealed the sordid mess concerning Shane, the bank could have serious problems. He had dug into the bank records to reverse any incriminating data, and felt he had covered everything, but if an army of examiners swarmed in, who knew what they might find? He wanted this patronizing bureaucrat out of his office—fast.

"What I can tell you about Caribbean banking practices amounts to very little. There are some places, such as the Caymans, that ask few questions about Yankee dollars. I suppose Panama would be another. Aside from that, I'm afraid I can't be of much help," Frank concluded and ushered Romer out.

Romer had accomplished what he intended. He could see the concern in Frank's eyes. He went immediately to his office and called his counterpart in Atlantic City. The office announced they were interviewing Stan Miller; the secretary would have the agent call Romer the minute he returned.

He still had no plan for recovering the money, and his superiors were making noises about incompetence. Letting the money slip away was inexcusable, but he probably would do it again given the same circumstances. He had trusted Frank O'Connor—had no reason not to—but the cutter's disappearance, and the fact that no one else knew the Stearnses had been allowed to leave the area, made the man suspect, at least to Romer. O'Connor's vague assessment of the Caribbean banking situation was bogus, he thought. Surely a man in his position would know a lot more about it than he had divulged.

Frank paced his office. Not much of what Romer had told him was news. He'd considered the risks regarding Stan Miller and Richard Stearns. Miller was a shady casino operator, and Richard was about to be imprisoned for years on a drug-trafficking conviction. Neither was to be believed. He was confident of that. He'd alert Rob Meyers just in case. Bank examiners were known to arrive with little or no advance notice.

THIRTY-EIGHT

RICHARD AND BROOKE WERE HELD in separate cells. They had been questioned several times and both were in a state of denial—this simply couldn't be happening!

Brooke was generally incoherent, sobbing throughout the interrogation sessions. Her demeanor ranged from staunch arrogance to rage and irrational rebuttal. She wanted to talk to Richard, needed him to strategize their assertions of innocence. The lawyer she called was an acquaintance from her days with Don Parker. Inexperienced in criminal defense, he agreed to refer her case to a competent attorney. It all looked hopeless; she feared for her sanity. In the long, lonely hours in her cell, she thought about how it all had come crashing down. What had gone wrong? The transfer at the Boston dock seemed to go precisely according to plan. They left the dock on their charter without delay or question. If the others had been seized, why had she and Richard been allowed to leave? Given her current circumstances, it was difficult to concentrate, but none of it made sense. They had been caught and the party was over. She could think of nothing else.

Richard paced his small cell. During interrogation he was evasive while trying to appear cooperative. His statements focused on one strategy: He had been coerced and knew nothing; others had organized the entire operation, and his wife had enticed him onto the boat. He knew nothing about any money; had assumed it was a pleasure trip to the Caribbean. He doubted they bought it, but he was fixated on finding some way out. Why they had opted for one more buy would haunt him the rest of his life. They already had all the money they would ever need.

His thoughts returned to the day on the dock. Everything had appeared normal: the transfer went off without a hitch; they left the dock and headed south, literally, but why had they been allowed to leave? It was so damned obvious—the money. But who? Probably the Feds, but they could have seized it on the spot. It became clearer as he pondered the whole episode. For whatever reason they were allowed to leave, the ultimate objective had to be their destination. It was where the entire bulk of their fortune was housed. If it was the Feds, how did they know there had been other transactions? And if they did, why assume we would park it all in the same place? The DEA was staffed with some savvy people, but not that savvy. It was obvious to Richard that they'd had some help. It wasn't difficult to establish who.

If he was doomed to life in prison, and it looked more and more as though that was the case, Richard was determined to implicate Frank O'Connor. He knew where the skeletons were hidden, and he knew enough about Shane's procedures to guide a skilled bank investigator to the closet. Small consolation, but he wasn't going to let O'Connor off the hook. Frank would pay a price for his betrayal. Maybe not jail, but he could lose his bank, and that would be a just retaliation. Richard looked forward to his next interrogation session.

FRANK O'CONNOR WAS DETERMINED to prevail in his encounters with Tom Romer or any bank examiner. He'd come too far to be thwarted by some bureaucratic tyrant. As soon as the funds were transferred to his bank's accounts, he would begin his conquest. No more second-tier bank—he'd be allied with the best in the world!

TOM ROMER WAS OBSESSED WITH RECOVERING the money. He called the Justice Department to have the FBI begin an audit of Frank O'Connor's bank. After his people interviewed Richard Stearns, it was obvious there was a history of some type of corruption. If what Richard told them was true, it went back more than three years. They'd have Frank O'Connor—and his bank— on charges of money laundering and criminal fraud. He just hoped the money was where he could get his hands on it.

IN HIS OFFICE IN THE CASINO, Stan Miller read all the accounts of the big drug bust. His interrogation by the local DEA had been a joke; his clandestine chores for Frank O'Connor and Richard Stearns untraceable. He was the only one who even knew the names of the people who'd performed the dirty deeds. The Feds were frustrated and totally baffled. He sat in his luxurious office at the La Samanna, pondering recent events. All the players were in jail. He'd banked a great deal of money, but the party was over. It had been a good run.

As he reflected, he opened his desk drawer. For reasons he couldn't remember, he had made copies of all the photographs and computer disks taken at Richard's office and home. The numerical maze was intriguing. As he sifted through the copies, it suddenly came to him: What Frank wanted from all the prowling through Richard's papers was an account number—the locations of the drug proceeds. And it must be a load of cash. He had no idea how much but he could guess. His digital mind quickly culled the nonessential information from the photos and hard copies, and he jotted down the name of the bank and all the security numbers. My God, he thought, the amount of money in this account could be astronomical!

THIRTY-NINE

FRANK O'CONNOR WAS DETERMINED TO GET on with the final chapter of his grand scheme. Rob Meyers and Don Parker would have to be apprised of his intentions. First he would begin the ponderous task of moving the money from Antigua through the dummy corporations and, ultimately, to his bank. He placed a call to the president of the Caribbean bank. A man named Julio Ortega was put on the line. His English was acceptable, and, after suitable introductions, Frank began his request.

"Mr. Ortega, we have deposited large sums of money in your bank over the past few months and we would now like to begin a procedure to move those funds. I'll be happy to give you all the necessary security information to allow you to commence the process," Frank said, and began reciting the lengthy litany of numbers. Ortega stopped him several times to verify the sequence. Frank could hear him pounding his keyboard. When all the data were entered, Ortega asked him to wait while the computer processed the information.

The time was interminable. After nearly ten minutes, Ortega was back on the line with ruinous news: the accounts he had entered showed a zero balance; all the funds had been removed three days earlier.

Frank shot from his desk, nearly dropping the phone. "What on earth are you saying? There was nearly $16 billion in those accounts and I'm the only holder of all the security passwords. There has to be some mistake. Check it again," Frank shouted. Choking, he loosened his tie. This couldn't be happening. He'd worked too hard, planned too long, taken inordinate risks. He'd suffered Shane's death. The money had to be there!

"I'm sorry Mr. O'Connor, but the accounts have a zero balance. I don't know what to tell you."

"This is insane, Ortega. Who had access to those accounts and who removed the funds? Where were they relocated to?" Frank demanded.

"You know I can't divulge that information. All I can tell you is that all the funds were removed three days ago. I'm sorry," Ortega said, and hung up.

Frank sat stunned. It wasn't registering. His mind was spinning. Who? It must have been the DEA. Romer was sharper than he'd reckoned. If it had been Romer, he'd never see it again, and he might have other problems. The Feds could be relentless.

AND SO THEY WERE. FRANK O'CONNOR, Richard, and Brooke would go to jail and would stay there for the foreseeable future. Frank's promise of a job did look a little dicey. Stan called for a one-way, first-class ticket to Barbuda, and packed his bags and golf clubs. He flew directly to the Caribbean, went to the bank, and moved the entire balance to the Cayman Islands: all $16 billion—a sixteen with nine zeros! That had been three days ago. He'd now have his very own casino. He could have his pick of the showgirls. Hell, he could have anything he wanted. Maybe he'd buy the Caribbean!